FOX – Betrayals

© 2013 Nick McCarty

ISBN 978-0-9554771-3-3

Text prepared by www.willowebooks.org.uk

FOX – Betrayals

by

Nick McCarty

Published by Kenelm

For Tiny, who knows how much he has done,
and for Susan, with love and so many thanks for
all she always does

PROLOGUE

John Fox peered through the rain as the dawn light began to glow over the rim of the mountains behind him. He was hungry, wet, cold and as happy as a bird. He knew that hidden under the morning mist, lay his target. After days inching through enemy territory among the hills and valleys of the skirts of the mountains he had found something that would interest his masters. More proof that the enemy was settling down into winter quarters and preparing the line of advance for the spring offensive after the snow.

Europe was in religious and political turmoil. The usual religious arguments that claimed to be about doctrine and practice were, in fact, about power.

Not that any of this mattered a damn to Sergeant John Fox. He was a mercenary with work to do, a life to risk. Shea, before he was killed, used to say 'Sure aren't we little dolls in the hands of Fate – pissed on by all and sundry and just used by power hungry kings, popes and such – God rot them all in hell, I say.'

But Shea had a way with words and was a deeply angry man. They had been partners working in enemy territory for four years.

Fox had admired the little broken-toothed Irishman above all because he was a ruthless survivor with the feral skills of a Connemara cat. He read the land as well as Fox and sometimes he had a sixth sense for danger that he'd learned off his mother. 'She had the sight, d'you see?' he'd explained. And Fox had learned to respect the gift.

The army had been all Shea's adult life. He was a regimental rat.

Fox had gone for a soldier years before. Seventeen years old and ready to leave the comfort of a home in Shropshire with a grieving father who was letting his barrel-making business fail.

When he had too much drink he was likely to lash out. The last time it happened, Fox hit him back. He never forgave himself for crushing the last of the spirit out of his father and decided to leave home before they destroyed each other. He had fallen in love with Alison who was destined for her cousin whom she hated. She had promised Fox she would not take her cousin to her bed but she also knew it was time for Fox to go.

'I'll wait for you,' she said on the day he left. She kissed him and walked away through the may blossom and the hawthorn, the dog roses lying pink and white in the hedges. A blackbird sang. She hadn't told him then that she was with child.

He rode away that spring morning down the river valley as far as Bewdley. On the hills beside the track, sheep were revelling in the fresh grass in the lower pastures close to the village. Some were already climbing up into the crags and valleys along the length of the Long Mynd where they would spend the summer and autumn.

Outside the white-painted meeting house, two of the older men sat in the pale sunshine and watched Fox ride by. He lifted his hand in farewell and they turned their heads away. Fox had been a troublesome boy and these quiet, religious men wanted nothing to do with him.

The dull clang of the rams' bells sounded as Fox went his way. In his saddle bag was a change of shirt, an old cloak, bread, barley and a cut of meat he'd stolen from the larder. He had an old leather bottle for water and a knife.

It was early the next morning when he came down into Bewdley. The houses across the river hid behind the tall warehouses that lined the bank. Even at this early hour, men were busy loading and unloading the barges at the water's edge.

Fox slid off his horse, stuffed what he needed into a leather bag and looked around for an old friend.

Two men lounging in the shadows by the last warehouse watched him for a moment. He took no notice. Then Alison's fat cousin stepped in front of him, grinning.

'Going are you, John Fox?' he mocked.

'If I am?' Fox said quietly.

'I know about you and Alison. I'll have her now and she'll learn who's master.' The young man laughed in his face and as he did so the two loungers stepped alongside Fox.

'You got permission?' the first asked him when he got close enough.

'Permission? What permission?'

'Didn't you know? You can't stop along here without you pay.'

Fox said nothing. He bent to fasten his leather bag. Alison's cousin still stood in front of him.

'So – turn out your pockets, boy.'

The first young man stood close to Fox's right side. Fox slowly stood up. He was yet to fill out into the broad-shouldered man he became but he was taller than the man threatening him. On his left and grinning stood the other with a stave in his hand. He went on smiling.

'You heard the man,' he held out his hand. 'Pay up.'

Neither expected what happened next for they were much too pleased with themselves. Stepping to his right Fox stood on the foot of the man on his right. Slammed down and turned his heel. As the young man screamed with the pain of his broken foot, Fox swung his bag into the face of the other and revealed the knife in his hand. He stepped close and put his knife to his attacker's throat. It was quick as spit.

'Tell your friend to hop off before I cut your throat,' he said.

He did as he was told.

'Now, undo your belt and let it fall.'

The young man hesitated. Then he felt the steel prick his neck and did as he was told.

'Now what have we here?'

Fox reached into the young man's jacket and plucked out a blade about eight inches long with a carved ivory handle.

'Pretty,' he said. 'Mine' he said.

The young man began to argue.

Fox leaned on the knife he held to the man's throat. He looked into Fox's eyes and held up his hands in surrender.

He lost his hold on the trousers and they fell to the ground. There was a snicker of laughter from a group of apprentices who were watching.

'Go!'

As the young man stooped to pick up his breeches Fox shoved his arse with all his force. He teetered on the edge of the quayside and then tottered and fell into the water.

Fox moved closer to Alison's cousin who was watching

gape-mouthed.

The blade flickered close to his face.

'If you go near Alison, I will come back and slit your throat. You understand me? Get on your knees.'

And the young man slowly knelt down. Fox walked round him and put his foot in the small of his back and shoved hard. He joined the other man struggling in the water. The apprentices roared with laughter.

Down by the riverside, barges and boats were loading bales of wool, sheep hides, and pallets of bricks from the kilns on the banks of the river. He left the old horse with a friend at the bridge in Bewdley who promised he'd take it back to his father for him next time he was going up the valley.

Fox worked passage on a boat down to Bristol. He'd known the bargee since he was a boy.

'Going away then?' said the boatman as Fox sat on a bale of skins in the belly of the boat.

'Might be,' he said. 'Might go for a soldier. I heard they were looking for men.'

'Always are, boy. I went once – got this there.' He held up his right arm. It had no hand on its end. 'Bugger soldiering.'

Fox shrugged and the water creamed under the hull of the boat.

'Know anyone?' asked the boatman and Fox said nothing. 'I know a good man might give a hint or two. Right place to look – the place you'll find recruiting men. In Bristol.'

Fox shrugged and stared across the reed lined banks. A swan glided out of the reeds.

'I'm in no hurry,' he said.

'I heard there was a girl, young Fox.' The boatman smiled.

Fox glanced at him and said nothing.

'I knew your dad, young man. He was a good man – once.'

Fox said nothing. His eyes held the boatman's who looked away and hauled in a sheet. The boat went faster. The boatman looked back and found Fox still staring at him. Dead-eyed as a fish.

'No offence,' he said and Fox nodded.

'I might look for a boat to take me to France. See the world a bit. No way can the two of us live in the same place together.'

The boatman nodded and spat.

'Ask at the Swan with Two Heads. They do pick up soldiers there. Or if it's a passage you want, go to the outer harbour and ask for a man called Terence Hawken.

'Terence Hawken? I've known Hawken since I was a boy. If he's still trading, I'll find him.'

'He trades from Cornwall to the other side. Brandy and wine mostly.'

For three years or so Fox worked the in-shore traders, mostly with Hawken, who was not much older than he was. He had a fishing smack he called *The Chough*.

It was a good life but Fox was restless. The two men eventually parted friends and Fox had walked into Brittany. It seemed a lifetime ago now.

Fox watched the farmhouse across the valley and smiled at the memory. He was still a boy when he found himself without money in Amsterdam. What's a young man to do? He had little choice but to join a company of soldiers. It was Tom Fairfax's company, and soon John Fox discovered what he did best.

So began a mercenary's life.

But now after six years working for Tom Fairfax he was beginning to feel restless again. He shrugged and rolled into the shelter of a grey boulder just below the rim. Times were certainly changing Fox thought.

He and Shea, the Irish gutter rat from Connemara, became a team. They scoured the territories between the lines and behind the lines of enemy forces. Spies. The eyes and ears of Tom Fairfax's company. They'd loved their life.

It ended when he found Shea skewered to a tree by a German dragoon guard a thousand miles from the wet green of Ireland that Shea had still called home. Fox believed he'd let his friend down. Not covered his back.

Time wasn't healing the wound of the loss of his friend even six months later. But maybe the disgust he now felt was for the killing, the rape, the burning and the violence he saw all around him. Sometimes he just felt that he was growing old.

The young officers who surrounded Black Tom Fairfax at headquarters never liked this dirty, ill-dressed, taciturn mercenary who was often seen before they were when he came to report back from an enemy city or from behind the enemy lines. If Fairfax needed information about the defences of a town, the health of an enemy army, or the whereabouts of an enemy commander, Fox would find it.

In his time wandering Europe he had learned French and Spanish and some German. His survival relied on country skills. He could read the land, understand the atmosphere of a place and by listening and looking and then by trusting his instincts, he honed his skills as Shea taught him. But Shea was dead and Fox had to learn to work with others. It was not the same. He felt that this would be the last time, the last foray into enemy land.

'Listen to your voices.' Shea used to say, 'And act.'

Being a soldier of fortune in the army of Gustavus Adolphus had been better than rotting under the rocks of the Long Mynd in Shropshire on the Welsh border.

But now he was bored. The end of the fighting season was nearly on them. He was bored and irritated by the routine of company life. Drill, practice and bedding down for the approaching winter.

For most of the rag-tag of infantry men it was a welcome time. They were fed, not in danger and had an ample supply of women and drink from the nearby town.

Black Tom Fairfax and Fox were near enough the same age. Fairfax was an officer and a gentleman and a Yorkshire man. Fox was none of these. He had been living off his wits since he was twelve for his father was no help to him.

This mission began when Tom Fairfax himself had called him into headquarters. Fairfax had given him a glass of wine told him to sit. Fox sat.

'You're ready to leave us, Fox. Am I right?'

Fox shrugged.

'Missing home? Got a woman to go home to after all this time?'

Fox nodded and looked at his commander.

'Will she have waited?'

'She promised me.'

Fairfax smiled.

'Has it been a long time?' his commander asked quietly.

Fox shrugged.

'She promised and she does not break her promises.'

Fairfax kicked the log in the hearth. Sparks flew up the chimney. It was a damn sight warmer here than in the lines under shreds of canvas.

'I could make you stay, order you.'

Fox smiled then.

'You might order me sir. But where would I be? Gone, sir. Vanished. It's what I do.'

Fairfax grinned and asked

'How are the men?'

'Cold, wet, hungry.'

'And ?'

'No "and" sir. They are not talking of desertion if that's what concerns you. You pay them regular enough. They had twenty four hours in that last place we took and looted what they wanted. So – now they're ready for winter quarters and a quiet time.'

Fairfax sniffed.

'Not quite yet if what I have heard is true. A last venture for you into no man's land.'

Fairfax got up and walked over to a rough map pinned to the wall. Fox waited.

'There are rumours of an advance from the Rhine, along this valley here. To the south.' He used a knife to point out the route on the map. 'They will need remounts for their cavalry and reserves of horses for their heavy artillery on their line of march. I want to know where these remounts might be. I want confirmation of the rumours about that advance. It's imperative that we get this information before we settle into winter quarters. How many men will you need?'

'One.' said Fox instantly.

'You have someone in mind?'

Fox nodded.

'The Welshman – Morgan is it? Troublemaker, him.'

'So am I, sir – when necessary.'

Fairfax looked sharply across at the young man sitting in the shadows cast by the firelight. He noticed that even here Fox found the shadows; never had his back to the door, was always alert. He had not touched his glass of wine.

'Good.'

Fox turned to go.

'I wish you'd stay with us, Fox.

'No, sir – thank you – enough's enough. To tell the truth, sir, I miss having Shea to guard my back. I miss him. It's like that, sir. You sort of lose confidence in the men you get sicked on you. I'll take Morgan. No one else.'

Fairfax sighed. 'Your choice, sergeant. If you need him. He's a troublemaker according to his lieutenant but then he may be what you need. If you don't take him I have no choice but to have him flogged.'

'I've asked about. Morgan was a good soldier. A natural and he was a friend of my mate – Shea that was killed.'

Fairfax nodded as Fox went on quietly, 'He's as quick as silver and has the killing instincts of a stoat.'

'Take him then.' Fairfax hesitated. 'There is another – a Dutchman or a Finn I'm not sure which. He's a cavalry man. You may have to take him. '

'A cavalry man'll find the going hard on foot sir, and if he can't keep up he gets left. It's how it is. We'll be moving fast – before winter sets in.'

And he walked out of the officer's quarters and back down towards the lines and the men. It was already raining harder.

Fox came to the punishment cell and found Morgan lying on filthy straw. He'd looked up at Fox, nodded and grinned. In the pale light his dark eyes glittered but there was little or no hope in them. He said not one word.

The flogging was to be at dawn. The square of soldiers lined up to watch one of their mates dragged in. Taken to a wagon that formed the fourth side of the square, lashed to the wheel like he was crucified.

His shirt torn from his body and the white flesh stark and bunched waiting for the first almost painless whistle of the cat across his bare skin. The pain came after the third or fourth whistling crack.

The drummer boy beating out the number of lashes, steady and remorseless. The lines of blood starting from the torn skin. The lash of nine tails was knotted and each knot tore into the flesh. As the farrier laid on the punishment the soldier would be biting on the leather pad in his mouth to stop him slicing through his tongue with the pain.

Fifty lashes were 450 lines of tattered flesh. And nine welts from the knots gave another 450 bloody welling wounds. Then cutting the man down and letting his friends throw salt on the tattered flesh of his back in the belief it might cauterize the wound. Men usually died of shock after that.

Morgan was a man to have on your side and at your back in trouble. Fox gave him the choice of coming with him or being lashed at the wheel for disobeying an officer. He chose Fox and a mission into enemy territory and was glad to. Morgan was a Welsh man, hard as nails, with a cold eyed ferocity when he was fighting.

'Better that than risking dying of poisoning from the filthy cat. And that bloody farrier sergeant hates my guts so he'd lay on the leather.'

'If the enemy catch us, they'll kill us,' Fox warned him. The Welshman grinned, nodded and said nothing.

'Morgan,' Fox said, 'Get your things.'

Morgan didn't say a word of thanks. He slid out of the cell, into the morning light, blinked, ducked his head and walked into the lines to get his meagre kit.

All around, the men stirred up fires, boiled water for a few old potatoes, ate stale bread and made themselves ready for what the day might bring. No one told the bloody infantry anything. No one told anyone very much.

Fox sniffed the air. He disliked the way men were dragooned into a sort of dull obedience. He liked nothing better than gathering information about enemy troop movements, the terrain over which the enemy might march, fortifications, possible ambushes.

He had revelled in it until Shea was killed by a German dragoon out in the field with him. Now he wasn't so sure.

He'd look at the lines of soldiers asleep by their little fires and wonder why he was there. He was paid and fed and watered but this was not enough. Orders irked him, particularly orders from inexperienced officers who thought they had the God given right to lead troops to their death. He hated them.

He walked out of the camp up into the hill overlooking their lines. In the distance a lark spiralled up into the silver sky, shrilling its warning song. Then another and another rose from their nests amongst the heather covering the hills beyond the camp.

The sour smell of the men followed him even as the autumn sunshine glittered over the wagons, the brass belts of the soldiers, the tripods over the cooking fires; the murmur of a thousand men gradually waking.

It brought to his mind the times when he was a boy and had climbed and roamed along the slopes and crags of the Long Mynd, looking down across the purple land from the huge rock seat called The Devil's Chair to the hills of Wales. He walked the banks of the Severn River down to Bristol and beyond. He hunted and speared salmon and trapped eels in the land of web-footed men and women in the mysterious water-filled Somerset Levels. And from time to time a web-footed woman might trap him.

He loved the pale yellow light of the Levels, the pale green willows stooped over the brackish peat streams, the slow even beat of herons flying low over the tufts of dark green grass. Watching the silent, immovable dagger-beaked killer standing to its knees in the cold water. He learned patience out on the Levels and above all he learned to be secret.

Fox lay still looking over the valley towards the horses penned on the other side of the stream that ran past the farmhouse. This last mission for Fairfax was using the skills he'd gathered since he was a child. He understood the land and what he didn't understand he had made it his business to discover.. If anyone could spot a good place for an ambush, it was Fox. If anyone could overhear soldiers' gossip in an enemy held town, it was Fox. If anyone knew the meaning of patience, of looking and watching, of listening and waiting in the shadows, it was Fox.

The rain began to ease for the first time in two weeks. He looked across at Morgan who lay asleep huddled in his cloak. Before they came on this sodden journey, Morgan had come up the hill overlooking the army lines, when he'd collected his kit. Fox hadn't heard him.

'Penny for them, Sergeant.'

He turned to find Morgan beside him looking down at the camp.

'All bloody fodder, Sergeant' said the Welshman quietly.

'You think we aren't, soldier?'

'No. I just think we got a better chance than they do. Led by clowns. Most of them.'

Morgan pulled his tattered shirt up and Fox stared at the sickening barely-healed scars and wheals across his back, nodded and looked away.

'That officer was out to kill me this time. I'm barely healed and another go would have done the job. It's personal, sergeant, before you ask.'

The same officer had confronted Fox when the two men walked back to their lines. He had an order for Fox.

Betz, a cavalry sergeant had been attached to him at the last minute and against his will. Betz had never been in the field behind the lines but the officer wasn't going to listen to Fox's objections. After all, Fox was a known troublemaker. Broken back to the ranks from time to time for insubordination or just on the whim of some green son of a rich man.

'Betz is a cavalry sergeant, Fox, and he knows what you will be looking for. We need more horses for the light artillery and he knows exactly what will suit us. Your work will be to locate a supply of horses for our cavalry and some of the light artillery.'

Fox shook his head.

'My orders are to check on the movement of the enemy forward lines. Are they planning a surprise attack?'

'Rubbish', snapped the cavalry officer. 'You've been listening to too many rumours. No one would advance their lines this close to winter. Old women listen to rumours.'

'Old women live to be old,' said Fox.

'You're not bandying words with me, Sergeant? Betz will be coming with you.'

Fox shrugged.

'Are you afraid? Is that what it is?

The young man was about to say more when he caught the look in the eyes of the sergeant. Dead, slate black eyes. Waiting.

'You will locate a source of horses. Sergeant Betz knows what we need. Then you will report back to me'

'Captain Fairfax is my line commander and he knows I never go with more than one. It's dangerous enough out there without an inexperienced soldier. Let alone a cavalry man .'

The cavalry officer snapped at him then.

'I am telling you, you will take my sergeant, Fox.'

It was pointless to argue.

'So long as he understands we are mostly on foot. We pass through their country and leave no sign. None. If we do they will know we know what they know. Tell your sergeant he'll be on foot, sir.'

They had left the lines in the early evening. It was raining. A week later it was still raining and was distinctly colder. Betz the cavalry man never stopped grumbling.

Fox looked to his right. Betz was leaning against a rock sheltered from the rain. He was staring at Fox. Betz was trouble.

The reconnaissance so far had been successful. All the three men needed to do now was to discover where the enemy were hiding their horses for the winter and then to extricate themselves from deep inside enemy territory, cross the open plains and head for the winter quarters where Fairfax and the protestant armies were settled.

Fox could report that the enemy was certainly settled for the winter.

Before climbing up into the foothills beyond the enemy winter quarters, Fox had infiltrated the bustling army lines and noted the regiments, the numbers, the strength and the morale of the men. He had noted the numbers of infantry and of cavalry. Names of officers, even. Details of the guns they were limbering into place, stock piles of cannon balls and chain shot.

He learned which roads were being prepared and where bridges had been strengthened and advanced observation posts set up. In short, Fox knew the probable line of the spring advance the enemy armies intended to take. Invaluable information.

He revelled in the threat and the danger of finding out secrets.

It might be a man calling up to a girl in a window, cancelling a meeting the next day. It might be a brawl in a tavern when men said too much; it might be the look of a field after troops have passed through it. It might be the brushwood concealing heavy cannons, the glint of early sunlight on the polished brass helmets of the enemy hiding in the shadow of a forest. Too much movement in a market, too little movement on the roads, all told their story to a trained eye and Fox could read the signs better than most.

In the occupied town Fox sat in bars and brothels, in canteens and near the parade ground. He walked with a crutch through the streets, as a soldier wounded in the name of the Catholic princes. He begged for bread which was all a wounded soldier could do. As often as not he sat quietly supping a free ale or a bowl of soup and appeared to take no heed of anyone.

He listened to officers boasting about their exploits during the last season of campaigning. They talked carelessly. Giving away names, the disposition of troops, and the number of wounded the morale of the cavalry. Who took notice of a man hunched over a bowl of thin soup stolen or begged from the suttlers' line? No one noticed Fox if he didn't want to be noticed.

And all the time Fox was hearing the cries of girls, the sobbing women and seeing terrible destruction by an army of occupation. Civilians terrorised, husbands killed for a look, mothers raped in front of their own children. Houses destroyed, children orphaned, a young and lovely girl, naked, surrounded by laughing soldiers. He walked away and heard her first scream.

At one time he would have shrugged it off as a hazard of war. Now Fox was not so easy with it. He heard Shea, 'Listen to the voice inside you, friend.'

What was certain was that the armies were going to settle into winter quarters and wherever they settled, the towns would suffer. Bars and brothels would appear on the most respectable streets. The officers had the use of the best of them and the soldiers made do with the camp followers and whoever the suttlers provided.

Fox took three days and then left the town as the light faded and rejoined Morgan and Betz who were waiting hidden in the ruins of old brickworks on the edge of the forest that covered the hills beyond the bridge. There they waited and watched.

Eventually they saw what Fox had been hoping for. Two men leading a string of cavalry horses heading into the hills along tracks that climbed into the mountain chain.

'We'll follow.' he said and the three men headed back into the foothills beyond the edge of the river valley. In the night it began to rain again. It rained for the five days the three men followed the strings of horses away from the enemy line and up into the dark hills.

The men were bringing strings of horses to the protection of the remote mountains where Fox and the others now lay watching from the rim of the valley.

The heavy horses used for hauling guns across country, smaller mounts for the cavalry and even a few fine looking horses for the officers were to be hidden in the valley below them.

Without fresh horses no modern army could move. These remounts would be well rested, fed on pasture and on the hay in the barns on the other side of the valley. They would be ready for action when the spring offensive began.

Fox and his team had followed on foot at a distance. Fox and Morgan revelled in the landscape, Betz never stopped grumbling.

Fox, Morgan and Betz could now look down onto the long wide valley with a stream running through it and beyond the stream a farmhouse and rows of barns. Two hundred or more horses were already behind paddock bars and as they watched two more trains of horses joined them.

The snow would come soon if Fox had gauged the weather right. A nagging plan was forming in Fox's mind.

A wolf howled. A sound that pricked the hairs on Fox's neck even now. The wolf howled again and then there was silence. The line of silver on the crags behind him began to grow. Dawn.

A hawk flew and vanished into the mist shrouding the lower slopes. When the mist had gone, every move they made would have to be made with care.

Morgan had climbed easily up the lower slopes and into the jumble of scree and rocks to their perch over the valley. Betz grumbled and moaned. He wasn't used to hills in Holland. He was a cavalry man not a bloody footslogger.

Nearly on the snow line the three men lay in the shadow of an old, ruined fortress

Fox wanted to create mischief amongst the enemy if he could get down to the horses unseen.

Over the steep grey slabs of granite rocks on the far side, the track wound alongside the fast moving stream and together slid into a narrow gorge which was the only way in or out of the valley.

The rain continued.

It had been raining for days and Fox knew that the other two had had enough. It was time to move out. The sound of that girl screaming, then her sobs, then silence and then soldiers mocking her depressed him.

He wiped the rain from his face. Now it was time to go home. But first a little mischief.

Tumbled stones from the old fort had found a new use in the farmhouse built against the rock on the other side of the stream. The three watchers could just see the house and the row of barns filled with hay and fodder for the harsh winter. The house was well concealed. It was built with a steeply sloping slate roof as were the outbuildings around the courtyard. The boundary walls for the pastures up at the other end of the valley were built from a mixture of cut stones from the old fort and the jumble of grey rocks littering the valley floor. The entrances to the paddocks were blocked by simple pine poles.

Behind these poles two hundred and fifty horses grazed on the last of the autumn pasture. More had joined them each day.

The three watching men could feel the cold seeping into their bones. Fox insisted they stayed watching the farm for one more night. He had one more thing to do.

Nothing moved down the valley near the outhouses and the

courtyard of the farmhouse. It seemed deserted but there had been a glimmer of light in one room. The woman was still there.

It was Betz who had seen her come out of the farmhouse. She had been silhouetted in the lamp light from the room. The three men watched her feed her hens and a pig in its sty near the midden. There was no sign of any man living there.

'She's on her own, Fox. A woman on her own will have a cold bed. We could warm her up first, eh?'

Betz giggled at the idea. Fox said nothing. It wasn't that he cared that much about what this fool wanted to do to the woman. None of them had seen a woman for weeks so that was understandable. A trophy of war, by any standards. It wasn't that.

The value of intelligence was that you knew and the enemy never knew how much you knew. It could be the difference between victory and defeat.

The Welshman was curled up in his cloak. Morgan understood it. Not as well as Shea had. But Shea was dead in a gully a long way up country and his bones picked white by buzzards and foxes by now.

Fox shut his eyes and wiped the rain away from his face.

'We're not going to touch her.' he said and Betz cut in angrily.

'We could have a night in the dry. And she's there for the picking, Sergeant. Or are you afraid of a woman?'

Even as he said the words he felt fear stir. He stared in Fox's eyes and saw nothing.

He looked away then and saw Morgan watching from under his cloak.

'You're a bigger fool than I thought,' said Morgan.

Fox hardly looked at the angry Dutchman.

'We could share her. Why not Fox?'

Fox spat on the ground at the Dutchman's feet.

'No,' he said. 'We'll deny the enemy the use of their horses. Then we're away. Before the snow comes.'

The Dutch man was about to argue again.

'You heard the sergeant.' The Welsh accent was strong when Morgan was angry and at the moment he had had enough of the miserable grumbling old sweat.

Betz shrugged and turned away, looking in vain for shelter amongst the tumbled stones. Below them the stream was gathering force as the rain poured into it and in the morning the rain was still falling.

Fox wanted Shea beside him

'Follow your senses,' he used to say. 'The only thing my ma left me was that. Shea, she'd say, if something breathes or whispers a feeling, a hint in the back of your mind, listen to it.'

Fox could hear a distant whisper even now.

Morgan watched him. 'Deny them their horses, Sarge? How?'

Fox grinned then and slithered away from the crest of the hill and stared down across the valley to the track down to the farmhouse. The early morning light was pale and slanting through the rain.

He trusted the little Welshman lying tight-coiled under his old cloak. Not the other though. He turned and stared down across the beautiful valley towards the farmhouse.

A door opened and a woman came out with a child. They were both tiny distant figures scattering food for the chickens.

Where the track came out of a narrow gulley came a flicker of movement. Fox counted five men riding at ease along the valley towards them with a string of twenty or more horses.

The horsemen greeted the woman. A mountain dog leaped up to the leading man barking eagerly. He pushed the dog aside and kissed the woman. They went into the farmhouse.

The others moved down into the fields and let their string of horses join the others. The man came out of the farm house, embraced the woman, ruffled the hair of the boy who stood with her and led the men out of the yard. They were obviously impatient to be off.

Fox slithered down into cover and waited for the others to join him.

Betz was grinning.

'It's easy. One woman and a kid,' he muttered and added, in his native tongue, '*Een vrouw en een kind*'

Fox shook his head. 'You don't learn do you? We came to get information not to tell the enemy we've been here. They must have no idea we've been here.'

'She can tell us who the men are, she'll know what they plan. Bound to do. One of theirs – you saw her and that soldier. All warm and friendly. I say we take her with us and the remounts. Or are you too frit for that?'

Morgan was whittling a piece of wood and whistling quietly

xvi

and tunelessly.

He looked across at Fox.

'Oh yes, and how d'you propose running over two hundred horses across enemy-held land?' asked Morgan. 'Prick!'

Fox looked up into the sky. The rain was easing off. There was a line of pale sky against the mountains where the clouds had lifted

'We know they're planning to come this way when they advance. We know it'll be after the winter now. They won't be back.'

'How the hell d'you know that?' argued the Dutchman.

'Look up. The sky. See – there's snow coming and this pass will be closed in two days. It's cold enough.'

Betz was furious.

Fox ignored him

'We wait for night-time and then we go down to the paddocks and we open them. We lead out two or three of the remounts and the rest will follow down the valley. It will look as if they made a mistake. They'll have lost two hundred and more horses all because they didn't fix the fences properly. No sign of us and no sign of the remounts either. And we get out of these mountains before the snow makes the going impossible. They can't restock before the snow comes. Back at their headquarters they won't even know the horses have gone,'

Betz said nothing. Morgan carefully stared over the edge between the stones. Fox joined him.

'We have to cross the stream and then come up the track where it passes by the first paddock. You open the gate there. It's a long way from the farmhouse and the dog worries me.'

Morgan grinned. 'I'll fix the dog. Leave it with me. I'm good with dogs. You got any of that rabbit left from the other night?'

Fox nodded.

'I'll use that. You'll see.'

'Not a sound, though.'

'Not a sound. And no sign neither. The river will take him.'

'So why wait?' the Dutch cavalry man asked. He was not happy. 'If there's snow coming we should get on our way.'

'We move down tonight. You open the third stockade and I'll take the one near the house. As soon as you get to your target open the gate and take out a horse to get them going. Then through the gorge and head across country for home.'

'In the dark? How are we to get off the mountain in the dark?'

'You frit of the dark are you?' Morgan asked, mocking the big man. 'Just follow me and you'll be safe enough.'

Fox leaned closer to the Dutchman. 'You do understand what happens down there has to look like an accident? Their carelessness.'

Clouds began to mount up against the distant peaks.

The wind began to carry flurries of sleet. Fox could almost smell the snow. An owl lifted over the scree, vole hunting.

Shadows chased across the rocks turning the mountains yellow and purple. As the last of the light was going, Fox saw Morgan for a moment as he crossed the stream. He vanished then slithered below the ridge line and joined them. He took his cloak and used it to dry his face and legs.

'Bloody cold, that water,' he said.

'The dog?' asked Betz

'Dead,' grinned the little Welshman, 'And in the river. Big animal. Seemed sad really. Simple rope ties on the gates.'

The moon flooded the valley with pale light then gathering snow clouds covered the moon.

Fox looked at the two men.

'Ready?'

Betz laid his sword on the rock with his cavalry cloak. Morgan was ready. Fox checked that the long knife that had once been Shea's was slung on his back.

'You know your target – once you get to the paddock, get in amongst the horses and get them moving. Then back up here and away.'

They crossed the stream, split up and headed for the paddocks. The horses were vague shadows in the dark; Fox lifted the first pole and slipped into the restless herd. They were edgy, spooked by the racing clouds and afraid of this new man amongst them. Fox slapped the horse nearest the entrance and slapped it again, took Shea's knife and pricked the animal in the rear quarter. It kicked out and raced for the entrance and as it moved the others began to flood after it with gathering speed.

The horses from the paddock down the line where Morgan had his work to do were already streaming along the track. One of the bolder ones crossed the stream and others followed running along the far bank, jostling each other and snorting as they ran.

Morgan came grinning out of the dark and watched them go.

'Where's that bloody Dutchman?' he asked. His paddock was still full of animals, crowding against the fence poles, eager to run.

Fox cursed and, using the dark shadow of the cliff wall as cover, moved with Morgan to the entrance of the last paddock, hauled the pole aside and stepped back as the horses raced after the others. There was no sign of the Dutchman.

They heard the woman scream.

'The bastard!'

Fox turned then and ran. The scream was cut short.

The door of the farmhouse was open and light from the fire and from a single lantern glowed out onto the yard. Chickens scattered. Fox stepped into the room and saw the woman crouched against the bed that was tucked into the wall like a crib.

Standing over her was the Dutchman.

As Fox came into the room the man leaned forward and ripped the dress off the woman in a single savage tear. She tried to cover herself.

'Get away from her, Betz'.

'*Loop naar de hel*, go to hell' said the Dutchman without looking round.

'Get away from her. You had a job to do.'

'Fuck off, Fox this is mine. You can have her when I'm done with her.'

He leaned down and slapped the woman hard across her face.

'You'll do as you're told, you foreign *hoer*.'

He shoved her back onto the bed and stepped in close, unbuckling his breeches and holding her by her throat. She was helpless.

The woman had her arms back against the blanket and pillows. Surrendering. She watched the Dutchman as he shoved closer. Then she pulled her hand from under the blanket and drove the knife she had hidden there straight into the Betz's right eye.

He reeled away from her screaming and plucking at the handle sticking out of his socket. Fox watched then as she pulled herself slowly away from the bed. The Dutchman crashed to the floor as she pulled the blanket around her and stared down at the writhing figure.

Fox was surprised at how little blood there was. The plucking fingers round the haft of the knife stopped. The body arched up and slackened.

The woman stared at Fox then. She waited.

Morgan stepped into the room. He hardly looked at the dead Dutchman. In his arms he held the bloody body of her child. The woman screamed, then. A howling feral scream. She snatched the dead child and held him close.

Morgan stepped past the woman to some pegs driven into the wall from which hung two saddles and bridles.

'I kept two horses back, Sergeant. In case we might need them'

Fox nodded. He hadn't taken his eyes off the woman .

'Get him out of here. Under the midden would be best. The right place for him. She won't see him there.'

'And her?'

'No one will be coming back up the track till spring. Too late then for them to do anything.'

'We could kill her, Sarge'

'No' said Fox. 'No point.'

For a moment he thought of Alison at the end of the track up to the Devil's Chair on the Long Mynd in Shropshire. It was a May morning and a blackbird was singing his heart out. She had turned and walked away from him between the hawthorn hedges.

Before him was the naked woman cradling her bloody dead child. He pointed at Betz's body.

'That carrion , lose it' he snarled at Morgan.

Morgan stooped and dragged the soldier out into the dark yard.

Fox stared at the naked woman.

'*Glaubst du an Gott glauben*?' she asked him. Fox wasn't prepared for that.

'Do you believe in God?' she repeated.

He remembered the German he had learned.

'Perhaps,' he said.

'I do – my child will.'

Fox looked around and could see no child. Only a body.

'Here,' she said and touched her belly. 'He will believe in God and he will believe in vengeance. One day. Before that day I curse you and yours. You have a woman? A loved one?'

Fox put up his hand to ward off the hate in her eyes.

'Each time you are with her – remember this.'

And she spat at him.

Fox left her, picked up the saddles and the bridles and stepped out of the warm room into the sheeting rain and the dark, running clouds. Morgan walked away from the midden wiping the blade and his hands on his jerkin. He took the bridles and saddled up the horses.

The rain had turned to snow. By evening the farmhouse would be completely cut off.

The two men made a slow journey out of the mountains, down the broken land and over old meadows, walking beside their horses as the wind pulled and tugged at their clothes. No armies moved now. No screaming hoards of men attacked villages and towns, no bayonets sliced into gut, no women were raped and slaughtered, no children orphaned. Nature held all that at bay for the season. Its time would come again when the land was not locked down by cold.

In the shelter of a dark forest, Fox and Morgan crouched by a small fire and tried to sleep. A hunting owl smoothed across the snowfields looking for slaughter. Blood spilled onto the snow. It was a desolate time in a desolate land. Nature never abandons killing. It's the way of things.

It was time for Fox to go home.

CHAPTER 1

Rumour filled the air in the tag end of 1642. Armies were moved into winter quarters in Oxford and London. Lord Essex had suffered a defeat at the hands of Prince Rupert at Edge Hill and was licking his wounds. Queen Henrietta had left her beloved little husband Charles and gone to Europe.

Autumn in the narrow London street was as busy as ever. The steel grey of the sky visible between the gables, pitched roofs, steeples and scaffolding-clad houses was a hint of the cold to come.

Women, carrying baskets of fresh fish up from the rickety quays on the edge of the Thames, hurried away from the muddy banks of the river and up the steps towards the markets.

Men drove laden donkeys with panniers piled with cabbages from the gardens across the river beyond the cherry orchards. Boys raced up the filthy cobbles, stole fruit from the stalls near the market, mocked the angry shopkeepers and went their ways, laughing.

The sun was barely up but the city was coming to life and the markets were busy.

Servants shoved through the crowded streets looking for fresh meat, fish and vegetables for their masters' tables. London may have an angry Parliament and be rife with rumour and gossip about the Royalist armies coming to take London, but life went on.

The stubborn King had moved his court to Oxford where he could appear to command his army. Parliament's army had regrouped beyond the city near Turnham Green just down the river. Volunteers, men and women and apprentice boys were fortifying London. And commerce went on.

A rich merchant flanked by servants and guards rode through the thronging streets. A closed carriage was shoved and pushed by laughing boys as its wheels spun on the slick cobbles.

London was loud and pushing. Everything in movement, rich men and poor men, dogs, preachers, mud-covered boys and pretty girls, rakes and whores, horses, midwives, old apple-faced ladies, carriages, soldiers, cattle going to slaughter, donkeys on the move.

A boy carrying a long pole on which were slung naked coney carcasses jostled a figure standing on a corner in the shadows. The boy cursed the hooded figure and ran on through the throngs of women carrying baskets of thyme and lavender, past the girls with posies of sweet-smelling flowers they offered to any passing man.

Under the outstretched arms of cloth merchants showing their wares, the boy with the rabbits hurried on.

A butcher's boy with a necklace of lights and tripes, still steaming, from a freshly killed sheep draped over his shoulders, was running to the pie shop. Bejewelled courtesans and the fur-clad wives of rich merchants, lawyers, motley soldiers looking for a friend, a woman or a drink, letter writers carrying their boxes of inks and sheaves of pens heading to the law courts where work was to be had writing briefs and letters and affidavits, girls hanging bedding out over the heads of the mob, yelling at each other as girls do.

And over it all the rich hum of a city waking to an autumn morning when the Council was in the Parliament House, and the King was in his Oxford parlour without his beloved French wife who'd left to raise support for her little husband. They could count their true friends in London on the ringed fingers of one hand.

The city was in turmoil. The apprentices were busy creating earthworks to protect the city. They hauled and carried boulders and rocks, pulled down walls and made them even taller and built a perfect protection behind which musketeers and bowmen could fire on any attacking force.

Women dug ditches to slow down cavalry and when not building defences, young men, carters and porters, cooks and coachmen, pot boys and candle makers, scriveners and butcher boys were learning military skills under the eyes of professional soldiers and mercenaries. They were in a hurry. The people of London were determined to keep the King's army and Prince Rupert out of the City.

It was such an autumn.

CHAPTER 2

In a corner opposite an insignificant watchmaker's shop, the hooded figure stood quite still in shadow watching the thronging crowds rising like a tide up the street past an old bookshop, a furrier's store, a spice merchant's emporium, then the watchmaker's shop. It was to the shop that the watching figure's eyes came back time and again.

Two men rushed past her. She did not move. A small and very dirty child came close and, looking up, whispered something to the watching woman. She nodded, crouched down, put an arm round the green-eyed child and hugged her.

Hidden by her own body she gave the child a scrap of paper which she instantly hid in the folds of her ragged jacket. The watcher kissed the child's mud-streaked face and whispered something more to her. The child nodded her understanding, smiled and turned and walked back into the tide of people. The watcher waited. The door to the watchmaker's didn't open.

Upstairs Master Thurloe was surrounded by papers. Pale faced black haired, the spymaster had the look of a man who rarely saw daylight. Small, soft hands steepled in front of his face when he thought. He was suffering from a head cold and his nose dripped.

Strewn across the desk, teetering in tumbling piles on the floor, on the wooden tables against the far wall and even on the window sill where, if he had ever opened the small window, the papers would have been in danger of blowing into the street.

Even now on the unseasonably warm morning Thurloe was rubbing his hands against the cold.

He leaned back and looked at the little man waiting in the doorway to a small landing. His face was small and perpetually worried. His small eyes behind the thick glasses were so pale as to be almost white. His hands were small – soft and sensitive. His dun-coloured coat covered a hunched back as if he was perpetually crouched over a book. He was carrying a quill as if he had forgotten to put it down and in the other hand was a letter that he held out silently to Master Thurloe.

'Well?' asked Thurloe abruptly, annoyed at being disturbed.

'Nothing,' said the little man. 'He writes about his uncle and the fishing on the River Wye. In Herefordshire, is that?'

Thurloe took the letter. 'You're sure it's nothing?' he snapped as he touched the wax seal. It was still warm. The letter had just been resealed.

'Sure as I can be. God knows I've opened enough of his letters to know when he is sending messages and when he is just writing to a relative or a friend about nothing. This is one of these letters. I resealed it. I assure you it can be sent on safely enough, Mister Thurloe.'

The little man looked up much as a dog looks for a bone or a sweetmeat, thought Thurloe.

'In future I see them all before you reseal them. But, Hans, you're doing good work. I'm pleased.'

Hans shrugged.

'I do good work because you pay good money. And because I like the work.' He smiled a dry smile, sniffed and turned to go.

'Do you never wonder what happens when we find something incriminating?'

'Never. Anyone who writes incriminating things in a letter is truly a fool. There is no way such a thing can be safe from hands like mine and eyes like yours.' Thurloe grinned then.

Hans was clearly anxious to leave. 'I will send it on its way then?'

'Do.' Said Thurloe. 'Have you enough work?'

The little forger smiled then. The light from the tiny window glinted on his glasses.

'There are always fools in the world. And the more powerful, the more vain and the more vain, the more foolish they become. There's always work for men like me.' he said as he dipped his head and walked away down the corridor.

Thurloe watched him go back to his small office. Not for the first time he wondered if anything apart from greed drove his master cryptographer.

He realised how little he really knew about him. He would

need to be watched. Never trust any living being, Thurloe thought as he turned back into the room, kicked the smouldering logs in the never-ending fire and shivered again.

'Damn the cold.' he said.

'You should come live with my soldiers,' the man in the shadows sitting in an armchair said as he stood up and walked to the window. Tom Fairfax was taller than the spymaster and looked out of place in this small overheated room. A soldier to his boots, he stared out of the window.

'It's no use looking again. Tom, the girl will come here when she chooses.'

'Damn her eyes, it's not her I want. I want – '

'Fox, I know. We both need him. You have no word?'

'None,' said the soldier. 'She may know. That Irish bitch down there may well know.'

'If she chooses to tell us.'

'We could make her tell us, my friend...'

'You know,' speculated Fairfax, 'I do wonder if we could?'

Fairfax shrugged, turned back to the chair, sat and almost instantly got up again. He peered through the tiny bottle glass panes across the roofs of the city and then down into the hurrying street.

His soldier's eye was still caught by the figure in the shadows. He said nothing. He turned back to Thurloe who was already making notes in his ledgers.

'What news then, Tom?'

'Nothing you don't know, I've no doubt. Essex is sitting with the army and blessing God and good fortune not to have been screwed at Edge Hill. That bastard Rupert is the best general the King has, that's sure. He turned the flank there with as pretty a cavalry feint as was seen on a battlefield. Essex was lucky. It's bad for the men. Bad for morale to be so nearly thrashed.'

'Are they restless?'

'Our men just thank God winter's coming and the end of fighting. They need to rest, train more and be hammered into a real force. This Cromwell may do it. Essex with luck might.'

'And you, Tom? Are you truly party to it? For or against us?'

The soldier looked quietly across the desk at the pale-faced man staring up at him.

'A test?' he asked quietly. 'Are you?'

Thurloe laughed aloud then and shook his head.

'Your wife? Is she well?'

Fairfax noted how this man always deflected an awkward question with one of his own.

'Aye and away from all this, back home where she thinks I should be. She has little stomach for politics and parliaments.'

'For the King and his little wife then?'

Fairfax shrugged and sat down by the fire.

'The Queen?' he asked as he steepled his hands and stared at the paper on his desk. The spymaster for the Parliament side carried secrets by the score. What to tell this blunt soldier?

'Looking for money and for weapons, we think. We don't know exactly. She seems to spend her time at the play house or attending masques. But she is no frivolous wife, this one.'

'Henrietta has history, my friend. She has background. Her mother a Medici. And we know what cut-throat, villainous, treacherous men and women they are. Looking for support from her father's French court and wherever she can find it. From the Pope and all his armies, no doubt. All against the godless English.'

Fairfax smiled wryly. 'She seems to have more balls than our little King then.'

Thurloe nodded. 'D'you have a mind to join her court?'

'Me, in court?' I'm a rough and ready soldier. I have made my choice.'

'For the moment,' said Thurloe. 'Tom – Tom, come on now. We both know everyone is jiggling and jostling for preferment, a place here or a position there. And we know your wife is no rough soldier. She keeps herself to herself in Yorkshire and watches over you like a mother hen. Bluff soldiers need such a woman. You are lucky in her, my friend.'

Thurloe stopped talking, turned over the sheet of paper before him.

'What will this Prince do next? Go to Oxford as the King has ordered him? What?'

Fairfax laughed.

'Rupert's a boy with all the eagerness of youth. If he was me when I was his age he will try to take London. He should be taking up winter quarters. His men will need a rest. But Rupert is eager for glory. It's a serious weakness in a soldier. Like ambition.'

He looked and saw Thurloe writing.

Fairfax shook his head.

'More bloody paper,' he grumbled.

6

He stood again, turned and glanced out of the window once more and picked up a book from the window seat. He grinned as he read the title on the newly-cut page

'John Cruso's Military Instructions for the Cavalry and a Treatise on Modern Warfare'.

Fairfax whistled softly in mocking appreciation.

'Never knew you had designs on a soldier's life, Thurloe. Have you read it?'

'Have you?' countered Thurloe. 'Know your enemy, I thought. Master Cruso is no fool.'

Fairfax turned a page.

'You could do worse,' he said and read from the book.

'Every good commander must have these two grounds for his action – '

Thurloe nodded and took up the quotation from memory –

'– the knowledge of his own forces and wants –'

Fairfax read on, '– knowing that the enemy must have notice thereof and therefore must always be studying for remedies if the enemy should come suddenly upon him.'

They smiled at each other now. Here was something they could agree on.

Thurloe relaxed a little and closed his eyes as if to remember then went on in his piping voice.

'The second is the assurance of the condition and estate of the enemy, his commodities and necessities, his councils and designs . Which is why you need men like Fox at hand, Colonel.'

Fairfax nodded and Thurloe read on

'Thereby begetting divers occasions which afterward may bring forth victories.'

'He's right Mister Thurloe. But men like Fox are rare as hens' teeth, hard to find and harder yet to keep close. They live on a free rein.'

Fairfax tapped the window pane and Thurloe was suddenly irritated again.

'God above, Tom be still will you? You distract me and I have work.'

'Papers!' The contempt in the older man's voice was clear. 'Work!'

'Intelligence,' Thurloe reminded his visitor. 'You'd be nowhere without it.'

He rummaged amongst the papers and extracted a sheet.

'A fair copy only. The original sent on. Read it. It might be important.'

'Unsealing letters, reading them, copying them, sending them on. It's bloody women's work, this.'

They had this argument every time they met.

'We need to know. The men and women who are a danger to the State must not know that we know their intentions. So I provide myself with a forger and a code breaker who knows only the value of money. He opens letters reseals them and no one can tell. What they say does not interest him one spit. So read that letter. It's why we wanted to talk with you and to see if Fox could help us.'

'Why Fox?'

'It needs a man with a grasp of languages, someone who has travelled and someone who can be discreet. And ruthless of course, if necessary. So Tom – is he working for you or not?'

Tom Fairfax shrugged.

'I'm not sure,' he confessed. 'It was the same when we put him in the field in Europe. Sometimes he would go absent, spend time in enemy towns, often alone. Either brave or mad. I don't know. But he always came back with the information we needed. He seems to have gone to ground.'

'Then find him. Bring him to heel. It's important. Read the letter if you please.'

Thurloe was not happy. He waved his thin hand at his visitor who grunted, stared at the letter and then, slowly, began to read.

When he had finished, he read it again and looked at Thurloe.

'Stuff,' he scoffed. 'Hints, rumours and a damned ragbag of conjectures. There's nowt there.'

When he was angry his Yorkshire vowels became more pronounced.

'Is this what you call intelligence? This behind the arras, so secret business you run. This cipher clerk in the back room, these agents about the country stealing letters, passing them to your hands and this cocanapes stuff. Rubbish is all you can find. My wife mislikes the work you do, sir.'

'Ah dear Lady Anne in Yorkshire,' Thurloe smiles like ice. 'Happy you said, to be away from all this. I could well believe her father would have had no liking for me or those with our ideas.'

Thurloe's face was still. His black eyes glittered and only

the slight twitch of a muscle beside his mouth betrayed how angry he was.

'She is a woman with her own mind. Soldiers are what she understands,' Fairfax said, 'And Yorkshire. Home.'

'Her father's opinions don't matter, as he's dead?'

Thurloe was blunt.

'My wife calls herself an orphan in a storm. She thinks the king is a bloody fool, his advisors worse, and the other side equally foolish.'

Thurloe smiled softly.

'Never, ever let her put those thoughts to paper, my friend. Never,' he said, still smiling.

Fairfax stared.

'Do I hear you right, sir? Would your little man in that back room dare to read – would you dare to thieve my wife's private correspondence?'

'If I thought it was necessary I would thieve my own wife's.'

'I'll tell you then that she believes this country is going to hell led by fools on both sides for whom she has nowt but contempt. And she hates what you do. It displeases her that I see your value and that we work together from time to time. Like me or not is not part of it. I am on the army list and will do my duty as a soldier. This is for our country's good, I believe, and for the King to be brought to common sense. Now, if you want to use that against me, try.'

Thurloe had never before seen Fairfax so angry. He was almost spitting with rage.

'Your secrets are safe enough with me in this office. Trust me.'

'I trust no bugger,' said the Colonel and kicked angrily at a smouldering log which had rolled from the hearth. It showered sparks up the chimney.

Thurloe took a moment or two, walked to the sideboard, poured a mug of water and drank it. He had never liked being thwarted nor even questioned. He was used to his own way and was still determined to get it.

'I want Fox in here. I want to talk with him.'

'On the basis of the rumour in this letter. There are always rumours of plots to kill or attack or remove this or that man or woman of importance. Times like this breed saft stories. This soldier – ex soldier – Campton. What is he?'

Fairfax waved the letter he had read.

'He is known to us. A courier for the King and also for his beloved wife.'

'The queen writes often, does she?'

'She has relatives, Colonel Fairfax. I'm sure you know that.

'I know sweet damn all about her save that she is our Queen and the King's wife and not accounted for much but that she puts backbone into him from time to time.'

'She loves him,' said Thurloe dryly. 'Whatever that is worth. And her father in France is a powerful king. She will do all she can to prevent Charles coming to harm.'

'And is to that end secure in Holland?'

Thurloe nodded.

'For the moment. With some of the crown jewels.'

He sighed and steepled his fingers as he watched Colonel Fairfax toss the letter into the jumble of other papers on his desk.

'Fox,' he repeated.

Fairfax stared for a moment into the cheerless face of the spymaster who served the Parliament side against the Royalists.

'Since he came back to England he has had a harsh time.'

Thurloe stirred impatiently.

'I don't give a damn for that. He works for us.'

'Hear me out. He worked for us after his wife was killed.

'Burned I hear. A witch, someone said – murdered, I heard.'

'Yes,' said Fairfax. 'And lost his daughter for a time. He may have had a touch of madness. He killed the man who burned his wife. I know that. Maybe two. Burned them, I heard. When he found his daughter, she was not able to speak. He took her north to someone. My information grows hazy. He is well able to conceal his movements.'

'Which is exactly why we need him?' Thurloe was impatient now.

Fairfax had regained control of his anger. 'D'you have any decent wine here?' he asked.

Thurloe, still impatient, took a bottle from a cupboard and put it with a glass near the soldier.

'Now, tell me what you can, sir.'

Fairfax poured a glass, stared into the red wine, drank it and refilled his glass.

'He has not surfaced since. Nor that girl, the Irish bitch, until yesterday noon. Outside,'

'I know she's outside.' Thurloe nodded.

'Why is she waiting? Watching? Do you know?'

Thurloe shrugged, 'Not yet,' he said.

'As for Fox, you may as well look for a needle in a haystack. And the girl has no love for us nor anyone,' Fairfax said.

'I have a mind to bring her in. She worked with Fox. Talk to her. Persuade her to tell us what she knows of him.'

Fairfax poured another glass of wine and shook his head.

'You try your games on her, you will regret it. I promise you. I also promise you will not find Fox through her if she doesn't wish to tell.'

Thurloe shrugged.

'No one can refuse. There are ways. Why hide him, anyway?'

'Happen she likes him.' Fairfax smiled. 'He was fond of her too, it seemed.' he went on.

'She's a whore of course, and a killer certainly. You know her for what she is, Thurloe. You've used her in the past. I don't believe they travel together any longer. He – he became softer. When he was under my command, we were soldiers, mercenaries together then. You know what that is? It was, no, *is* a bond, Thurloe. Men at arms, brothers in a way. It's not like your world. It's hot, dangerous and you look out one for another. Maybe he marches to a different drum now.'

'Spare me,' Thurloe put up a soft palm to prevent the other going on. 'It would be a favour, Colonel, if you could put the word out for Fox into the grapevine you will know so much better than I. There is money in it for him.'

'There is bugger all in it if you want him to look at that letter and to look over the tales and tittle-tattle there. The sweepings of any barrack room or bar or brothel – gossip about what?'

Fairfax laughed in Thurloe's face and went on.

'A hint that there may be plans afoot? There are plans afoot and we know them for what they are. Plans to kill Essex, Cromwell, my lord this and that, me or you even. I don't listen nor lose a wink of sleep over threats. Meat and drink to me.' He lifted the letter from the others on the desk.

'You'd do best to burn this and forget you ever read it.'

Thurloe smiled and plucked the letter from the soldier's hand.

'I'll be the judge of that, my friend. Put the word out. Tell him you need him. He'll be intrigued. Hook him for me, Tom. Hook him for me – again.'

CHAPTER 3

Across the street the hooded figure still stood patiently in the shadows.

Fairfax looked down from the window over the watchmaker's shop and looked again. The figure was gone.

As he watched, he saw Thurloe's little cryptographer hurry from the watchmaker's shop carrying a small leather satchel. He looked neither to right nor left as he stepped across the gutter running with blood from the butcher's shop and the stinking slops of a hundred pails thrown out of the houses up the cobbled hill.

Fairfax lost sight of him as he turned into a narrow overhanging alley.

'I will do what I can,' he said to Thurloe and walked out in to the autumn chill.

The cryptographer hurried down the narrow alley and across another busy road. He then turned left down towards the river and slipped under an arch into the yard of a lodging house.

He stepped briskly across to a narrow doorway and unlatched it. Then he almost skipped in eagerness up the stairs and along a landing. At the end of the landing was another door. It was ajar.

On the bed was a girl. Green-eyed, smiling a welcome as the little man latched the door and turned eagerly towards her. He threw the leather satchel onto a chair which already held the dark cloak the girl had been wearing. He was eager for her but not so eager that he didn't take off his glasses and lay them carefully beside the bed.

'It's good to see you again, Hans,' said the girl. 'In her voice was a hint of Irishness. Did you bring what I told you?'

He grunted as he tore off his shirt.

'Plenty of stuff – mostly gossip. Nothing.'

'Nothing is nothing in these times, mister. If you live by your wits as I do, you'd know that well enough. Anything that's worrying your Master? Why was that oaf of a soldier there?'

The little man shrugged off his breeches and kicked them across the room.

'They're looking for someone.'

The girl shrugged.

The Dutchman tried to get onto the bed but she sat up suddenly and pushed him away.

'Tell me what was said.'

The naked man stood trying to hang on to his dignity.

'It's hard to hear through the door. I think Thurloe insisted and I know your friend the soldier seemed to think this man'd be hard to find.'

'Who?' she snapped.

'He was called Fox. Does that mean anything to you?'

She shrugged. 'No, What did they say?'

The girl lay back on the pillows and folded her arms across her ample breasts.

'Go on,' she said. 'Then you can do what you have to do.'

'They said – he said, my master said – no. The soldier said that the information they had was too thin.'

'Is it?' she snapped. 'Too thin?'

'It's in a letter from a minor English courtier in Amsterdam. He wrote to his cousin in Somerset or I don't know where – anyway he was writing about the boring life at the court. No one there in The Hague nor in Amsterdam wants much to do with the English courtiers surrounding the Queen, it seems. Henrietta's an embarrassment.'

The girl laughed as he went on.

'She brings her daughter to meet her husband but the Prince of Orange was not expecting his mother-in-law to stay and to go about her business in his state. It's not comfortable for him.'

She shifted in the bed and laughed.

'Go on,' she said.

'No one wants to take sides, but she's a hard woman to like. Petulant and mean, they say. Surrounded by English men who behave as if they were in their own homes. Not liked. The letters make that plain.'

The little man looked eagerly at the naked girl. He was

14

feeling the cold of the upstairs room.

'What else? There must be more,' said the girl. He stepped closer to the bed. She pulled the sheets across her white body and lay back on the pillow. Her auburn hair framed the beauty of her face. The little man was almost crying with anticipation.

'What else?' she repeated.

'He writes all this which is very indiscreet of him. He tells his cousin in England that Her Majesty is bad tempered all the time; they eat poor food and have worse lodgings. The usual domestic stuff everyone writes. She is looking for a market for some jewels, it seems.'

He reached for the naked girl. She shoved his hand away.

'You swore we'd make love.'

She laughed then in his face.

'Love?' she said. '*Love*? No sir! We may make the beast with two backs, but love is not part of our bargain. And you have not yet fulfilled your part of the bargain by any means. What was it in that letter that interested your master?'

The little man sighed. His hand wandered to her breast and she took his hand and bit it hard.

'Later. News first. What lit lights for your master? If you can do no better than this, I may have to inform your master he has a traitor in his employ. Then what would become of you, little Dutchman?'

She began to get out of the bed.

'No, wait... I have more. This courtier wrote about people meeting in secret. A powerful group. Quite small.'

'Why? What was the meeting for?'

'I don't know.'

'How many – their names?'

'Six. I don't know their names. One maybe; Harry Morton. The writer was afraid of him. His temper.'

'Did he describe any of them?'

'Nothing. Harry Morton came from Derbyshire.'

She interrupted him. 'Tell me about Harry Morton'

'Cruel to his wife, it seems. Cruelty seems to be something he enjoys.' The woman nodded and closed her eyes a moment.

'Dark or fair? Tall or short?'

'Dark I think and not of any party. Not part of the old inner circle. Not liked. Except by the Queen, it seems. So a powerful man.'

15

'Indeed. Good, good. And your master was eager for this man Fox, after he read that?'

'No. Before that. When he read about a secret group – then.'

'Good. You've done well. You'd better take your pay, friend. I have fish to fry. So hurry.'

'But you said we'd have a night together.'

'Did I? You're a better forger than lover my little Dutchman. Take your pay and be done. And be silent about our little trade my friend or you'll find yourself with your throat slashed and lolling on the mud flats below the Tower. Understand? But if you continue to work well – who knows what we might do together?'

And she laughed in his face then as he reached for her.

'Maeve,' he said his voice thick with lust.

'Get on with it,' she said. 'I'm losing patience.'

CHAPTER 4

A MENACE OF BIRDS

The heron was quite still in the water, its left leg cocked and drawn almost out of the mud under its grey body. The yellow of the cruel beak held steady, balanced for the kill. The shallow water moved a little and whirled as a fish surfaced, snapped at the dawn rising of the midges and subsided into the brown water. Unerringly, the heron stabbed beyond the still whirling water. The craggy bird lifted his beak out of the water and laid back his black-streaked head. The fish still moved and as the heron lifted his head back yet more and opened his throat the last of the fish was the still moving tail.

In the early morning mist that rolled up the river the heron settled again. The water in which the bird stood was still. Slowly the early morning light shadowed the water and lit it pale rose and grey.

Watching from the cover of the reeds, a tall man crouched and waited with as much patience as the bird. In his right hand he held a line.

He waited. Intent. Watching the bird he could just see through the river mist on the opposite shore. His eyes flickered to where his line lay on the surface. The water beyond rippled a touch and at that instant the man flicked. A slash across the water as the fish took the hook.

For a moment the heron cocked his head and watched the whirling struggles of the impaled fish. Then the bird rose in one easy movement away from the water. His dark wings hung across his body, flapped once and he moved, a dark shape against the elm trees, looking for a quieter fishing ground.

The young salmon broke the surface of the water again, jumped, flickering in the morning light and crashed into the water, jumped again and was drawn steadily towards the man where the water rippled under his feet. He bent, lifted the line and the fish flapped once, then he thwacked its skull with a stone from the riverbank.

The fisherman moved away from the river and into the cover of a small copse of scrub oak trees. He searched his saddlebag for a sack of oats and fed the horse a handful as it stood quietly in the shade. Then, turning away, he crouched to the fire that smouldered between two logs, picked up a small pan and laid it on the heat.

He gutted the fish, filleted it, sprinkled it with oats and laid the fillets on the pan to cook. He sat for a moment reflecting that this was what he had done so often as a young boy. He had often wandered the Levels in the land beyond the Severn, miles from his village home up in Shropshire and the border land between Wales and England. His father had taken a belt to him often to try to stop him wandering. Useless. It had taken Alison, his wife to stop him and she had died.

He checked the fish, flipped it over in the pan and sprinkled it with salt from his saddlebag. He sat and waited. It was patience that ensured he lived, patience and being alert to danger.

He looked across the river to the jetty that was half hidden by tall grasses and brown tufts of bulrushes.

Then he heard the soft sound of a paddle on the water. The man crouched a little and watched as a tiny boat slowly emerged from up river where the village of Brentford stood.

He cursed, went back to the small fire, took the pan off the flames, threw clods of earth on the fire and made sure no smoke rose to betray his hiding place. The fish was cooked.

He crouched quite still watching the boy in the boat as he came to the jetty. He was about 14, thin, poorly dressed, and easy with the boat. He sculled it into the reeds and the boat was hidden. He stepped out of the boat, tied it to the jetty and took up a wicker frame. He also took a metal trident and a net.

'Eeling,' thought the watching man. 'Just as I did when I was a lad.'

As he began to eat his fish he watched as the boy laid the trident and the net on the bank and took three wicker baskets out of the boat. He walked along the edge of the river then stepped into the reeds and began to hunt. He went about the business of laying the eel traps. The silver of the early morning mist was clearing now.

He returned to the boat with three dripping traps he had laid the night before. He was grinning with delight. Writhing yellow and grey eels squirmed in the wicker traps.

The boy took a knife from his belt, tipped an eel from the first trap. Held it down with his foot and cut its head off. The body continued to flay about but already the boy was onto the next. The man counted fifteen.

When the boy had killed them all he went back to the boat and climbed back up the bank with a wet sack. He shoved the eels into it and wiped the blood and slime off his hands and the knife on the grass.

The watcher smiled. The boy took the sack back to the boat and then climbed back up the bank and cast a line into the water.

The sun was warm on the watcher's back. The boy was wasting his time fishing now. It was too late. The early morning rise was done. The salmon would be resting in the dark shadows at the edge of the river in the faster flowing water. Maybe the boy was after something else. A pike perhaps.

Then the boy heard something that alarmed him. He stopped fishing, hauled in his line and crouched in the reeds.

The man knew the sound for what it was. The steady approach of a troop of cavalry men. Below the bend of the river there was a ford and they would cross there. On the far side the watcher saw the boy begin to run towards Brentford. He'd abandoned his eels and the small boat in the reeds and ran for his life.

The troop clattered onto the boy's side of the water. The royalist banner fluttered ahead of them as they rode along the river through the now lifting mist towards the village. They were nothing to do with him. He had no wish to have any more to do with soldiering. He had other work to do.

He drank from his water bottle, buried the fish bones and the ashes, rolled up his cloak and slung across his back his long bladed curved knife.

The cavalry soldiers rode in good order out of the mist towards the Parliament foot soldiers who were barricaded inside the village. They were the front line before Turnham Green where the main army under the command of Lord Essex camped. They were fresh from defeat at Edge Hill. These Parliament men were standing by for the autumn end in fighting. They would not expect an attack by Royalist cavalry now.

. John Fox saddled his horse and watched the troop as it vanished along the lanes and fields towards Brentford.

Brentford commanded a river crossing and so was important. Cow parsley and nettles swayed a little after the horses had gone by.

He shrugged his shoulders and was ready to ride on. These horsemen were not his business. The war was not his business. What could he do against a troop of cavalry men with their banners for the king?

Fox had other fish to fry.

He heard the rattle of gun fire and the thunder of hooves muffled by the rising mist. It wasn't long before it lifted enough for the watcher to see desperate soldiers running for the river bank from the barricaded village. Chased by dragoons, cut down or captured, kneeling asking for mercy, chopped down mercilessly.

Some managed to reach the water and tried to swim across the Thames. Many drowned. Others were shot for sport by the victorious soldiers. Soon they turned from their sport and back into the village.

Fox knew enough of soldiers to know that these had been promised an hour or a day to loot the village they had captured. He could hear them as they began a systematic rampage through the houses.

Still he waited and did nothing. The terrible screaming, the tolling, desperate cacophony of church bells, the crashing of walls and smashed timbers were a chorus of familiar sounds. Then he saw the boy running along the path away from the chaotic noises of pillage.

He spurred his horse towards the ford and into the path of the eel boy who was blinded by fear and panic. He leapt from his horse into the shallow water and held the boy fast.

The boy struggled. 'Let me go,' he yelled, 'Let me go.'

He beat with his fists but slowly gave up and stopped struggling.

'Tell me what you saw,' said the man quietly.

'My sister – they had my sister – what could I do?'

'Run,' said the man. 'No need to die, boy. No need. You did right.'

'They – I saw my sister – she's a baby – they threw her into the water. They laughed and threw her into the water; I'm going back. I'll go and kill – '

'No!' said Fox. 'No, you won't do that. Not yet. They're soldiers and they are mob-handed, boy. There is nothing you can do. It's a sick and sorry business and worse when brother fights brother, father fights son – it's sick.'

The boy stared and saw, to his surprise, that the man had tears in his eyes. Holding the boy he moved back into cover.

'You're crying. Why?'

'Because – because I know what happens next. What's your name, boy?'

'Peter,' said the boy and suddenly turned away and was sick as neatly as a cat. He wiped his face on his sleeve and looked round at the man who was watching him gravely.

'Who are you?'

'Fox – John Fox,' he said.

'I have to go back – my mother – my granddad is there – in there.'

'The soldiers are still there,' said Fox. 'You will wait. We will wait.'

They could hear the sounds of metal on metal, occasional gun shots, screams and the roar of the soldiers and over it all the bell sounded louder and more and more erratic and still it sounded. Then there was a terrible silence. Black smoke began to rise over the village.

'Come,' said Fox. He lifted the boy onto the horse and rode away from the noise and the smoke and round the bend of the river and crossed on the ford and slowly, carefully inched his way back to his camp. He let the boy drop to the ground, tethered his horse, still saddled, in the cover of the trees.

The boy was staring back across the river and seeing the column of smoke spiralling into the sky.

'They promised – the King promised there would be no more fighting. My mother told me that.'

'He can promise what he likes. Soldiers don't listen to kings' when plunder's to be had. They had a reason for coming here and not just plunder. Stay and watch and wait, boy. There is nothing we can do.'

The boy was angry and frightened and wanted to go back to find his family.

'If you go back now the soldiers will take you. They may kill you. Men like that let loose in a town lose all idea of right and wrong. They kill you as soon as spit, boy. They'd kill you for sport.

'Now, we sit fat here and wait. We'll find your mother. Believe me. You'll get a chance later.'

Fox knew he was lying. The soldiers would leave no one unharmed. The boy stared at him and then shook his head.

'You're lying mister, aren't you? I'm not a fool. We had two men go for soldiers from Brentford. Went to France or some such. Foreign anyway.'

'One come back. Jem Harding. He come back. One hand gone. A cutlass took it off. He said he was lucky not to be captured. Said the other side was bad men. English he said, but bad.'

Fox looked at the boy then and saw he was just talking so he didn't have to think.

'Catholic or protestant army?' Fox asked quietly.

'I dunno. Catholic maybe. He said the others were bad men. I don't think he cared what side it was cut his hand off. Nowt to be done, he said. But he didn't stay in Brentford long. Went up London looking for work. Who gives work to an old soldier with one hand, my grandad said? No one, do they? Going for a soldier's a fool's errand, my mother says.'

Fox nodded

'Was she right, mister?'

'She was right, boy. I went for a soldier, lost my wife and my daughter. My wife dead and my daughter – well – needed help after that. Nothing a soldier can offer even his daughter. Rebecca's about your age maybe.'

Tom stared at the man's gaunt face in the shadows of the bushes.

'She alive then?'

'I think so. I hope she is.'

'Then I do hope she is too,' said the boy. He held out his hand and Fox took it. It was a simple, kindly act that moved him.

'What are you, mister?'

'One time sergeant in an army in foreign parts too. I never lost a hand though.'

'You killed a man?'

Fox nods and stares across the river.

'Many?'

'Enough,' said Fox. 'You don't count and you don't talk about it after. It's not easy, son. Never easy.'

He found he was still holding the boy's hand. He looked into the upturned face and tried a smile and the boy let his hand go and lay back on the ground.

'You going to find her? Your daughter?'

'If I can, I am. Yes.'

'A sort of quest. Like King Arthur. My mother told me stories about him and his court at Tintagel. She come from Cornwall when she was a girl, to marry my father. She tells such tales.'

The boy smiled, remembering, 'What did you do in the army?'

'Mostly I went looking for information – where the enemy was hiding, what their plans might be, who was taking command when would they march – where to? Stuff like that. Spying. Mostly alone or with one good friend.'

'Is he still there? Your friend? With the army?'

'No. No, he's not.'

Fox didn't want to talk about the way Shea had died.

'I fish salmon and eels. Dry them with my mother.'

'I saw the traps. I did that when I was a boy in the West Country. I'd run away from my father down to the Somerset Levels. Marsh country – eel country.'

Fox remembered the men and the women on the marshy levels where he'd live in the marshy villages with the hard little men and their web-footed wives.

'I learned to make the traps and set them.'

He remembered the high grey skies and the waving reeds as far as he could see. The brown peaty watercourses and ditches, the high call of the curlew over the secret water world. The booming call of the bittern.

The boy looked away from him. Buried in thought – fear.

Fox was sorry for him. The boy would be changed when he and Fox went across together to see what was left. However much Fox wanted to escape the old life he knew he'd go and look, glean what he could in what he knew would be a shambles, before moving on.

Why had the Royalist cavalry chosen to come this close to London? Surely they should be headed for Oxford and winter quarters? The fighting season was done as near as damn. He'd find the answer if he could and perhaps pass on the information when he had the chance.

CHAPTER 5

Fox leaned back against the bole of a stunted oak. Across the river he could still hear soldiers yelling, doors being shattered, windows and bottles smashed. The boy lay wide eyed, listening.

'You took salmon and eels then?'

Fox was quietly whittling a stick as if nothing was happening. The boy nodded.

'Nets or traps?'

'Both,' said the boy. 'I never used but proper nets. No ericks – not allowed for they take all the fry and young of eels and salmon and round here no one likes that. When the salmon run I sometimes take out my grandpa's fish spear and try that.'

'Fish spear? I never used one.'

'Not for eels. Only for salmon really.'

'Your grandpa taught you?'

'Yes. He's too old now. He lives alongside us though. We sit him outside when the sun comes up. He likes to see the river.'

'Old men have old habits, boy. T'will come to all on us, no doubt. This spear, was it wood or iron?'

'Iron,' said the boy. 'Two prongs with barbs to stop the fish sliding off once speared. It's better sport than netting.'

'Your father?' asked Fox and the boy looked away and shrugged.

'Gone away,' he said quietly. 'My mother said he had wandering feet. I dunno. I never hardly knew him. My sister knew him. She misses him more than me. Knowing him like she did.'

'Not easy having no father. Women have a hard row to hoe, boy.'

He stopped whittling the stick and put it aside. The noise from across the river was more confused and even louder now.

'Wait,' Fox whispered.' Be still, boy. Patience is a hard game, boy but be still. Listen. Wait and listen. We'll go soon enough.'

'You'll come too?'

Across the river towards the tall elms that stood along the bank two herons swept across the brown water, turned upwards and feathered back their huge wings, thrust out their long legs and settled into the piles of sticks where they nested, brought up young and now settled, half-camouflaged by leaves that were showing hints of autumn colours. Another bird dropped out of the trees and swept along the river, its bony breast just clearing the water. Hunting.

CHAPTER 6

It was in the heat of the forenoon that a boat put out from the far bank There were four soldiers rowing and a fifth was paying out rope. The boy slept in the shade.

Fox watched as the men hauled the rope across and then strained as the rope became chain. Concealed in the bushes along the edge of the river, he knew why.

Thirty minutes later, three barges lumbered round the long sweeping bend past Richmond and the salmon curing racks near Isleworth Church towards the flat land where the old abbey had stood and where Syon House glinted in the sun on the Brentford bank.

It was only when they rounded the bend that the bargemen would hear the din from Brentford. Too late to stop and turn the unwieldy craft. They'd have to run past as best they could.

Fox could see a number of small cannon chained to the decks and beside them were piled round shot and chain. In the holds would be powder and more shot. Essential stores for the Parliament armies.

These heavily loaded barges were the real target for the cavalry squadron that was even now raping Brentford. Fox glanced across at the boy who was awake now. He put his finger to his lips.

They could hear the curses of the oarsmen as the barges passed. They had heard the screams and the clatter of battle on the left bank. They oarsmen tried desperately to steer across the river to the shelter of the far bank. On the Brentford side musketeers waited until the first of the barges hit the submerged chain across the water. The first barge slewed across the track of the next and the third tried to stop but could not. It was chaos, and then the Royalist troop on the river bank opened fire. One lucky shot hit the powder in the leading barge. The explosion roared out across the wreckage of the barges and flung dead and dying crewmen into the water. It whipped the trees and bushes and debris from the barges fell where Fox and the boy lay. Then they heard the screaming as wounded bargees tried to swim for safety. On the Brentford bank the musketeers reloaded and fired again and again at the desperate men in the water. The Thames ran red for a moment, and then the noise died away.

Fox heard the cheers of the cavalry men. They had denied the defenders of London vital munitions. He grinned slightly at the thought of Tom Fairfax's language when he heard.

In Brentford the bell continued to toll erratically.

Fox sat close to the shivering boy. Nothing he could say would prepare a fourteen-year old boy for what they would soon find.

Beyond them, in the thicket, a blackbird began to sing.

It was three hours later that the officers restored order into their men and formed them up to ride away.

Out of habit Fox counted the number of troopers and officers, noted the colours they wore and the images on their standard.

They watched as the cavalry troop rode away from the burning village clattering through the ruin, laughing and boasting as soldiers do. Some lifted bottles of wine and drank in mockery, at the bodies they left along the river bank. Someone began to sing and the officers made no attempt to stop them as they rode away.

Peter suddenly got to his feet, ran along the bank back to the old Roman ford and splashed across the river.

Fox led his horse after him. He had no wish to see what those soldiers had done. It would be no more nor less than he had seen before. All he wanted was to go north into Derbyshire to find his daughter, Rebecca. He had left her there in the gentle care of a woman who had once sheltered him.

He stood a moment in the swirling shallows and looked down the river to the peaceful curving stretch of the river and then he looked towards London and saw the jagged ruins of the village and the bodies of men and women stretched out along the bank where they had been chopped down mercilessly.

He wanted so much to talk to Alison.

Revenge had been a cold pudding as she would have told

him.

The flat black flight of a cormorant whipped across the water and distracted Fox. He looked up into the afternoon sky which was the wiped out colour of a blackbird's egg.

He led his horse out of the shallows. The boy would need help and maybe Fox could see to that. Now he had a small mission before heading north to the Derbyshire house where he had left his daughter.

The boy ran towards the smoke and flames. He disappeared behind the walls of the first house, on the edge of the village. A dark pillar of smoke rose in the middle of the cluster of houses

Fox led his horse into an old byre surrounded by a small clump of trees on the outskirts of the village.

He had passed two men with shattered heads and a half naked woman with her throat cut. He looked away and saw, beyond the walls of a house, the wooden door hanging on its hinges, smashed.

He stepped inside, stared round at the shattered home. Pottery plates smashed, glasses shattered, lamps and bowls thrown against walls, a table upended and an old man lying under the heavy rough chest with his face a bloody mess. Nothing moved.

Fox reached over his back and took the long-bladed knife that was always there. A legacy of Shea who had died in silence so long ago to protect him.

He moved quickly now from house to house, smashed doorway to smashed doorway. A small shop was a chaos of fruit and wine bottles, a cask in the corner staved in, vinegar running onto the ground to join the blood of the dead girl whose body covered that of a dead child. She too, was naked.

Fox stepped into the square in front of the church, and breathed in the stench of death, fresh blood and eye-watering smoke.

Raped towns are dangerous places for a stranger. Everyone is the enemy. The soldiers had been given an hour by Prince Rupert destroy, steal, rape and slaughter as they wanted.

Five bodies lay on the edge of the square and already there were dogs snuffling and tearing at them. A cat dragged a trail of bloody offal into a corner and began to eat.

Fox stepped into the church and in the debris, a man knelt before the altar. Fox walked down the aisle. The soldiers had left the windows unbroken and the light shafted through in yellow and green slanting arrows leaving crimson pools on the slabs of rough stone.

The priest was praying. As Fox came closer he stopped, looked round and held out his arms in surrender.

'Kill me too. If you're a merciful man, kill me too.'

Fox shook his head and crouched down by the old man.

'The killing is done with,' he said gently.

'They showed no mercy, none. They laughed in my face when I told them what sinners they were. They told me to pray. They killed so many helpless... They refused to leave our cattle, our stores.'

'Yes,' said Fox. 'And you have work to do, priest.'

'Work, what work? What can I do?'

'Get off your knees,' snapped Fox. He had to make the man understand. 'There are many who will need help. They may have escaped the soldiers but they will need to be told what to do when they come back. They are ruined – in their heads they are beaten. They will need a leader. You, your God – I don't care which but get off your knees, damn you. You must help them begin again. Your duty.'

'How? How can I?'

'Begin by burying the dead. Get the women to clean up the wounded then you can pray if you want to. Just do it for them or God or yourself. Do it.'

He put a hand under the old man's arm and lifted him to his feet. The priest looked into the cold, unflinching mercenary's eyes.

Fox left him and went to search for the boy. He kicked two dogs out of his way as they tore at a carcass. He stepped into the square as a villager with an old cavalry sword, rushed screaming at him. Fox stepped back into a pool of blood, slipped and the man came on at him roaring with anger.

'You bastards, I'll kill you all. You killed my dear wife you bastards.' He lunged and fell, suddenly tangled in a net.

Fox saw the boy hauling as hard as he could on the weighted fishing net, like a Roman gladiator. The man thrashed about like a netted fish and the boy could hardly hold him.

Fox was up and across to the man, blade in his hand.

He turned to the boy.

'Tell him I am not one of those men. I had nothing to do with this. Nothing . If you know him, tell him.'

The boy shouted.

29

'Abel – leave it be. This man is a friend. Let it be.'

Slowly the man stopped struggling. The boy carefully began to untangle him from the net. The man was weeping now.

Gently Peter put an arm round his shoulders.

Fox watched as the man fell to the ground in his grief.

'I know,' Fox said. 'You've never seen such things nor ever want to. You've lost everything. I know that too. I have something for you to do.'

The man looked at him, not understanding.

'There are dead and dying here. Some will need tending, bandages, splints for them. The dead and yes, even your wife, needs to be buried decently. Tell the priest in the church. Tell him you'll help him. They need graves dug and prayers said. Go. Tell him. Go.'

A moment and then the man stood, threw aside the old sword, turned heavily and walked through the dark door of the church.

Fox turned to the boy and put out his hand.

'I owe you, Peter.' They touched hands briefly.

'Have you been to your home?'

The boy shook his head. 'I saw, I saw all this and I dared not. Nothing's moving in our little street. Nothing. There are fires burning in some of the houses down there. I dared not go home. What can I do?'

'Face it. It's never as bad as what you see in your head. Come with me, Peter,' said Fox.

The boy bent and took up the cavalry sword, gathered in his salmon net and nodded that he was ready. Fox grim-faced, made him go in front up the cobbled track from the river towards the cluster of trees behind the church.

The smashed tables, benches, old chairs, curtains, bowls, copper pans, new coils of rope, jugs, bent pewter, cloth, casks of wine still emptying their sour contents across the cobbles, and, apart from the tearing and growling of dogs, no sound.

A huge elm stood over the village and a clump of beech trees loomed beyond the houses.

In the dark shadows along one side of the narrow street they passed doors hanging open, in one doorway a man lay staring sightlessly into the dark house. A cat ran over his body trailing a gleaming piece of offal, leaving a trail of slime and blood. The man didn't move. The boy stared at him for a moment.

'You knew him?' he asked and the boy nodded and looked away.

'He was a good friend of my mother. Always helped her. I liked him. David Ames.'

Fox put out his hand and moved him on.

The two came to the end of the cobbles and the boy stopped. He looked round at Fox,

'Here?'

The boy nodded once and said nothing.

'I'll come with you.'

They stepped into the gloom of the room where a fire smouldered in the hearth. Fox stared about. The boy drew in a breath and Fox looked into the corner of the room and saw a woman lying there. He stepped to her and pulled her dress across her nakedness.

'Who?' he asked the boy. 'Your mother?'

Peter shook his head.

'Your aunt?'

Peter nodded. He looked around wild-eyed and wiped his sleeve across his face to hold back his tears and stared at the closed door beside the fireplace where a log still smouldered.

'Your mother's room?'

Peter nodded.

Fox opened the door and faced a narrow staircase. He went up fast and stepped into what had been a pretty room. A bed by the window was smashed to matchwood. A small table and some lace and a candlestick smashed too.

The boy came up and stood in the doorway. He looked at Fox.

Fox shook his head. The room was empty. Peter came in and looked at the table by the window. He inched closer. Afraid of something. He looked under the table and shook his head.

'What is it, Peter?' asked Fox and as he asked the question they heard something crash downstairs.

Fox, knife in hand, moved fast past the boy and thundered down the wooden stairs. In the room he found an old man crawling across the floor. He was badly wounded. A rough sharpened cavalry sword had taken him below the breast, and the swordsman had twisted it to get it out. The old man would die soon

Fox didn't stop the boy when he rushed to the old man and

took his head in his arms and kissed him. He knelt beside the two and touched the boy gently.

'Easy Peter, easy.'

'Grandfather,' said the old man. 'Don't hurt my boy.'

'I'll look after him, mister. Where's his mother and his sister?'

The old man shut his eyes.

'They took his sister.'

Then the boy moaned his grief and buried his head in the old man's shoulder.

'They killed her, my boy. It was best. They made me watch. Your mother is gone. I made her go. I told her I'd find you, tell you what I could.'

The old man shut his eyes for a moment.

'Gently, old man,' said Fox softly.

'I have to tell him before I die. I'm no fool, mister. Peter, she took something from her room. The cross she had from her family down Carnwald way. She said she'd find you down there. She was afraid to stay, afraid. Find her, Peter, if you can. Down West Carnwald. Padstow mebbe. St Merynn was her village, I mind that. You must too.'

The dying man lifted his hand and put it on the boy's head.

'I got nothing for you, my boy, 'cept my love. Remember that. And do sommat for me, Peter. Find her and take care on her. I do love her and you. And leave me now and go. 'Tis dangerous now for the scavengers will be about soon as the soldiers have gone. They'll come and take what they can glean. They have no more mercy than do soldiers.'

He looked up at Fox.

'Mister – there was an officer. Black haired, pale face rat's eyes, cold. He took my granddaughter. A cruel man. Should you find him and should you have the way of it , kill him. Vermin him. Harry he was called. Go now, Peter. And you mister – guard him, for he's a good boy.'

As he spoke blood welled up into his mouth, he spewed it over his chest and died.

Fox waited in the doorway. Already he saw the flicker of men and women as they came cautiously towards the ruined village. The camp-followers, the scavengers, were here and ready to go about their business. Taking what they could, killing those who survived, stealing trinkets, gold rings, small things left by the soldiers. Another came boldly down the street towards Fox.

Fox hated these feral animals forever in the wake of soldiers. They disgusted him. The man at the end of the street walked towards the body of Ames. He crouched over the dead man and took out a gutting knife. Fox stepped to him, Shea's knife raised and took his hand at the wrist and left him screaming.

Peter stepped out of the house with a small bundle and his fishing net wrapped around the salmon spear. He said nothing. Stared at Fox and waited.

'You done what you had to do?'

The boy nodded.

'One more thing. Will you want to come back here again? Ever?'

The boy stared at him and then shook his head.

'Wait,' said Fox and stepped into the small house.

He was only gone a moment or two before coming out to join the boy. The crackle of fire inside the room drove out a cloud of flies. The flames would hold.

'Best,' he said. 'You can say a prayer if you want.' The boy stared at him and slowly shook his head. He said nothing. Fox nodded and walked down to the riverside and the clumps of trees were he'd left his horse.

They walked to the ford and there Fox washed his hands and the boy washed the blood off his hands and face where he'd kissed his grandfather.

As the two walked slowly away, Fox looked back and saw, up in the village, beyond the church, a new plume of smoke rising over the roofs.

CHAPTER 7

They travelled west together on old drovers' paths and forest tracks avoiding villages and small towns along their way to Bristol. Peter didn't speak.

They rode Fox's horse sometimes but for much of the journey they walked. Fox taught Peter as much as he knew about living off the land and passing through it without leaving a trace.

They were as invisible as ghosts as they trekked across open country. They passed any settlements they came to at night.

From time to time in the distance they saw signs of unrest and war. Troops of irregular soldiers burning crops, harrying farmers and tearing down homesteads. Fox marvelled at the natural skill the boy had in reading the lie of the land. And worried that Peter had not uttered a sound since holding his dying grandfather. Fox had no idea what he was thinking. Peter was burning from the inside and Fox could not think of any way to help.

He had explained that they would travel together as far as Bristol. If Peter was intent on going on south to Cornwall, then he would have to travel alone. Fox was going home. In truth he was going to Bristol for the boy's sake. Fox had friends there and, if the boy was determined to look for his mother down in Cornwall, Fox wanted him to have protection and he knew that in Bristol he could arrange that.

He would turn north then and up the remote border land along the Wye valley and into Shropshire. He was determined to find his daughter at the remote Elizabethan mansion, in the Derbyshire Dales where he had left her in the care and protection of Elizabeth Morton, who had nursed him there through one long winter.

Fox told Peter he could join him if he wanted to but the boy had shrugged and walked on silently.

They passed through forests following ancient drovers' tracks up onto the high plain which folded over the land like billows of cloud. Here had once been vast forests and ancient settlements. Now the land was cropped by sheep and the forest had long been cut and used for houses, fuel and forts.

Some of the land was terraced and strips of poor earth held crops of corn and barley. These terraces stepped above the small hamlets crowded into the sheltering folds of the land below. They lay in parallel lines beneath ancient earthworks that lay on the top of every piece of high land.

The two passed across these uplands without going down into the villages. Fox had his reasons for travelling secretly but above all was his love of being alone in the wild land. It gave him time to think.

They walked steadily and at night, slept where they found shelter. Fox's horse carried all they needed. From time to time if the boy was tired, Fox let him ride. Peter never asked where they were going nor did he ever complain. He was learning all the skills he would need to survive alone in the wild. The way moss grows on one side of trees which give an idea of direction, how to use the lie of a tree to gauge direction also, when it was better to walk low down in the hidden valleys and when to take to the high land, where to find wild food and what to leave alone.

Above all, how to stay out of sight of people. Making shelters from fallen stones or the occasional tree branch covered with bracken if the weather was too harsh to sleep under the stars.

It was always primitive cover that he'd destroy the next day before they set off. Their passage continued to leave no marks. The boy used his net and fishing spear to take small trout from streams and Fox snared small animals and birds from time to time.

Peter was afraid at first to sleep in the hill forts or against the sheltering barrows that dotted the land. They held a primitive power. They passed the remains of the wooden henge near Avebury, and passed quickly away from yapping dogs up onto the higher land.

The close cropped grasses were a sign of sheep passing, driven by men who knew the land better than Fox. The last flock had passed this way only a week before from the signs of hooves and shit along the track.

Headed for Bristol Fox guessed. Or maybe down to

Salisbury market. Peter said nothing but walked steadily to the west.
.

Skylarks flickered up in little leaps and then soared overhead shrieking alarms .It was cold and bright up here and remote from any danger.

They moved on past the city of Salisbury miles in the distance. They tracked across the land, three specks in a vast upland of folding hills. Then the track dipped down, curved around a soft bluff that led into a forest. They moved along the track and came out of the trees into the open as the light began to fade. Ahead a long line of trees marching up from a remote valley, lay directly across their path.

It was almost dark, then they stopped. In the cover of the bushes at the edge of the trees, Fox made a small fire, fed it with dried sheep dung and the small branches they had foraged.

Peter walked towards the sound of running water not far away, taking his fishing net and their water bottles with him.

They ate fresh trout and made themselves comfortable out of the wind. They lay on their old cloaks on the soft turf. The hint of winter coming was growing stronger. Every day the ground felt colder.

Peter sat by the small fire and began to whittle at a long stick he had gathered three days before down in the valley. Fox watched him as he worked. The silent boy made a sharp point on the stick and pushed it into the embers of their fire. He turned it and turned it again and then took it out of the embers. He cut away at the point and again pushed it into the ash and turned it again and again.

'Another fish spear?' asked Fox. The boy stared at him and then took the stick from the fire, plunged its sharpened end into water he had emptied into a horn mug.

'You're hardening it, Peter? Who taught you that? Your grandfather?'

The boy stared at Fox for a moment, nodded and shut his eyes. It was time to talk.

'Your mother escaped that attack. You know that. Your grandfather knew that before he died. You said she was from the West? Is that right Peter?'

The boy nodded reluctantly, after a moment and looked away. A star flew across the bright night sky. The land was silent, then an owl hooted once, and the boy looked across at Fox who was no longer looking at him. He went on for he knew he had the boy's attention.

'Cornwall – some place there? Am I right, Peter?'

He said nothing.

'You and I, boy, are going to Bristol. I have a friend to see and a journey up the river there past my old home. And then north to find someone. My daughter, Rebecca.'

He waited. Peter looked at him.

'I told you before that you can come with me, if you want? No need to say yes or no. Not yet. But if you want to go west down into Cornwall you'll have to go alone. Can you do that?'

The boy lay back and wrapped his cloak around him and stared into the glittering sky. The edge of a sickle moon began to show low across the land below them.

'You think on, Peter and tell me when we get to Bristol. I can find you passage on a small boat down the coast to one of the fishing villages down that way. You know where your mother comes from?'

The boy nodded and said nothing. Fox sighed.

'Maybe, later we can find a way to make you talk again. Maybe?'

The boy shut his eyes. The quarter moon rose a little on its back and its horns were sharp points in the night sky.

Fox had grown fond of the boy and wanted him to speak again but knew healing takes such a long time. He lay back and for a moment had a flash of a woman he remembered. The Irish woman, Maeve, was standing in the shadow of the trees, on the far side of the bowl of soft land where they had lit their fire. He saw her pale face and the flashing green eyes and a mocking half smile, then she was gone.

The next morning before the sun was up, Fox and Peter, leading the horse, stepped through the line of trees. The sun had just tipped over the edge of the land.

The trees were black under the pale yellow light and standing stark, mysterious and tall was a ring of huge, capped stones standing beyond them. Stonehenge, magical, powerful, awesome, bathed in the dawn light.

Fox and the boy stood there and waited a moment, watching the shadows of clouds flying across the faces of the rough cut pillars of stone. High over them in the still dark sky the moon lay pale silver on her back.

The boy looked at Fox and then in wonder at the stones

'Druid stones, Peter,' he said. 'The priests come here secretly out of Wales, across the border and high up here to worship the rising of the sun and the moon. It's a holy place. Christian priests curse it and tell us it's evil. I never believed that. I never met one of those old priests but I never heard they did harm.'

'I knew a woman once who understood their ways and beliefs. She was a wise woman and cured sickness in men and cattle with her simples. Some people, priests and the like, were afraid of her and cast her outside our village. She died too. Killed for a witch by men who called themselves God-fearing men.'

The boy stood on the outer circle under the lintel perched on the top of the huge stones. He took Fox's hand and slowly they walked in to the centre of the circle. Looking up they could see the sun piercing the gap in the distant hill and the light shafting across the dark plain towards them.

Distantly, an owl hooted and choked back its sound as it went in for a kill. A moment later and the single scream told that a rabbit had died under the soft cloud of feathers and the razor claws of the killer.

Time to move on.

Behind them the sun lit up the vast stones capped with their massive lintels. The boy looked back once and shook his head as a dog shakes his head after swimming. Fox laughed then and, clapping the boy on the back, stepped out into the morning light on the soft tussocks of grass and began to whistle.

He had not whistled for months. Not since he had left Rebecca with Elizabeth in Derbyshire to go working for Master Thurloe and Black Tom Fairfax, and to avenge his wife's murder.

The days of spying were done.

CHAPTER 8

A distant bell chimed the hour. It was already dark and the street was empty. Behind closed doors men and women were singing, arguing, eating their supper. Children cried and refused to go to bed, lovers made their usual noises. Across the narrow street the heavy wooden door alongside the small window of the watch mender's shop opened.

Mister Thurloe, heavily wrapped in a cloak and gloves, shivered as he looked into the shadowy street.

A dog walked slowly across the street, down towards the river ferry. Apart from that, nothing moved. The pale-faced man locked the door and, as he turned back into the street, a tall man limped towards him. He was carrying a staff and had the scarred face of an old soldier.

Thurloe stepped away and the tall man settled himself down to guard the door. Thurloe took no chances with the secrets behind the doors upstairs over the watchmaker's.

He walked down the street towards the river. A cat skittered across his path. He stopped and waited. A small, filthy figure stood at the corner. A child, he saw and a girl at that. Her hair in filthy locks uncut, her clothes equally dirty and ragged. She was barefoot and the cloaked man shivered. He moved on down the cobbled street. The girl stepped into his path.

'I got sommat for you mister.'

Thurloe felt for the short dagger he carried under his cloak. 'Yes?' he said and watched her and the shadows behind her. It was sensible to take care.

'She said you'd pay me,' and the girl stared up at him from grave, grey eyes. Under the dirt and grime this was a beautiful child. Not much older than his own daughter.

'Did she now? And what am I paying for?'

'Pay first, see after.'

Her smiled at that and took a small coin and showed it to her. She nodded and handed him a twist of paper.

'She said it was urgent. Come from a connection, she said. I dunno what she meant. She made me learn it,' and she reached for the coin.

He took the twist of paper and flipped the coin to the child. By the time he had untwisted the paper the girl was gone and he was left alone with a message.

He read the paper once then turned away from the river and up past the watchmaker's shop, into the city. He had a man to find urgently.

The two men sat in a room at the top of the stairs in a small inn tucked in a courtyard beyond St. James's Palace. A discreet place for discreet meetings. Lovers, mistresses, secrets could be unravelled here.

'Danger, she says. Danger, she means. But not our business, Mister Thurloe.' Fairfax poured more wine.

'Fox is one of your people. I thought you should know.'

'Why would the Irish girl concern herself?'

'Maybe she's fond. Maybe she wants to protect him. How would I know what a woman does?'

'You're a married man, Thurloe, surely you have an idea.'

Thurloe shrugged

'My wife is not an adventuress, Tom.'

'No, indeed not. I know what my wife would say.'

Thurloe sipped his wine and waited.

'Never trust a whore, she'd say. So, what is there for her in this titbit she's thrown you?'

Thurloe shrugged and began to stand. Fairfax lifted his hand.

'I'm not saying we should not heed her. If our man is in danger then we can but tell him, and he poured another glass. Here. Drink.'

'If we can find him,' Thurloe murmured quietly, sitting down again. 'We want him anyway. He has work to do.'

'If he wants to do it. When he wants to be absent he is absent.'

'As we know to our cost. So now he's a target for someone

– does she say who ?'

He opened out the crumpled paper on the table between them.

'Fox is at risk. There is a contract to kill him,' Fairfax read and crumpled the paper. He sniffed. 'Hazard of his trade. You don't make friends doing what Fox does.'

Thurloe stared at the red wine in his glass and saw blood for a moment. He shook his head.

'It's a lonely business, his trade.'

'Some men like that,' said Tom and drank. 'He was born to it. He understands the dangers. We will only find him when he wants us to find him. That's the fact.'

'So what do we do about the threat to his life?'

'Put the word out with old comrades. There are places in London. The best is an inn at Seven Dials that serves as a post box. I'll get the word put out that there is a message for him from an old comrade. It may get to him. And if the girl comes into sight, tell her what we are doing.'

Thurloe glanced away.

'Her? Was it she sent the message? Are you so sure?'

The young man shrugged and sipped his wine. He drinks like a girl, thought Fairfax.

'God's blood man, was it her? If it's her, it's serious. He's truly lost if she can't find him.'

Thurloe shrugged and dismissed the thought.

'There are other men we could send,' he said.

Fairfax was pouring another glass. He whirled on Thurloe.

'You may think me cold and hard, my friend, but I respect a good soldier and I respect that man above most. He never lied and he never failed me. So, I owe him. If she is the source then I have to take it seriously. Find her too. Tell her I need to speak with her. She too has her ways.'

Thurloe had never seen his companion so concerned. Fairfax was right to think he was seen as a cold-hearted man.

'I want to get to him before this killer finds him. I will do what I can, Thurloe.'

The two men drank their wine and a little later, Thurloe stepped into the courtyard and was given an escort to his home along the river near Cherry Pickers' Gardens.

This part of the city was busy. All around him young men hurried through the silent markets, along the line of the old Roman

41

walls and down towards the Tower. From all sides flares lit the route.

More lights flared over the groups of men and women working to build the defences of the city. Men with hoes and spades, and women with strong baskets, moving stones and wood and mud into position.

Thurloe watched them working with dogged determination. London was prepared to keep the King's army out, come what may.

The King himself had chosen to move his court to Oxford, which hardly made him popular with the people. If Prince Rupert took London, or tried, with the impetuosity of youth, it would do even less for the people's regard for their king.

Like all astute political men, Thurloe was already working out how he could play on both sides in the battle that was unfolding.

He ducked down to the bridge near the Tower, and hurried across it for home.

All around him the noise of the busy citizens as they worked. Some singing, others silently determined as they built barricades of rock and mud and wood.

In the inn, Black Tom Fairfax sat over the bottle and re-read the message before touching the paper to the candle flame. John Fox was on his own.

CHAPTER 9

It was late when they came into Bristol through St John's Gate. The gates inside the archway were shutting. Within the city flares lit up the market stalls and the main shops along the streets leading, eventually, down to the dockside.

The stableman agreed terms with Fox and offered him a glass of brandy and the boy some beer from a cask in the corner. He was anxious for news from the country.

'Sithee master, one gets little enough here just now. People are not coming into Bristol without good reason. They'm frit, to tell the honest truth on it.'

'What are they afraid of?' Fox asked, quietly sipping his drink.

'Not knowing.' said the stableman. 'Listen, this town has come down on the side of the parliament for whatever good that might do. 'Tis all the same for common folk. The council, the aldermen, the lawyers and the rest say that we are parliament men. Not for me to understand. I am no way no bugger's man. I want a quiet life. I seen enough of what it can lead to when I was fighting in Prussia, or Sweden or wherever. You know how it goes, having been a soldier.' Fox nodded.

'Trouble is master, no bugger trusts another. 'Tis the truth that our city governor has the reputation of running with both sides in the matter and when the fighting season begins again he could as soon hand the city over to Prince Rupert and his men as stay with parliament. No one trusts anyone.'

'There's religious mad men and women running wild through the place. Men proclaiming the second coming and others saying Christ will not come to papists and others just plain dog barking mad for God. Add to them people coming in from the

43

country, afraid to stay out because there's already bandits running wild. There's always someone looking for his own gain and if it's a bit of rape and pillage whose going to protect them that suffer? People are afraid and come into the city to be safe. Winter's coming and there's no place to sleep for half of them.'

'Are they any safer?' asked Fox. The old soldier shrugged.

'Bristol's as dangerous a place to be as any city and more than some. Have a care when you leave here and stay on the lighted streets. No short cuts. Stay out of the shadows, my friend.'

He promised to rub the horse down, feed him and take care of the saddle and other tack. Fox took the leather saddle bag and the scabbard in which he kept a Papenheimer cutlass.

Peter had his cloak wrapped around his fishing net slung on his back and he still carried his fishing spear which he had refused to leave behind.

The two left the stables and stepped into the cobbled street. It was a lively, noisy, constantly moving wave of people. Fox looked about him and began to understand what the old soldier had been saying. These were people on the edge, scared, exhilarated and at the same time anxious and confused.

New arrivals carried bundles on their backs and the women were already looking for a roof. Their men had the strained eyes of hunted men. Tempers were frayed and sudden raised voices and sharp slaps told their own tale. Children cried and mothers tried to hush them but they were tired and afraid in the shoving mass.

The smell of cooking reminded the two travellers that they had hardly eaten that day. Fox bought a pie and handed it to the boy. They boy took it and ate without a word.

They pushed their way through the crowds thronging the streets under the smoking flares. The sound of music seeped from a tavern. Men, women and children, like a huge flock of sheep, clattered along the cobbled streets.

Fox stopped for a moment and pointed over the nearest gable roofs to where the dark spikes of masts and the network of rigging indicated the dockside. The smell of pies and cooking began to give way to the smells of cinnamon, cloves and the spices brought by the ships from all over the world.

Down through a narrow alley leading to the quayside, he welcomed the familiar smells of tar and spices, timber, exotic fruits, cordage and rum. Sudden spurts of flame from forges that were still at work providing tackle for the ships. In workshops behind the vast warehouses, the scream of wood saws never ended. Here was a port which even at night was vibrantly alive.

Two girls, arm in arm, stepped into their track and suggested a price. Fox laughed at them and refused and the boy said nothing when one of the girls kissed him and walked away, laughing.

Sailors stepped lively along the cobbles and into the alleys where they might find a bed, a wet and a whore for the night.

Those who'd been paid off couldn't wait to spend it all. They walked with their ditty bags on their shoulders and swaggered into the inns and ale houses along the way.

Here were the sailors, whores, porters, workers, tally men, chippies, riggers, rope makers, pie men, crimpers and the flotsam and jetsam of any busy port.

The boy was amazed by it all. The stink of molasses and the salt smell of curing barrels, the tang of exotic fruits and tobacco leaf, the jumble of marlin spikes and chains, wet weather clothes and boxes and ropes in the chandlers' shop windows and corridors.

Fox strode through it all. He'd done these walks from Brest to Leghorn, from Rotterdam to La Rochelle, from Brittany to Paris and he trusted no one. His eyes flittered endlessly to all points of the compass. From time to time he'd double back up an alley and walk back on his track to emerge a quarter of a mile further on or on a totally different quayside. Anyone following would have been giddy with it.

He kept the walls and windows of the shops on his left leaving his sword arm free. The walked down a long alley where the smells changed again into pine and fresh cut wood – men and boys were hammering metal rims onto half finished barrels inside one of the workshops – the flame of the furnaces and the battering of metal on metal was deafening.

Peter watched, waited and then followed Fox.

Around a corner came a small procession. Women in grey hooded robes, carrying wooden crosses strode through the crowds who parted to let them pass, the women singing a hymn as they walked. Their leader, a tall pale-faced young woman with her hair covered by a black shawl, was not singing.

They stopped at a street corner and the woman turned to her flock and began to talk quickly and quietly to them. People, mostly women, gathered to listen to her. Fox watched as she spoke. Her voice grew stronger with gradually rising force. As she spoke, her shawl fell back to reveal long black hair that came to her shoulders.

Her mouth was full and ripe but it was her eyes that caught the gaze. These were eyes full of passion, full of determination. Blazing eyes. Dark blue, almost black eyes that held the gaze of anyone who happened to catch them. These were the eyes of a fanatic.

She preached of damnation and the Popish whore in Rome. She preached of fear and anger and the coming of the Antichrist to England. People crowded closer to hear her. The group of women at her feet listened in rapt attention. From time to time they raised a hosanna and each time the preacher grew stronger, louder, more angry and eventually she was preaching hate.

Fox stopped in the shadows of a narrow alleyway. The boy watched for a moment then turned away. Fox stopped him.

'Patience,' he said softly. 'Learn something, boy. You see something not quite usual, you watch and wait and sometimes you learn something. It might even save your life one day. Wait now and see.'

The tall woman was preaching hatred of Rome hatred of any other belief but her own. Hers was the severe certainty of the fanatic, a message about suffering and the second coming, About godlessness and the armies of the devil let loose in the world. People pay for their sins. Only faith can save.

Fox leaned down to Peter.

'This is a dangerous woman. She spits hatred. There is no love in her. See her – ice cold.'

Fox was no believer but he waited and watched the woman who went on while some of the youngsters in the crowd began to jeer at her. They were silenced when she looked at them out of her black eyes. They were afraid of her and she knew it.

'Your king on earth says he is appointed by God. He lies. His wife is a whore to the Pope in Rome. They are an abomination to the Lord who will come to the city. We know this is true. He may even already be here. These are terrible times, terrible times. When men will kill brothers, sons kill fathers. These are an abomination to the Lord and he will come to stop this violation. If we don't let him into our hearts then the righteous and the sinner will be flayed in hell with Charles and his whore.'

And as she spoke under the light of the flares along the street, the women again answered her with amen and hosannas. The preacher was about to turn away when she saw Fox watching her. She caught his eye and spoke almost as if to him.

'There are evil men abroad not just in this city where we

shall be loved and blessed by the coming of the good Lord. He will come. He will come and stop the abominations of the Queen, harlot of France and her consort the Pope in Rome. Charles her husband is a part of the war of the Anti Christ and should be abominated.'

One of the women from the group stepped across the street and came to Fox with her hand outstretched.

'A little something for our Lord's work, master?'

Peter was astonished when Fox gave her a coin. The woman in the black shawl had stopped speaking and the crowd was melting away into the shadows. She walked across the cobbles and stood looking into Fox's face.

'You're tired, I see. And anxious. We can help you if you will only hear the word of our Lord.'

Fox shook his head. He had stared into her eyes and saw darkness there. Something heart-wrenching in its loneliness.

He put his hand on her arm and she flinched.

'No harm,' he said as gently as if he was talking to an unbroken pony. 'I am not your man. I have other things I must do.'

She continued to look into his face. Eventually he turned away from her. She smiled then.

'Bless you, son. You could join us if you wanted. You can find us at the crossing by the White Swan and Dog Alley. There is our house. If you want peace, somewhere away from the abominations of the world. Vengeance is the name of our Lord. I see death in your eyes. Death in your heart.'

She pulled her shawl over her hair, turned and the women gathered around her and, lifting their crosses, they walked slowly away singing. No one mocked them any longer. They were soon lost amongst the crowds in the market.

Fox shut his eyes and opened them on a square full of hucksters and noise. Tinkers selling potions, men showing off their skills for hire, women with posies of white heather for luck, knife grinders and sharpeners, women with baskets of vegetables for sale, a fire eater belching gouts of flame, a fiddler tuning up, a drunken man lurching across the square and by a miracle, not hitting anyone, a hurdy-gurdy man playing a merry Italian dance, groups of men with ledgers gathered around their master in his lawyer's robes, two girls no better than they should be making eyes at every man they passed to the irritation of the wives.

Noise, bustle and life vibrating throughout the square, a man shouting after another about a debt he owed, another running with a dead chicken dangling from his hand and a woman chasing him crying, 'Thief!' Children running wild, playing tag, hide and seek or lifting sweetmeats from a stall, shrieks and laughter as they were chased by the angry stallholder while behind his back another child took what she wanted.

Fox put his hand on Peter's shoulder and they stared together about the square. Standing by the market cross was a tall figure in rags with a huge wooden staff. His hair matted about his head and down his back. The boy stopped, watched and listened as the man with blazing eyes in a pale ivory face preached his message.

'He is coming to scourge the ungodly. He will toss you sinners into the pit and scatter the unbelievers and the filth of this city. He will bring the armies of the righteous Lord to tear the sinners limb from limb and the end of the world will be there. You will feel the pincers and the fire, you will cry out and nothing will save you – you are all an abomination. Our Lord will have no mercy on sinners.'

Half a dozen drunks began to shout abuse at the man who leaned on his staff and ranted his faith into the smoking night.

They went on yelling abuse at him and then he lifted up his face and stared at them and they saw madness in the white, sightless eyes and were silent.

Fox shook himself and turned away from the lights. He'd heard this sort of madness before. Women predicting the second coming, men pronouncing the arrival of the new Lord, men and women together beating and scourging themselves in the name of their God.

Fox remembered his home then and the quiet of the simple wooden building were villagers gathered and worshipped in silence. No God had saved his wife from the flames. If these sad women wanted to delude themselves; if this poor man was deranged by his faith. it was nothing to do with Fox. The pale faced girl with the black hair was something else, dangerous. Mad, maybe.

Fox and Peter turned down the street that led back to the quayside and the comfortable smell of rope, tar, old pitch and salt water.

Directly in front of them a cargo ship was unloading timber from the Baltic. It was being winched over the side on a small gantry and lowered to eager hands below. Further up the quayside men and boys rolled barrels away from the side of the quay and straight into a vast dark warehouse. The sour stink of old spilt wine came from the huge open doorways.

At the other end of the jetty, sacks of spices were perched in piles on huge carts ready to be hauled off to the same row of warehouses. All along the dockside men stood with tally sticks checking the depth of grain, of spice or brandy in the kegs and bags and sacks that emerged from the holds of the ships berthed alongside.

In the shadows behind them lurked groups of women who'd swoop on any broken barrel or split sack and scoop up what they could until they were beaten away by the merchants' men.

Under the flickering flares and lamps, men sweated to empty the holds of the ships so that the masters could move their vessels to another berth and wait for morning to begin loading with empty barrels, lengths of sailcloth, spars and cordage for their next trading journey across to the Indies or to the Baltic and the shores of Russia and beyond before the winter ice closed those northern routes.

In some ships the holds were open and the unmistakable stench of rotten flesh and ordure hung over the area. Into the holds of these ships were loaded barrels of glass beads, badly made hatchets, knife blades by the bushel, bottles, wire bangles, copper bangles, kegs of cheap wine, lumps of pig iron, for the African trade.

Here were men of every colour, belief and creed from Africa or the Indies, Asiatics from the Far East and men who were a mix of all races and colours. This was a place where the world met.

They drank and whored and worked together in the unending quest for wealth. Fox watched them and remembered his time working in the wine trade for Alison's uncle. He grinned sourly at the memory. He had been lucky to escape with his life.

He looked round into the alleyway behind them. Nothing moved there but he was suddenly sure he was being watched. Shea used to say, 'Listen to the suspicion and it might save your life one day.' It hadn't saved poor Shea. Fox reached under his cloak and felt his knife.

Nothing moved in the alley.

In front of him a cask swayed and fell out of its sling. The rich smell of rum swept over the alley and by the time he'd blinked, the women were already scooping at the dark golden tide. Laughing sailors and eager women together sopped rags, dresses, old kerchiefs in the liquid and sucked them dry. An old toothless hag cackled as she sucked up the spilt rum.

A woman behind her shoved her aside and like bedlam, in an instant, there were women grunting and hitting out at each other

Fox shoved through knots of men already doing deals under the watchful eye of the merchant trader with his tally stick. And always beside him his most trusted foreman watching everything and everyone. No one would cheat or rob his master or even try.

Huddles of merchants compared trade with friends before moving off to their homes. These men of affairs travelled together for safety against the eagle-eyed crimpers who roamed the streets looking for likely men they could kidnap and hustle onto any ship needing crew.

Market boys were already huddled under the carts trying to sleep. They'd be up early taking fresh produce to the markets. Trade was unending in the port of Bristol. It was a rich city with rich pickings for whoever controlled it,

As far as Peter could see there were masts and spars hanging in the clear sky as the sun finally went down. Gallows-like gantries hung against the night sky dangling their hooks ready to haul the loads off the quay into the upper store rooms.

This was the port of Bristol in the year of our Lord 1642.

As he turned a corner Fox checked, doubled back. The boy dashed after him trying to keep close. An old man sitting on the cobbles watched them, spat a stream of tobacco juice onto the pavement and getting up, walked quickly away into the darkness.

Fox grinned at Peter. 'We're almost there, boy,' he said. 'Hungry?' The boy nodded.

The two of them slipped into a small paved street alongside the inn. Fox kicked aside a pile of rotting cabbages, stepped quickly across the cobbled yard, down a side passage and straight through the back door of the old inn, through another door and along a narrow passage

A serving hatch in the passage was open. Fox looked through it into the back of a large and crowded bar. Men shouted for wine, maids hurried between tables carrying pots of beer, flagons of rough red wine, plates of meat and cheese and bread.

The men pawed some of the girls and were promptly slapped. Others tried to go without paying and were met at the doors by suitably hard-face men, whom Fox knew to be old soldiers. Fox grinned. Patrick Shea still ran a tight ship.

Here was an inn run by one of the few men Fox could trust.

Pat had been a soldier like his brother but then became a suttler for Fairfax's command and made and kept enough to get out and buy this place.

A huge hand clamped Fox's shoulder and spun him round. Peter kicked the big man hard and he spun about to deal with the lad who threatened him with his fish spear. The huge man began to roar with laughter at the sight of this angry boy.

'Peter – Peter it's alright – Pat's a friend,' Fox yelled. 'Don't do that.'

The boy looked from one to the other and was only reassured when the two men hugged each other. He lowered his fish spear. The huge publican tousled Peter's hair affectionately as Fox grinned.

'You did well, boy. But back off now, back off. Meet Patrick Shea as good a friend as a man could have.'

The huge old soldier held out his hand to the lad and reluctantly the boy extended his and they shook.

'Peter, that your name, boy?'

'He doesn't choose to speak. I have hopes, but he has good reason, Pat.'

The innkeeper called through the hatch to a pot boy, 'Wine and a plate of bread and cheese and meat and some of that chicken pie – and quick about it. In the snug and no one to bother me there. Tell my wife.'

They walked into the inner snug bar and Shea kicked the old oak door shut. Fox looked quickly about the small room. The dark settle near the fire, the window behind it shuttered against the cold. A table in the corner and another carved oak chair where Fox knew his old friend did the accounts each day. He was a careful man was Shea and the habits of a suttler die hard.

Shea laughed as he watched Fox.

'Old habits die hard, my friend,' he said as Fox continued to check the room.

'And them as forget die young,' retorted Fox noting the one door into the room as he sat on the settle with his back to the fire and facing the door. Shea laughed again. The boy inched to the fire to warm himself.

There was a knock on the door and Shea opened it for the merriest faced serving girl to flounce into the room with a tray of food and drink and behind her the pot boy with a bottle which he put on the table.

'Get out, boy.' Shea said, and the pot boy left.

Shea put his arm round the merry-faced girl.

'My wife.' he said proudly and she smiled. 'This is my oldest friend, John Fox. Trust him,' he said.

'And this lad would have killed me when he thought I was attacking my friend here. So trust him as well.'

The young woman nodded and smiled at Peter.

'Get some ale down you, boy and eat. You look like we should've brought a sheep. But eat and drink and welcome to our inn,' she said, and left closing the door quietly.

Fox leaned back against the wooden panels behind the settle. His Papenheimer rapier was in its scabbard leaning by his side and Shea's old knife lay on the table.

Patrick shook his head at Fox.

'God's teeth, but you're a suspicious sod,' he said. 'For ever on the watch.'

'I am,' Fox agreed, 'But then I'm a living suspicious sod not a dead one, so that's something.'

Shea looked at the curving hilt and guard of the rapier and nodded at it.

'New?' he asked.

Fox handed it to the old soldier who drew it from its scabbard gently.

'Plenty don't like it. I do. That hilt protects the hand. In close combat it's as much a weapon as the blade.'

Shea held the sword and moved it through a thrust and parry exercise. 'Old skills,' he smiled.

'Never lose them, friend. A yard of blade, light weight, flexible, fast. Cuts and drives, rapier and cutlass in one. It's not heavy and the grip is wire bound over wood. See? The pommel is steel like the guard. And I can use it in either hand. Perfect.'

He looked across at Peter as he sat staring at the plate of food.

'Eat,' he said and took a piece of pie.

The boy began to attack the food. The two men watched him and smiled.

'Well?' asked Patrick Shea. 'Bristol again. You going home, Sergeant?'

'Not Sergeant any more,' Fox said. 'Those days are over. You've done well here.'

'I have always told you, John Fox. You're welcome to join

me. I'd be glad if you would. You could settle down, find a – '

He stopped . He knew about Alison and what she had meant to his old comrade. It was personal territory, that.

'Drink up,' he said and poured more wine.

Fox leaned closer.

'I'm here on account of the boy.'

Shea stared then at the hard glittering eyes in the boy's pale face as he wolfed food without a word.

'I have business further north.'

'With our old commander?'

Fox stared at his old friend.

'You know too much, soldier. What d'you know?'

Patrick drank from his tankard and shrugged.

'From time to time I have my uses, John,' he said. 'An inn like this is a place for passing messages, for passing news, rumours. Gossip. Sifting it all and passing it on from time to time.'

'Passing it where? And what gossip?'

'Nothing about you, John. I assure you. Trust me. On my brother's life I never pass anything about you. People ask from time to time if I have seen anything of Sergeant Fox and I lie. I respect Fairfax and I loved my brother as he loved you. So, be easy on that, John. But the word is in the exchange, you could say, find Fox. Me? I've never seen him.'

Fox relaxed a little, took the sword from Shea's hand and slid the silver black blade into the scabbard and nodded.

Shea lifted his goblet. 'To my brother,' he said simply and Fox lifted his drink and they drank the toast in silence. A log fell across the hearth in a shower of sparks, Peter went on eating.

'I declare the city is full of madness,. I've never seen it so. Never felt it so edgy. Like a nervy colt ready to fly in any direction.'

Shea nodded agreement.

'Bristol is filled with ragged arsed mad men and women who preach the second coming. And hate.' Shea laughed.

'And they believe it, I declare. There's one old army sergeant claims he is Jesus Christ. He's surrounded by believers. Madmen.'

'And women,' said Fox dryly. 'They have a church by the Cross down by the river – mad too? Their leader's young and pretty enough. Sad she's a bride of Christ or thinks she is.'

Shea shrugged.

'Maybe she is. It's the time we live in, friend. Brother agin brother, sure that's madness too. Father against son – madness – King's men against Parliament men . What's the sense in all that, for the love of Christ? You've seen war. I have. What'd it ever do except make hills of old bones and burned hopes and hunger? Did it ever solve a jot? Be buggered if it did. We know – we've seen it. More widows and more orphans. Sickness to infect everyone. Even that madman who thinks he's John the Baptist in the market. Ragged arsed and mad. Lost souls. Like your boy there, maybe.'

Peter had fallen asleep, his head in his arms on the table.

'He needs to find a way south, to Cornwall. He thinks, maybe his mother went there. Back home. There was nothing left in Brentford for her. Nor him. He got lost in the – you know how it can be. Chaos. She ran for her life. He watched his grandfather die. Held him. Not a word out of him since.'

Shea nodded.

'He could stay here. There's work – my wife would take care of him. We've no children ourselves.'

Fox looked across at the boy who was awake looking at them. He had heard what the big man said. Peter hesitated and then shook his head once and dropped his eyes. He understood.

He dropped to sleep again.

'I want him safe to Padstow. Near his mother's village called St Merryn. You heard of it?'

Shea sighed, 'I heard of Padstow. The King's men hold Cornwall as I hear it.'

Fox ate a mouthful of cheese, drank more wine and sat back.

'I want him safe there. He's seen enough. He needs to go there to find his mother if he can.'

Shea nodded.

'I have a friend who trades across the channel from time to time – you know how it is? Brandy and wine and stuff. You understand me?'

Fox nodded.

'What's his name?' he asked.

'Hawken,' Shea answered.

'Terence Hawken of *The Chough*?

'You know him?'

Fox smiled at that. Peter was listening.

'When I was a nipper,' Fox laughed, 'I would come down the Severn when my father was in a mood to thrash me. I'd run off for weeks at a time. I shipped with Hawken a time or two. Is he still alive then?'

Shea nodded. 'He is alive alright. He's in the outer dock tonight. Taking the tide in a day or so. He goes down the coast – He'll take the lad. I've a share in his enterprise, John. He'll do it for me and the boy can work his way. You can do that, boy?'

The lad nodded and ate more cheese. Shea walked over and stood looking down at him.

'I've taken to you, Peter. My wife did too. I saw that. If you find your mother never made it home, you get back here, boy. You hear me? You'll be safe here with us. I'll tell Hawken. You understand?'

The boy looked up at the wide smiling face of the old soldier and nodded seriously. Shea turned to Fox.

'So, you're going north?'

Fox nodded.

'If anyone asks you still haven't seen me. Unless it's the Irish girl.'

He picked a chicken leg and gnawed it as he thought for a moment.

''Twill be as well to hold our tongues I think, my friend, when King and Parliament men get to fighting as they mean to. I was at Powick Bridge and that was ugly enough. But what comes soon will be savage.'

Shea nibbled a heel of cheese. The light from the fire threw shadows about the small room. Outside the streets were quieter. He shook his head.

'True enough. It's going to get worse. The King is hag-ridden by a froggie Catholic wife with clowns for courtiers.

Fox wiped his sleeve across his greasy mouth and took a pull at the wine.

'Treason, my friend,' he said and Shea smiled.

'I heard all that,' Fox said. 'Nothing to do with me. I've my daughter to find and to bring up in peace and quiet and not anything any longer to do with the bloody whorehouse mess we live in here.'

Shea mocked him, or maybe it was the wine talking.

'You'll find your daughter and settle down to church and a tad of land and bring up sheep? You! You know we used to call you the Preacher. Not to your face of course, but on account of your religious woman who wanted to settle you down. I know it hurts to talk about Alison but you were never suited to that life. When my brother died we heard you'd gone soft.'

He went on.

'Listen to me, John. Listen to that madman preaching in the market square. Listen to the women talking about the second coming. There's a man at the cross says he's John the Baptist and he's an old soldier. John Taylor was a friend of mine but he got religion and now preaches that he is the Son of God. He believes it, poor sod. Bristol, everywhere is going mad. True. Go and find your daughter by all means, man, and be sure she is safe. But there is work with Black Tom. The word is out for you, John. I'll tell you now that a friend came by and left a message to say Fairfax wanted you badly. Needed you.'

Fox shook his head. He slammed his fist on the table.

'Bugger all that. I'm done with it all. Let the world go screaming to God in a handcart on the way to Hell. I am done with it.'

Shea spoke quietly.

'There is war coming to England such as we have never known. Tom Fairfax needs you. Who are you to turn your back on him?'

Fox stared at the Irishman who had never talked to him like that before.

'I don't want more of it, Patrick. I am tired of it.'

'You'll be tireder in the grave, boyo. And longer there too, mark my word.'

Shea shoved his seat closer to Fox.

'Listen, boyo, you speak French like a Frog, German like those bullet-headed guardsmen we hated and Spanish when necessary. You are Fox. Sergeant Fox who'd take on any man in single combat, armed or unarmed, knife, sword or single staff. My brother would never have let you walk away when the colonel asked for you. And he's asking. You are the best intelligencer he has. See him.'

Pat Shea was as angry as Fox had ever seen him.

'I have to be sure my daughter is safe. Then maybe. I don't know.'

Shea nodded. He knew what a torment Fox was in for he knew Fox's worth. It was a bitch but Shea would not let go.

'Sure you want a quiet life and peace. You can have that in the grave. When my brother was killed you lost something, spirit maybe. You were there when he died and could do nothing. Not your fault. He died. Soldiers get killed. It's what they are paid for. Will I tell any messenger that comes by that you have gone for a quiet life, looking for your daughter? My brother would be ashamed.'

Fox was angry at first but then he remembered the woman, alone and naked in a mountain farm, near as spit, raped by a soldier under his command. A woman with a child who cursed him as he rode away.

War.

CHAPTER 10

Outside the inn, on the corner near a small water trough sat an old woman huddled in thick skirts, old shirts and scarves. She had a bundle of white heather on her lap. Two men passed but she didn't try to sell them heather for luck. She watched the inn and waited.

The room in the back of the bar was quiet. The boy was fast asleep with his head in his arms beside the remains of his meal.

Outside, the woman had gone. A man lay in the shadows between the water trough and the cold stone wall. He was wrapped in an old piece of sacking and appeared to be asleep. His hand clutching the sacking was thin and veined and from time to time shook with cold or fever.

Overhead, the stars went out one by one as heavy clouds gathered adding to the deep shadows all around. There seemed to be the promise of rain. The man pulled the sack over his head leaving only a narrow slit where his eyes glinted. The lights in the inn went out one by one. Somewhere a dog howled.

The moon lit up the sky as the rain had passed and the cobbles were slick with water. There was a slight movement in the alley as Fox moved past the front of the inn, keeping in the shadows.

Even in the dark he was sure of his way. The man lying in the dark shadow cast by the water trough, lifted his head and watched.

Fox headed across the basin which was filled with trading ships. Lights showed through the portholes of some and in others the cabin doors were open and the mutter of men could be heard.

A sweet tenor voice singing an Italian song came from the deck of one of the ships on the other side of the moorings. Suddenly two men shouted in German and Fox froze. The men were arguing about a hand of cards and a bet made. They appeared on the deck of a coaster silhouetted in the light spilling up from the cabin. They yelled at each other for a moment more. Then someone called to them to shut up and they stopped, shook hands drunkenly and went below.

Fox moved on. Behind him a slighter figure followed, hugging the shadows.

Fox stepped across the ropes holding ships to bollards, avoiding spars and piles of crates, nets and old floats strung along the quaysides. Past rusting chains and piles of boxes and barrels, he eventually came to the outer basin. He checked along the smaller jetties and found what he was looking for.

He went quietly aboard a fishing boat, tapped on the cabin door and waited. After a moment the door opened, light spilled out, and Fox hurried inside and shut the door.

On the quayside the figure who had been following, ducked into cover provided by empty fish barrels and waited. The moon was up now and pale light spilled over the fishing boats moored in the outer harbour. A smaller shadow hid, watching *The Chough*.

Fox sat hunched on a bench screwed to the bulkhead. The cabin was neat. A bunk at one end, a table screwed into place with a bench along one side, wet weather clothes on hooks. A gaff, various floats, lengths of coiled twine for mending nets, lines of fishing hooks already tied onto long coils of line. The only light came from a small lantern on the table and over it all the powerful stink of old fish from every quarter of the old boat.

In front of Fox a large glass of brandy and a bottle. Opposite him a rat-faced, hard-handed, eager-eyed man leaned back and yawned. He had few teeth left and those he had were yellow or broken.

Terence Hawken, owner and captain of *The Chough*, had spent his life on or around the sea. He and Fox had known each other when Fox was a boy as Terence reminded him with roars of laughter.

'And you were already running ashore with cargoes no one should ask questions about,' Fox smiled.

'So what changes?' asked Terence. 'You? I heard about Alison. Sorry for that.'

Fox said nothing and the sailor poured a tot into the glass.

'Bad business. You married?' Fox asked his old friend and

the sailor grinned.

'In a manner of speaking.. Married in Roscoff and in Padstow an' all. Well, m'lover, a man has needs and when you get older it gets harder to charm they beauties like we used to. You'll find it, m'lover,' he said quietly.

Fox drank.

'I've got two lovely damsels for daughters so. One Breton and one true Cornish.' He laughs again. 'Two families is nice enough. Two warm havens to head the boat to from time to time. Neither one knows of t'other, which is comfortable.'

He offered Fox another tot. Fox put his hand over his glass.

The flickering light from the lantern on the table lit Fox's face for a moment and danced shadows over the wall of the tiny cabin. Hawken looked into Fox's eyes.

'You must excuse me talking about myself. 'Tis not often I get the chance, but that's no excuse.'

He waited a moment. Fox said nothing but toyed with the glass in front of him. Thinking.

'You look troubled, John. Can I help?'

Fox told Terence about Peter who needed to go to Cornwall. He wanted him gone but not alone across country for it was too dangerous for a young lad.

'There is a problem, he don't speak a word. Not dumb, just won't speak. This bloody fighting.'

'Don't begin me on that. They're all as bad as the other. The Parliament men looking for one thing and the King's lot wanting that bitch Henrietta to have her way and the Pope sitting in parliament more'n likely. I got no time for any on'em. I goes my ways, John Fox, and minds my own business.'

Terence went on angrily

'Cornwall is slipping into Royalist hands and the lads are being recruited, forced often as not, to fight for they know not what, the beauties. They should all hold their noise and say nothing. I did hear you was doing work for some soldier or another. Information gathering work.'

'You heard that did you, Terence? Nothing but lies, my friend. I have a damsel, as you say, of my own to look after now. I'm going north to find her when I have the boy seen to. Will you take him on down to Padstow? His mother comes from thereabouts. He might find her.'

The smuggler nodded. 'No need to ask, John. I remember

one time – we was both much younger and you were in Roscoff and you'd heard tell of a rumour that there were them as would stop me beaching my cargo. It was down Newlyn way. You come with me that trip and a merry battle we had. Remember? '

Fox nodded. Not smiling now. The little man went on,

'Bring him aboard. I'm sailing tomorrow on the tide. He'll work his passage.'

The two men drank up and Fox stepped out onto the deck of the coaster, walked down the gang plank, stepped over the old ropes warped over the ancient rusting bollards and didn't look back. Good friends, no questions much and doing what is asked for friendship's sake. Fox knew he was a lucky man.

The moon was hidden by a curtain of cloud as he stepped along the quayside back towards the inn. In the looming shadow of a huge ship he heard to his right a faint scuttling then, on his right again, a barrel toppled into his path as ahead of him he saw a figure blocking his way.

Fox stopped and waited until the man on his left revealed himself. He was carrying a belaying pin in one hand and a blade in the other. To his right, Fox was aware of the man who had tipped over the barrel. He was tall, fat and grinning. Fox was alone. He'd make an easy mark for the crimpers men. They'd have him aboard a boat and he'd be gone in an hour.

Another men appeared round a pile of logs. Pine from Poland. Fox waited. They had lost the element of surprise. They'd come for him. It was no accident.

Fox wrapped his cloak over his left forearm and plucked the blade from the sheath on his back. Even as he did this, he moved quickly to the man on his left. He checked, made a move to evade the man on his right and as the man turned to him, Fox changed direction and closed to the man with the belaying pin.

He slashed his blade across the man's face and opened a wide wound across his forehead. Blood poured down his attacker's face, blinding him. Fox kicked the man's legs from under him and stamped hard on his kneecap. The man lay screaming as Fox turned to take the man behind him with a slashing backhand from the long curving blade. The man had come too close and the blade slashed the upper arm as Fox stepped in closer and smashed the advancing man between the eyes with his forehead. Welcome to a Bristol kiss, thought Fox, as his opponent dropped like a felled ox.

The third man, armed with a cavalry sword, hesitated and

then saw that Fox was staggering. He came in fast and clumsy but sure of his ground, swinging his sword, fooled by Fox's feint. Like a lark tricking a fox by pretending a broken wing. Fox ducked under the swinging arm and sunk his short blade into the forearm holding the sword, tore it upwards and slit the muscle. The sword dropped and the attacker screamed in agony.

The last attacker was huge. He came in fast and light as a dancer and Fox kicked an empty barrel that lay on the quayside into his path. It spun across the charging man's track and he hesitated. Fox feinted right and left and then slashed the man from chin to ear and opened up a second mouth. Blood poured out of the wounds. He dropped his sword, turned and limped away, dripping blood as he went. Fox stood watching him and at that instant heard a voice scream a warning.

'John behind you! Fox, behind you, Fox!!'

Fox turned and had no time to protect himself as a fifth man came at him with a sack hook in his hand. As he swung at Fox's head the man stopped, scrabbled at his back and pitched forward. Between his shoulder blades stood a salmon spear.

Fox looked across the quayside and saw Peter. He leaned down and felt for the pulse of the man on the quayside. He was dead as mutton. The boy came over to join him and Fox put an arm around his shoulders.

'You called my name, Peter?'

The boy nodded. He spoke hesitantly as if surprised he could.

'You were in danger, you were going to be killed. Is he dead?'

Fox nodded and hugged the boy to him.

'I owe you, Peter – again,' he said and the boy began to cry.

Fox knelt and felt into the big man's jerkin and took a rough portrait of himself on paper, a seal skin sheet in which were wrapped coins and a leather pouch which held gold coin.

He wrenched out the salmon spear, rolled the dead man across the quayside and into the black water.

'I never killed a man before,' Peter said eventually.

Fox put his arm round the scared boy as they cut through narrow alleys back to the inn. Once there, Peter was given brandy and Patrick's wife put him into a warm bed.

She came back ten minutes later.

'He's sleeping. He'll be right as rain in the morning. I'll see to him.'

And she wished the two men goodnight as they talked.

'He could be in danger, Patrick. Seen, maybe. Can you get him to Hawken's boat secretly? He'll take the lad.'

Patrick smiled. 'And you?'

Fox shook his head. 'No. I still go north. I have a daughter to find.'

'Were they crimpers men?'

Fox shook his head and showed him the drawing he had lifted off the dead man.

'They were looking for me. A contract on me, maybe?'

'They'd've crimped you if they could. Made coin from whoever gave them the picture and from the captain who'd got another crewman. They'd only to sling you onto any one of the ships moored in the lanes and you'd've been shipped out as crew. You were lucky.'

'You'll get the boy away?'

'Listen man, for the love of God, find Fairfax, take work. There's someone looking for you. The enemy who set on those crimpers. Paid them. The others walked away?' Fox nodded.

'Limped I'd say and they'll not work their trade for a time. I hear you, Pat. I'll be on my way.'

'When?'

'Now. Tonight. If I stay in town I'll be picked up. They'll be watching if they want me. I go now. Bring my horse tomorrow. Up on the downs. Clifton Hill.'

'Can you get out the city gate?'

'Why ever not?' grinned Fox.

At last he felt the blood stir in him. Things were happening.

'Tell the boy I'll find him . Give him this.'

He handed over the heavy leather purse.

'Tell him he's earned it. Tell him I'm proud of him.'

Fox picked up his cloak and took his leather saddle bag from the floor, stuffed a lump of cheese, some bread and a piece of ham into his bag.

He stepped to the door.

In the corridor the two men shook hands. Shea snuffed the candle before Fox opened the door to the yard.

'Take care, friend,' he said and Fox was gone into the night.

CHAPTER 11

DERBYSHIRE

The high dales were bathed in early morning light. Frost glittered in the trees and across the land.

In the distance the higher hills rolled across the country up by the lakes. Before them the dales undulated like a great green and brown sea. Outcrops of rock broke through the vast swathes of forest and untamed land. Valleys were dark gashes and huddled beneath the uplands villages and hamlets were tucked where little or nothing had changed over generations.

Whatever went on in London and Oxford hardly touched the people here but lives were about to be changed. Death and war and pestilence would follow one after the other as men who had no interest in ordinary lives used ordinary peaceable people to settle the quarrels which had nothing to do with the people they would maim and rape, murder and pillage. In the name of God maybe, or land, or more usually, power.

The horseman rode carefully below the crest of the slopes. Fox had come through the trees where he had spent the night and onto an open slope. He looked back. No one following him.

Below the edge of the valley was a glitter of water and lower, beyond the curve of the hill, Fox knew there was an ancient stone bridge. Above him the scree-covered hillside was almost a cliff. The loose grey shale was like a wave waiting to crash down into the green valley and onto the stands of trees and the occasional dry-stone wall that marked the edge of the path.

Fox made for a small copse of trees that grew close to the lip of the land which he knew fell away into a high hidden valley.

He left his horse and spent an hour working his way to the edge of the high land and looked carefully across and down to the path by the river that tumbled along the valley. Painstakingly he checked and checked again. Nothing moved. No one was waiting in ambush.

A curlew mewed down over the grass and rock. Sheep moved across the turf. Fox watched the black shadow of a hawk as it swooped over this desolate land.

Land that had been carved out by ice and was now a fertile, almost secret place. In the distance, at the end of a valley stood the manor house.

It was here that Fox had left Rebecca, his daughter, in the healing hands of Lady Elizabeth Morton. He trusted her. Had she not nursed him, wounded, back to health through a savage winter? She had been lonely, abandoned by her husband. After time, as she came to trust him, they had become fond of each other. She had told him that her marriage was an unhappy alliance.

One of the servants told Fox that her husband had bought up her father's debts and demanded her as repayment. It was solely for appearances' sake and to get a son and heir. He was not interested in her and seemed to prefer younger flesh. He was hated by the tenants.

Harry spent everything Lady Elizabeth had inherited on her father's death and sold the properties and land, apart from the Derbyshire home and that would go next. Then he had gone abroad to find employment among the restless courtiers who lived there and worked for their own interests and those of the King. Elizabeth had been lonely.

They had both known Fox could not stay, for the master of the house might come back at any time. They had been locked together by snow. The whole house knew that he and their mistress slept and loved together. They hated her cruel, harsh greedy husband for what he was.

Fox also had been lonely. When the winter snows melted and Fox left her, she did not weep until he had quite gone from her sight. When he returned with Rebecca, his daughter, she took her into the household for his sake. Elizabeth promised to care for the damaged, motherless girl. She would do what she could for her while Fox went about Black Tom's business. Now he wanted his daughter back.

He rode down off the craggy top and quickly vanished into a rocky cleft. He appeared lower down and rode out onto the old drover's path amongst the trees. He avoided the little village at the end of the dale.

Dusk was setting dark shadows across the folds of the hills. To left and right the top of the valley was grey scree lying in unstable waves. He reined in his horse in a stand of trees near the stream and dismounted. This was as close as he wanted to ride.

He tethered the horse and armed only with Shea's knife, he stepped into the shadows and made his careful way along the edge of the peat brown water of the stream. It was full and ran fast, flashing white over slabs of limestone rock.

Fox was worried. It was too still. He stopped and looked right and left and then behind him. Nothing moved but he felt he was being watched.

He moved along the river bank to the single arch of the old pack bridge. Mosses grew in the niches of the brickwork, yellow lichen stained the top flat surface of the ancient grey stone.

Beyond the bridge was a bend on the track and beyond that bend was a small, stone shepherd's hut. Fox moved up the bank and into its cover. Behind him a jackdaw screeched and fluttered into the trees. The sky was growing darker and streaked with yellow. There was a hint of autumn in the air.

Fox rounded a buttress of rocks and looked down to the end of the dale and the old grey stone house. It stood four-square in front of a rising hillside and before it a long open view down the dale.

The house stood on the site of an old monastery. Red brick chimneys and mullioned windows caught the afternoon light. Stone from the monastery had been used to extend it.

There were huge barns and alongside them a walled garden. A small orchard with a long line of fish ponds necklaced the house following the gentle slope towards the end of the valley. A row of stone pillars with broken arches marked the line of a ruined cloister and the remains of a vast arch showed where the main chapel had once stood.

The last of the sun glinted on the attic windows. The other windows were shuttered. There was no light, no movement – nothing. The gates at the end of the courtyard were chained. No one was there.

For an hour Fox watched the house. Patient as ever, he waited another hour and finally moved in a wide circle around the house and the ornate gardens. There was no sign of life.

Dusk was falling as he walked along the bank of the stream to his horse tethered in the stand of trees.

He lit a small fire, took a hand line from his saddle bag, tied on three hooks and three lures. He tied the line to a stone and left it in the running water. Back at the small fire he took bread and cheese from his saddle bag, ate his meagre supper, drank fresh water and slept, wrapped in his cloak, until the morning cold woke him.

He knelt by the stream, washed his face with icy water and checked his line. Two good sized trout. He gutted them and wrapped them in dock leaves and tucked them into the embers of the fire. A blackbird sang in the hedge up by the track.

Fox ate, buried the bones and poured earth over the fire. There was to be no sign of him passing. He saddled his horse and rode without a backward glance up the valley on a track that took him back to the high dales over the ridge.

He had a man to find and when he did he might find out what had happened at the house. He rode up into the next valley and saw below, beyond the rocks and stunted trees, the heather and gorse, what he had hoped to see. A thin curl of smoke rising like iron-blue thread into the early morning sky.

Two dogs announced him as he clattered into the shippen yard. An ancient, single-storey cottage made of limestone blocks that seemed to grow out of the land. The yard in front was made of more limestone slabs and a low dry-stone wall curved around the ancient house.

The figure in the doorway shaded his eyes against the early morning sun. Fox came out of the sun as of habit. The watcher would not recognise him. Fox stopped, dismounted and fussed the dogs who no longer growled.

They lay, tongues out, watching him as he walked across the yard and took the hand of the man in the doorway.

'I wondered when you'd be by,' said the man quietly. 'Come in.'

CHAPTER 12

Fox was angry, 'Gone – gone where?' he demanded. 'Where has she gone?'

They had eaten bread and ewe's cheese in silence. Peter was, like many shepherds, not unhappy to sit in silence. But his friend was hurting and would hurt more when he learned what had happened.

'Where did they go?' Fox repeated quietly. 'Is my daughter well?'

Peter smiled. 'Much mended, John. Near perfect and as wild as you told us she might be. But my lady loved her as we all came to. She even tamed Rebecca a little.'

'Were did they go, man?' Fox asked urgently now. ' I need to know.'

The shepherd shook his head.

'They don't tell us 'owt my friend. One day they're here and gone the next. It isn't natural but is the way things are with men like Harry Morton. He come back a week or two after you left your girl with us.'

'Did she and Elizabeth – were they friends?'

'My lady took her in as her companion at first but when her husband came back she put her with the other maids. She had her good reasons for that.'

'What reasons?' asked Fox.

The morning light filtered into the dark brown interior of the cottage. Old rough cupboards and chests lined the walls and made the room even smaller. Hanging on the walls, traps and an old fowling piece. A blade or two and a beautiful carved crook. A cured leg of mutton hung by the chimney and another swung in a net on a beam. Fox could see jars of preserves in the store at the back.

A stack of wood lay by the hearth and outside Fox had noticed a huge stack of cut wood for the winter.

Water was in a large pot and mugs on a shelf near a small ale keg. All neat and clean but without the redeeming touch of a woman's hand anywhere. It was comfortable enough for a simple man with simple wants.

'Why was it best?'

Peter shifted uneasily and looked away.

'My lord, God rot his soul, likes young meat. He likes to hurt things, animals and even people. My lady thought it best to have Rebecca out of sight. No one looks at a maid, do they?'

'Has he touched her?'

'She said not when we talked last. Rebecca knew you and I were friends. She was afraid of him. He's a vicious, dangerous man to tell the truth. He hits my lady, her maids do say. And them too.'

Fox's mouth tightened.

'And men?' he asked. 'Does he hit men?'

Peter shook his head.

'He's a coward. He brings his own men here when he comes. They lord it about the place for a few days. They beat the servants from time to time. Shout at them. Mock them for country bumpkins. Some of them leave. Some stay for the sake of my lady. The young maids didn't stay long.'

Fox stared into the flames of the fire and was silent.

'I need to get my daughter away from him then?'

'And my lady Elizabeth, like as not.'

After a pause. Peter added, 'She had a son, you know?'

'What? A son?'

'Yours, John. A son. Before her husband came back but the boy was born dead, by good fortune.'

'Dear God – her husband?'

'He knows nothing. No need for him to know anything. Her maid, maybe Rebecca and me. I saw to doing what had to be done.'

Fox sat silent.

'She was very happy with you,' said the shepherd. 'And when your daughter came she was happy to take her in and protect her for your sake.'

'She never told me.'

'No. Nor will she. God's will she said to me. God's will.'

'She never spoke of it after?'

'No one told her husband about – me and her ?'

'She is well loved. No one in the house told. And now she is gone with him. To join the Queen who is abroad.'

Fox sat and closed his eyes for a moment.

'Abroad?' he asked.

'With the Queen's court.'

'Why did he take her?'

'He shut the house, sent the servants on their ways. I would have been sent away but he needed someone to care for the flocks. The rest is closed because he has no money left to keep it up or to pay our keep. He has used her dowry on drink, rich friends and debauchery.'

'So he took his wife and my daughter?'

'She had nowhere to go, John. My lady took her as her maid for her own sake. Maybe he ordered her to take her.'

'And he likes young flesh, you said.'

Peter nodded. 'Yes,' he said quietly.

'When did they leave?'

'A month, six weeks – I don't know exactly.'

'Hell!'

The two dogs moved, sensing the anger in the stranger's voice.

'You can stay here, John. Rebecca said she would be back, if she needed to be. She is a remarkable girl.'

Fox laughed mirthlessly

'As her mother was. This man tries her he'd do well to guard his balls for she always carries a blade, hidden. She'll not be afraid to use it.'

The shepherd stood up and removed the platter, took two wooden mugs and drew off ale from the small barrel on the dresser.

'There's one other thing you should know. A woman came through here a month back. Just after they left. She was looking for you, she said. Said she'd find you in Black Tom's place.'

'Black Tom?'

'I have no notion what she meant. She left me that message for when you came by. She said you'd be here.'

'What else did she say?'

'She said no more than that. She was a strange one. When she came the dogs kept away from her. She calmed them some way. They never like strangers and yet within an hour they were sitting at her feet.'

'What did she look like? Red hair?'

'Yes. Pale faced, green eyes, I think. They changed colour.'

'Young – ?'

'Youngish. Twenty five perhaps. I have no way of judging. She was angry when I told her that Rebecca had gone. I told her something about Harry Morton and she cut me short. She said she know about him and his habits. She was very angry. To tell the truth she made me afraid at first. And then, I don't know. There was a calm about her, it charmed my dogs then me, I suppose.'

'What else?'

'No more than that. She was a strange one, that.'

'Her name is Maeve. I know her.'

Fox walked to the door of the cottage. He turned back, his mind made up.

'Black Tom's place, she said?'

The shepherd nodded.

'There was something about work to do – abroad. I don't remember any more.'

'Abroad. Good. I'll find my daughter, my friend, I'll go now.'

'Not yet, John. There is more. No one in the house told Harry Morton about you. Someone down the valley told him. He beat Elizabeth black and blue and swore he'd never free her to whore about. She'd pay and so would the man. He would pay. It's what he shouted at her. Her maids heard him.'

Fox sat silent in the dull light that filtered through the window.

'He told her she'd go with him, he told her if he cared to humiliate her, he would. He told her that her life was going to be a living hell and he'd glory in it. She said nothing. No one saw her utter a word to him after that.'

'He told her he'd put a price on your head in the village. Any man who killed you would be paid well, any man who informed him of your whereabouts would be well rewarded.'

Still Fox said nothing He stared across the room without seeing. She'd born him a son, she'd cared for his daughter.

'Rebecca? Does he know anything about her?'

'No one in the village knew who she was. No one told. As far as he knew she is merely a maid to his wife. She's a lovely girl. So he kept her with them.'

Fox could feel the anger churning in his gut.

'I'll go now.'

'Go later. Avoid the village. Avoid men until you're well away. There are plenty would betray you for the gold on offer.'

'The girl, Maeve – how long ago did she come by?'

'A month ago. You know her well?'

'Yes. Very well. She looks as if butter wouldn't melt, yet she has killed a man. She is slippery as an eel, as cruel as a hawk, vicious, magical, to tell the truth.'

'Your mistress?'

He smiled at the idea.

'I have owed her in my time Peter. And she has power. That power over the dogs, you. There is more in her, something old. If Alison my wife had met her, she would have said she was an old soul. Maeve can see things. I can't explain her to you.'

'You are fond?'

Fox stared at the shepherd then and shrugged.

'I don't know. I know I have to listen to her. There is old wisdom, old ways – something of magic about her. Fond? I don't know. I do know I am sometimes afraid of her, like you. She will find me when she wants to find me. I tell you if so much as a hair on Rebecca's head has been touched, I'll geld that husband of Elizabeth's before I slit his throat.'

Peter nodded.

'Go before dawn on the high path. Safest that way.'

High overhead a hawk quartered the sky. It stilled and suddenly, stooped to the kill.

CHAPTER 13

Stars glinted between the clouds as John Fox led his horse away from the old shuttered house at the end of the valley. In the courtyard the fountain that once fed the fish ponds down the hillside was still.

Fox skirted the walled garden where he and Elizabeth had been so happy.

Around his neck he still carried the half melted silver cross Alison had concealed in her hand when they built her pyre. It was Maeve who had found it in the bare earth where the stake had been driven. Maeve had been frightened by the power she felt in the twisted piece of silver.

He rode away up the narrow track behind the elms. It was only because he had taken the path so often with the shepherd that he knew it well enough to follow even in the false dawn that was beginning to filter through the night sky.

Fox quickened his pace. He had to be clear of the valley and over the top ridge to be sure no one looking for him should see him from the village.

As he came to the ridge line he moved to the right and into a clump of stunted trees on the crest. He moved down the far slope and joined the drovers' track.

The watcher standing in the dark shadows of an outlying pile of huge boulders smiled as the man suddenly vanished from view. It was half an hour before the watcher moved.

Dawn rolled slowly across the land in waves of shadow and light. Silver undersides shone on the darker clouds and sulphur yellow where the rising sun tipped the top.

The watcher checked the back trail one more time and then moved on. The figure ahead was climbing steadily across the rolling grassland up a steep slope cropped short by successions of vast flocks.

Fox rode on searching out cover in the long folds in the ground. He never hurried his horse. They had a long way to go and he wanted him strong in case he needed speed to avoid an ambush.

By mid-morning they were hidden in a long curving valley carved by a series of streams that tumbled over the edge of high pastureland into a rocky gully. He stopped by a long pool fed by a fall of peat brown water.

The watcher just below the ridge line amongst a pile of random boulders the size of a house, waited, puzzled. Below, Fox had taken off his shirt and dipped water out of the long pool as he sluiced his pale body, face and neck.

He looked around for a moment and then stepped naked into the icy water. He ducked down into the pool and gasped at the shock and shook his head. Droplets of water sprayed about him.

Slowly he clambered out of the water, took up his cloak and dried himself.

The watcher shook with silent laughter. To take such a risk and at such a time. To be naked if an enemy arrived; Fox had not lost his willingness to gamble.

Along the curving open land behind the watcher there was no sign of any followers. Far away a buzzard coasted on the updrafts that were beginning to swirl off the land.

The sun was burning off the distant haze. It was going to be one of those warm mornings, bright with sharp light. The buzzard dipped closer and the watcher raised a hand with the first and last fingers forked to ward off evil.

An hour later, Fox moved away from the stream and up through a copse. Below him the watcher saw a cluster of mean roofs and the tower of an old church .

Fox saw to his right and just under the ridge which sheltered it, the ruins of a small cottage. Smoke billowed in a thick pall from its shattered shell. The fences that had enclosed a shed and shelter for cattle were smashed to matchwood.

Standing staring at the ruins was a man. He didn't look up when Fox dismounted and walked quietly to him. He didn't even look at him as he spoke.

'They took my son. They came and took my son. Soldiers came, they said looking for recruits. They took my son and my cow and then killed my chickens and rode away laughing in my face.

They took my son for a soldier. Just came and burned down my place and – I don't give a damn who they were fighting for – King or God or Pope, do I care? Parliaments – they all lie to us. They burned my home. Why?'

He didn't look at Fox once. Fox walked silently away, mounted his horse and rode off. Still the man didn't look but went on scrabbling in the ruins of his house, covered in black soot searching for he had no idea what.

Fox didn't look back. Nothing to be done.

The sun was nearly at its height when the watcher came down to the house and waited as the man pulled out of the ruins a chair, a long charred beam, a table – two iron pots. Useful things for beginning again.

He looked up the watcher who asked,

'When?'

'Two hours. three. They went that way,' he pointed in the direction Fox had ridden.

'How many?'

The man stared at the figure on the horse and raised a hand.

'Soldiers?'

He shrugged.

'Who knows? No uniforms, no banners, God knows what they were.'

The man went back to listlessly scrabbling in the charred ruins.

Fox stopped as the light began to go. There was plenty of sign of the passage of four or five men driving a cow and two extra horses. Broken bushes, the head of a cockerel, dollops of cow dung. The animal was slowing the men up. But they had time and didn't care for there was no one to see them or to stop them as they marauded over the countryside. Not soldiers he guessed, but men taking a chance. England was already sliding into anarchy.

Fox unsaddled his horse, laid the saddle in a mossy circle of boulders, collected dry wood from alongside a nearby stream and built a small fire. The watcher waited.

Fox sat patiently on a rock with a lure on a line in the water.

By the time he had caught two fish, the embers of the fire glowed. He moved the ashes of a fire off a pile of flat stones, wrapped the fish in a handful of wild garlic leaves put them onto the hot stones and covered the makeshift oven with the still glowing ash. And now the watcher stepped out of the shadows.

'You took your time coming to the surface,' she said quietly.
He didn't look round.

'Maeve,' he said. 'Fish?'

She crouched down by the fire.

'There's no one behind you. I've been with you for three days. Since you left the house in the Dales. No one followed.'

Fox brushed the ashes off the trout and handed her one hot parcel.

They sat quietly as the sun dipped in the sky.

'That burned house?' she said.

'Yes. I know,' he said. 'nothing to be done.'

He smiled at her then and she nodded. He looked into the pale face and the mass of auburn hair that tumbled about her shoulders. Her eyes were a shocking green and danced in the light. There had been times with her – he shook his head and she laughed in his face. She could read uncannily what went through his mind.

'We have other things to do, my friend,' she said. 'Thurloe insists you are the man he wants. Fairfax promised he could find you. All you have to do is agree to meet them. What's that to you?'

'And what do you get out of it?'

'Me?' she asked innocently. 'I get a measure of excitement and to tell the truth I'd as soon be out of this pox ridden country for a few weeks.'

'A man?' he asked.

'In a way. Yes,' she said. 'A man. I'm going to sleep.'

She pulled her cloak about her and slept. Fox wasn't sure what he felt about seeing Fairfax. He was more concerned now about Rebecca.

The next morning nothing had been resolved. They rode on across country and heading north.

'Why does my old general want to see me, Maeve?'

'I'm the messenger, John Fox. No more.' She went on., 'Look boyo, it's a way to get to Europe and close to the court. That's all I know and you want to get to there to find your daughter and nothing wrong with that in a father. Though God knows she's seen little enough of you these past few years. Not that that's any handicap, from what I know of fathers, mine having gone absent when I was a spit and a scream. Bad luck to him.'

Fox was about to answer angrily but nodded an admission.

'It's pay back time, isn't it?' he said quietly

'Sure don't I know that? For Alison and the harshness of the world and sure, a father should protect his daughter. Sure it is all that. And a mission for Black Tom might add a little spice too.'

He said nothing and she went on.

'It's a way, John Fox, for you to get close to the court in Europe. You'll need help there for no one's going to let you sniff about those men with the Queen. Not without you've got good reason or a friend at court. Those coxcombs who preen about Henrietta's court. Even in Amsterdam and The Hague. There. Your man. Harry Morton will be there sure as rats suck hen's eggs. Trust me. I know something of him. And soft, loving Elizabeth his wife will be there with him, no doubt of that.'

Fox shrugged.

'You're a stubborn man. Come and see your old leader for old time's sake then. It's not out of your way. He's at home in Yorkshire.'

Fox and spurred on his horse. 'And Thurloe is coming to see him there?'

She said nothing.

'He calls the tune, Maeve. Will he be there?'

'He hates the country, does Master Thurloe. He hates open spaces. He's better suited to a hot room in a quiet street near the river.'

'I'll be wasting time.'

She sighed, gave up and rode quietly on.

Fox rode alongside her.

'I'm not working for Tom Fairfax again. I'm looking for my daughter.'

'Sure you are, Sergeant Fox. All that spice of life is dead and buried.'

She did not even look at him. Fox was angered by her indifference.

'Scared is it? Afraid is it? Lost the love of spice, is it?'

'What d'you mean by "spice"?'

'I'm a provocative bitch,' she grinned. 'Nothing changes with me, John Fox. 'Tis a shame you've lost the edge for life. Is that not the truth?'

By now they were riding side by side again.

'What d'you mean by "spice"?' he asked again

'There's a man to pay back for his cruelty. A cruel husband who thrashes his wife with a dog whip needs seeing to. More than that, I can tell you, in all honesty that man is a vicious and a wicked man.'

'Will I ask how you know that?'

Maeve reined in her horse. The track climbed through a line of stunted hawthorn and old elder past the ruins of an old drift mine. Piles of spoil covered with grasses and wild flowers stood in front of the dark empty openings into the shallow diggings where fifty years ago, men risked their lives mining silver.

In the valley they had passed through the ruins of a village abandoned when the workings ran out.

As silent as a grave with its own ghosts. Shadows darkened the valley ahead of them. She sat quite still on her horse and looked into Fox's eyes. After a moment he put his hand on hers. Her horse twitched away.

'Don't touch, John. Don't.'

'What did Morton do?'

Maeve sighed and moved away and then turned back to the still man.

'Not him only. There was a time, John, when I was a child. You don't want to hear this.

Fox dismounted and waited for her. Slowly she too dismounted and stood gentling her horse. She whispered into his ear and he snickered, put his nose close to her and she gently breathed into it. The horse stood still, quiet. Distantly there was a slow trickle of a tiny stream and even further way the rhythmic sound of an axe on a tree.

She stared at the ground.

'I was fourteen, John. Out of the bogs, you might say. Left home when my mother died of hunger. She'd left me with nothing but old lore, old wisdom, old beliefs. Born when the moon was on its back and the sky was clear as silver. Maeve Aherne. 'Make your way in the world' she said and died on me.

'The English were there and about from time to time. Cruel, some of them. Liars, most of them. I believed one that offered me a place. I was cold, I was hungry and I had no one. He and his friends, that man and his friends. One was especially bad. No need to ask who'

Fox stood silent, a dark shadow against the twisted branches of a blasted hawthorn.

'You may ask as much as you wish, my friend. What can I tell you? I was with your friend, the shepherd. He had a dog whip there that he'd been told to mend by Harry Morton. Your man would use it not only on the hounds, it seems. I took it in my hand. You've seen what sometimes happens to me when I touch powerful things. Your wife's cross. Powerful things. Dear God, I'd never touch a thing of that man. I knew then who used it. No one had to tell me. I could see him. Just holding that whip, I knew. Harry Morton, as cruel and vicious a man as I have ever known has an appointment with me.'

'Vengeance is a cold mistress, Maeve,' Fox said quietly.

'No doubt,' she said. 'And you had yours one time and now I have my chance of mine. But now you know all I need to tell you. Don't talk to me of cold mistresses, John.'

She remounted, kicked up her horse and went ahead of him. He left her alone as she toiled up the narrowing track onto the high dales. From the coarse grass along the track, larks flew spiralled, singing a warning high into the pale blue of the sky.

Later he came on her in a circle of trees. She had a pile of mushrooms and wild garlic, a rabbit already gutted and skewered over a small fire. She'd spread her riding cloak and a saddle blanket on the ground and was sitting there reading from a small, very old, leather-bound book.

She didn't look up when he tethered his horse alongside hers and walked to the fire.

He threw down his saddle bag, put down the long-bladed knife that was once Shea's and the Papenheimer rapier beside it. He turned the spitted rabbit and Maeve, not looking up from her book, held out her hand and poured a stream of salt for him to add to the cooking meat.

'What are you reading?' he asked.

'A book of simples. There was an old woman, you remember her? A wise woman. Up near the Devil's Chair, remember? I took nothing but her medicines and her old books of balms and simples.'

Fox remembered they had buried the old woman when they cut her down from the hawthorn tree. They had laid her under rocks to keep the carrion eaters off her.

They ate, drank fresh water, lay on her saddle blanket and talked into the night about the past. It was not the time to make love, they both knew that. But they were comfortable together, not making demands. They slept easy and woke early.

'Your man will be with Fairfax?'

'Thurloe hates the countryside. He will want you in London.

Black Tom Fairfax will be there. He'll tell you what you need to know. Well? Will you talk with him?'

'We have business to see to, you and me. We'd best not disappoint him. Our business, Maeve, not theirs.'

CHAPTER 14

There were dogs everywhere. In the parkland beyond the main walks of the solid stone built mansion's gardens, in the courtyard and in the stables.

Fox was alone when he rode into the courtyard. Maeve had not wanted to see Fairfax.

Fox had never been to Fairfax's home. It had been inherited through the his marriage to Lady Anne. A Yorkshire grandee's home. Yorkshire stone, mullioned windows and as comfortable as an old glove.

Fox dismounted and led his horse towards the stables. Two lads came out and nodded a greeting at him.

'Sergeant?' said the first. Fox nodded and saw that the man had lost a hand at the wrist.

'Cavalry sword?' he asked.

'Yes, Sergeant.'

'You know me?'

'I've heard of you, never saw you before. I never really believed what I heard.'

Fox smiled then and passed him the bridle.

'No, well – maybe you were right. I spent more time out in the field than around the sergeants' mess. He looks after you well?'

They had stepped into the cool of the stable. The old soldier was already unsaddling the horse.

'I'll not hear a word against him.'

'No, well – apart from his being an over-hasty, over-eager sort of a bastard. I might agree.' Fox laughed.

'I see you know my husband well, sir,' said a quiet voice behind him.

Fox turned to see Lady Anne Fairfax gentling a horse in the

81

stall nearest the door. She was laughing at the confusion and embarrassment on Fox's face.

She nodded at the stable boy and took Fox across the yard and into the house.

Even now in the main hall where Lady Anne stood in the light cast from the high windows down the polished stairs and onto the stone flagged floor, he felt embarrassment and she was smiling.

The old family house had been passed from father to son over time, added to, changed by whim of fashion and of need, a place comfortable within itself in Lady Anne's hands.

Fox was reminded of his dead wife's old home.

It was curiously embracing. The polish, the flowers, the huge table so like the one in Alison's house in the long valley up to the Shropshire hills.

Bigger, richer of course, but with the same care and love showered on it that Alison had showered on her home, his home. Once.

Lady Anne coughed a little and he was reminded of his manners. He made his bow and she smiled at him.

'What can I say, my Lady?'

'Nothing to say. There are very few of his sergeants he talks of, but John Fox is different. He was expecting you tonight.'

Fox was still embarrassed.

'I'm sorry, my Lady, I should never have spoken as I did about him.'

She laughed in his face.

'You spoke as you find. Nowt wrong wi'that, Sergeant. We call a spade by its name in Yorkshire. And you are right. Don't think any more about it. I was expecting two - you were coming with a lady?'

'She chooses not to come, Ma'am.'

'This woman?'

'Maeve Aherne. She had to persuade me here. Having done that, she prefers to absent herself.. She, she is not easy my lady, so.'

'But is formidable, I understand.'

Fox laughed then.

'Your husband makes too much of both of us, I think.'

'Indeed?' Lady Anne cocked an inquisitive eye at Fox.

'She is her own person. Not a tame lap dog like other women, is what she would say.'

Fox saw the laughter in her eyes and laughed himself.

'She is not easy, my lady. And now she is angry with herself and with me.'

Lady Anne gestured to a chair and they both sat.

'She is – a very private woman.'

'You like her?'

He shakes his head.

'More. I admire her. And to tell the truth sometimes she frightens me.'

'Why?'

'I cannot say.'

'Will not? Cannot?'

'Both, my lady.'

In a dark corner of the room a tall clock ticked. Its case newly inlaid with elm and pear wood, glowed with polish.

He looked about him and noted the main door and two doors below the curve of the stair.

'Sergeant, excuse me. A drink? I have ale or wine.'

'I was once a wine buyer in France. When I was very young.'

'My husband tells me you speak French?'

'And German and Spanish.'

Anne Fairfax was a well bred woman and at ease with men. Not stupid, not light, not ill favoured. A serious woman. Used to her place in court when she was there and used to her place here on the estates that were her dowry and which she cared for

Fox watched while she poured the wine. The light sparkled on the glasses.

'I think you will like our wine, sir. My father liked his wine well enough. I have something I want to ask you.'

Fox looked at her in surprise. He picked up the etched goblet and looked at the dark wine against the light. He tried it. It was good.

Lady Anne Fairfax continued.

'I will be indiscreet. I am not happy with the work my husband does for that man Thurloe. You know him?'

'Hardly. I know your husband and I'd trust him with my life.'

'Rightly. But these are not normal times and he is an impetuous man you said, I think?'

Fox sipped his wine and said nothing for a moment.

'Some of his younger officers would say so when we fought

those wars together. It was a time ago, my lady. We have all grown older. More discreet.'

'Perhaps,' she said. 'I want my man to come home and stay here in our place. He comes from a line of soldiers, well and good, and so do I. Tom has done his soldiering in Europe. But to fight here, on home soil. King's men against his own subjects. It is not right. The world flies topsy-turvy and it concerns me, Sergeant.'

'It concerns us all that have seen war Ma'am. Though we're not yet at the fighting. A little light skirmishing so far. Nothing yet. Except for Edge Hill which was bad I'm told.

'Please God it doesn't come to anything more.'

'Amen to that. But it will come, be sure of it.'

The hall was suddenly filled with excited dogs yapping and prancing and Black Tom Fairfax strode into the room, nodded at Fox, kissed his wife, fussed his dogs and hurried to the chair by the fire. He was followed by a young man who was not introduced.

'Sergeant – you got your orders then?'

'I was told you wanted to see me.'

'Oh, cold Sergeant. Lost our eagerness have we?'

'I have other fish to fry, Sir. I'm no longer in your army.'

'Mr Thurloe needs you, Sergeant.'

'I think I don't need him.'

The young man lounging by the window snapped round.

'You forget your manners, Sir.'

'I don't think I know you,' said Fox so quietly the man had to move closer to hear what was said.

'You will do as you are told,' snapped the young man.

Fox turned to Fairfax.

'Tell him he forgets himself, whoever's son he is. Wet and green and a fool to boot.'

Fairfax puts his hand up.

'Michael, hold your tongue if you please.'

He turned then to Fox and asked him quietly,

'So why are you here?'

'To listen. I said I'd listen. That's all.'

Fox saw the anger rise in his old commander's face. No one gainsaid Black Tom with impunity.

Fairfax stared at Fox as his hounds crept closer to his chair and the fire.

Anne stood up then and walked to the young man.

'My son, Sergeant, sometimes wants to stand up for his

father.'

'Then he did well my lady and I meant no offence to my old commander. I speak as I find. I thought that was the Yorkshire way of it.'

He smiled at the young man who eventually grinned back.

Anne nodded approval and kissed her son.

'Here's a man knows his own mind, Tom. I will see what the kitchen is preparing.'

She smiled at Fox and walked to the door.

'Wine to your liking, Sergeant?' Fairfax asked

'He used to deal in wine in France, Tom,' said his wife as she swept out of the room to see to food and beds. 'It was a pleasure to meet you, Sergeant Fox.'

Fox stood as she left the room. He turned to face the man watching him. Fairfax's Irish wolf hound lay beside his master.

'Where's the woman?' Fairfax was still in a high temper.

'I thought you'd know, sir,' said Fox.

'I'm asking you. She brought you here, after all.'

'I'm here, sir. To listen.'

'Do I take it you are willing to do what we want?'

Fox shook his head.

'Who, sir? You or will Master Thurloe be my master in this enterprise?'

Fairfax snapped 'That's of no importance, sir.'

'If I knew what you wanted, I might give you an answer, sir. I'm no longer in the army and so will do as I wish.'

'You'll do as you are told, Sergeant.' The young man could not stop himself. Fox stood and Fairfax saw then something he had never seen before in his old sergeant's eyes. That dark emptiness. Here was a dangerous man.

Fairfax put his hand on the wolf hound's head and the dog rumbled a low growl of warning.

Fairfax laughed.

'Michael, please leave it. Well, Sergeant not changed, then? It's why Thurloe needs you. I told him as much. We need a man of independent mind, a man who understands what he is doing, a man willing to take on danger. A man who speaks French and German as well as you do. I know, I know, I flatter you and flattery sometimes works. Not with you, by all I have heard. But you have served me well in the past.'

'In the past, sir, it was another country. It was another army, it was other people, sir. This is different.'

The pale faced young man by the window snorted at the idea. Fox stepped closer to him.

'You ever seen a man spitted? Seen a woman naked set up for rape? A man lose his nose, an ear or worse? Have you? A girl screaming for the men to stop using her? You seen that have you?' The young man shook his head.

'You play at war in your offices and parliaments and fine halls like this. Out there is what war is. Houses burned down, women raped, children spiked on bayonets. Oh yes. You send men to do that. Against the French or the Spanish or the Prussians, well and good. But this is our own people as I understand it. I am heartily sick of such a war. Even now, before it really begins.'

Fairfax knew the value of a man like Fox but was not prepared for the anger he saw in front of him at that moment. Sergeants were not expected to have attitudes. His wife's father would have had Fox flogged for it.

Times were changing. But his son had needed to be told and here was a man whose experience was what made him the best spy Fairfax had worked with.

It had taken him a long time to convince Thurloe, that pale, cold-blooded man in his overheated room near the river crossing, to the Cherry Pickers' Orchard bank near the Tower, that Fox would best respond to his old military master and not to a man he'd regard as a clerk. Fairfax understood his men well. He leaned forward and put his hand on the wolfhound's head.

'Sergeant, sit you down. I will tell you what we want you to do. My son sometimes has an unfortunate way. But soldier to old soldier, maybe I can help you understand. Tell me what the woman told you.'

Fox sat then, glanced at the young man and then at Fairfax. He said nothing.

Fairfax was not amused.

'He's my son, Sergeant.'

'It's my life.'

Fox turned to the young man.

'I mean no offence, believe me. But sometimes it is best that the fewer people know what a mission is the better for all. The safer I feel. One careless word, you see, and I could end up doing the hemp jig or lie dead in a ditch with my throat slashed. So no offence, but – '

He left things hanging. The young man looked quietly at Fox. The wind-burned face, the long dark hair and the dead, still, eyes. He sat, the boy noticed with his back to the wall and opposite the doors. Across his back was still slung a long curved scabbard holding a blade.

His hands lay still on the table and only the faintest twitch of a nerve under his left eye gave an indication of the tension in the air.

The boy walked to Sergeant John Fox and put out his hand. 'No offence, Sergeant, none taken.'

The two of them shook hands and Fox smiled softly.

'Your father's son. Take care of him and remember sometimes it is best to think before opening the mouth. That way you keep friends and confuse enemies.'

He watched the boy walk out of the room and then turned back to the business in hand.

'That was gracefully done, Fox. Thank you.'

Fairfax poured more wine.

'The matter is simple enough. The Queen has left the country. It is said she has gone to take her daughter, Princess Mary to her husband, a Prince of Orange. That is a bit of smoke to hide the fact that she has taken some of the royal jewels. Not just her own jewels, but Crown property that belongs to the State. Huge diamonds, a gold collar with rubies that was Queen Elizabeth's. Crown property smuggled out, we believe, to buy help from relatives and friends in Europe.'

'And the King?'

'Immediately it seems he intends, if Thurloe's intelligencers have it right, to take Hull back for the Royalist cause. It depends on who last gave him advice. With the Queen out of the way in The Hague, or Amsterdam, he is liable to bend to the last word from one favourite or another.'

'So who knows which way the wind will blow? What does Master Thurloe want from me?'

'Confirmation that Henrietta is trying to buy allegiances to the King. It may be possible that she is trying to raise money to pay for the King's army for the coming war by the sale of crown property.'

'Yes?'

'We believe she is trying to buy arms, muskets, powder, cannon, everything an army might need. We need to know if she is, who is providing it, when it will be shipped, by whom, in what and to which part of the English coast.'

'Is that all?'

Fairfax lowered his voice.

'No. It is not all. There are rumours that she is planning to sweep up soldiers from the mercenary armies about Europe. Young English and Scottish officers who have gone for a soldier as I did. She wants them back in their King's service. Men with ambition. Their skill, experience above all, would be a danger to the Parliamentary army.'

'Ambition? What's the threat there?'

'The queen can promise them advancement in the court if they come into the King's service.'

'Or hers?' Fox murmured.

Fairfax looked up sharply.

'What d'you mean by that, Fox?'

'She seems to be a formidable woman. In Europe on her own. It depends of course on whether her party wins.'

'My wife believes she is the backbone of the King. But she believes all women are the backbone of their husbands.'

Fairfax drank more wine, offered the jug to Fox who shook his head. Fairfax poured another glass as he went on, 'She is only a woman and she is trailing the usual group of courtiers and King's men with her. I think Thurloe is imagining shadows in the dark. But he wants to know what she is promising the men who are coming to the King's standard and who they are. Names, Fox. Their names and connections.'

Fox shut his eyes and was silent for a moment.

'You want me to go to The Hague or Amsterdam and to bring back the answers to those questions?'

Fairfax nodded.

'You will be well paid of course.'

'Yes. I will. When would you want me to leave?'

'First you will go to London, see Thurloe.'

'Why?'

'He may have a contact for you in the court. Close to the Queen.'

'I mislike Thurloe.'

Fairfax smiled.

'Not an easy man, sergeant. But loyal in his way, I think. He wants to speak with you.'

CHAPTER 15

Maeve and Fox sat together in the back room of the Sign of the White Horse where the usual whirl of business went on.

'Liar! The bloody old liar. It's the half of the truth for God's sake.'

Fox had ridden down from the north. He'd been alone. Where Maeve was he had had no notion. But he knew she'd find him when she wanted to at the Sign of the White Horse.

He had agreed to see Thurloe but first he wanted to talk with Maeve.

He had sat looking down across London in the dawn light. Smoke and mist were clearing from the mass of buildings, the homes, the churches, the towers and roofs. It swirled about the warehouses and the masts of tall ships in the berths up the river. The great river Thames wound in from the countryside and through the city.

The water in the river sparkled where the mist cleared, like diamonds. It was an illusion. The river was putrid with night soil, old vegetables, dead dogs and even corpses trapped against the pillars of the bridges. There were patches of green and choice land held by the richest merchants and the aristocrats.

The drums of war were already sounding and the men of power continued to twist and turn the fates of people whose lives they held in their hands. The poor living in the rookeries and slums were to be fodder for what was coming. At its heart the city was decaying and rotten as a corpse in a charnel house.

The great men and women, the merchants, the bankers, the powerful, the great and the good lived in splendour alongside the citizens who lived without hope. The gardens of the rich smelt sweetly of herbs and flowers.

Everything was for sale here. Pepper, power and people, diamonds, debauchery and death were all to be had for coin.

Down there in the huggermugger of streets, Thurloe and his intelligence men, sweeping up all snips and snaps of information about their enemy.

But the enemy was English men and women. Fox had done his work behind French or German, Swedish or Prussian lines. He'd scavenged information in enemy cities, bought traitors, killed turncoats from time to time. Men and women had died, for sure. That was his trade but never amongst or against his own.

The work for Thurloe was a price he had to pay to get close to the court around the Queen where his daughter would be.

Fox rode down into the stinking city to find that mysterious, bitterly angry Irish woman whose beauty still astonished him.

'No man owns me, John Fox.' She'd told him as much the first time they had lain together. It seemed so long ago now.

She came into the back room of the inn five minutes after he had arrived. They sat opposite each other in the snug bar and she was flashing with anger.

'The bloody liar,' she said again. She stared in disbelief across the table puddled with ale and swirled about with rings stained into the scrubbed oak planks.

'Bloody men. You astonish me, John. You do astonish me. To believe that story about a few men being recruited and a little money changing hands for weapons. You think it's that they want to know about? What's the truth of the business, John? Not what he's told you, that's for sure, my friend. That Thurloe's a deep and dangerous player so have a care when you meet him. Which side is he playing on? Don't ask him, watch him and those about him.'

In the room beyond the snug, men were singing, others were shouting for ale, a girl slapped a man's face for getting too familiar with her backside. A sudden flare up of noise as two angry men stood, a table went flying and chairs were knocked over. A woman screamed and there was the sudden thud as two men who had set to with fists were clouted by the publican with the axe handle he kept behind the bar for keeping order.

A girl was called to refresh the tankards and the noise rose up again. Life went on at the Sign of the White Horse.

Fox walked back from the jakes through the men packed around tables, huddled on settles, standing by the barrels along one wall. He stepped past two girls who thought he might be interested in what they had to offer. They had few teeth left. Not enough between them to make a mouthful. They stank of old ale and grease.

He passed them without a look. A tall man stepped into his way and refused to stand aside.

'You got a drink for me, mister?' the man asked as another man moved in behind Fox.

'No,' said Fox as he stepped forward, picked up a pot of ale from the nearest table and slung it into the face of the advancing man.

He turned as he stepped closer and smashed his elbow full force backwards across the bridge of the nose of the man behind him. Bone smashed and the man went down in a welter of blood. Fox kicked him in the groin then turned back to the tall man who'd taken him for a fool.

He came at Fox fast with a knife in his right hand. Fox stepped in closer, took his wrist and elbow, flexed the wrist down and the elbow up and slammed the forearm across the back of a bench. The wrist broke with a click like an old stick broken for firewood.

No one moved for a moment and then the inn keeper shoved through the crowd of men with two pot boys.

'Get that filth out of here.' He ordered.

The man with the broken wrist was moaning in pain.

'Next time,' said Fox. 'Choose more carefully.'

Fox turned then to the inn keeper and put his hand out. One of the pot boys picked up the bloodied man on the floor and the other shoved the man with the broken wrist out of the inn and into the street.

The inn keeper called the serving girls.

'Get a pot of ale here. Seems some has been spilled.'

No one looked at Fox. Slowly they went back to their drinks.

'Every time you come here you attract trouble, sergeant.'

'If you keep a recruiting house you attract troublesome men,' said Fox. 'You making good trade?'

'Good enough. There's trouble brewing and work enough in England for them with the skills and the experience, sergeant.

The Sign of the White Horse was a post box for mercenaries. For thirty years and more men had come here to find work in European armies as Fox once had.

'Will it get to real war, d'you think?' Fox asked.

The inn keeper nodded.

'Not one to get mixed in, sergeant. Not one to take a side on. War is my business I suppose and the business of most here, but war with brother agin brother is nothing but sorrow and sadness.'

He went on. 'You should know two men came looking for you. A month since. I told them I didn't know who they were talking about. But they had come looking. Unlikely men, well spoken, angry men. Not mercenaries at work. One of them slapped one of my girls. He said she spilt drink on him as she passed by with ale for my customers. He slapped her hard. Man to man is one thing. Slapping my girl is another. The two went their ways then. He was not pleased and I can tell you they meant you no kindnesses.' The inn keeper grinned.

'I owe you,' said Fox. 'Tell me, if I was to go to Holland looking for work – army work, soldiering work – do you have a contact you trust?'

The innkeeper looked at him sharply. 'You could sign up here.'

'Not here. Not fighting in my own country. A name?'

The Innkeeper considered a little, looked across the drinkers and the men in the room. He leaned closer to Fox.

'In Amsterdam you'll find an old Dutch soldier from our time in Black Tom Fairfax's regiment. Pieter Stalhorn's the man you want. You find him in the Inn of the Two Windmills, along the canal not far from the docks in The Hague. If he's not there you'll find him in some painter's studio in Amsterdam.'

Fox looked at him in surprise.

'He lost a leg or an arm, I dunno which, somewhere in North Germany. He discovered he had a good eye for colour. He mixes paints and assists some painter. Rembrandt. I think that's the name. In his studio. He knows people. Ask for him. Tell him Michael sent you from the White Horse. He'll help.'

Fox nodded his thanks. 'I've a friend in the snug bar. I should join her. Thank you for the name.'

'I'll put the word out about your daughter. I remember you see, John. And have a care. '

Fox turned back to the room that was pulsing with noise and drunken singing once more.

He walked into the small snug bar. It was empty, Maeve had gone.

CHAPTER 16

It was late afternoon. Fox walked warily across the filth and detritus of the streets. Heard the sounds of men and women, children laughing, a girl shouting at a lover, two women bargaining over a piece of fruit or a cabbage, soldiers lounging in ale shops and clerks and merchants walking grandly about the streets to meetings in back rooms and old haunts. The Parliament house was busy with barristers and clerks with ledgers as they went about their business.

London was forever changing. On the river and down stream, masts stuck sharply into the sky over the tiny buildings that housed the myriad workers whose skills kept the navy afloat.

Fox turned back on himself, switched to a side lane, emerged into a tiny courtyard, stopped and waited. He stepped back into the narrow lane and into the flow of citizens past the watchmaker's shop on the slope of the hill leading down to the river.

He stepped into a shop that sold blades and bought a small knife. He walked out of the back of the shop into the alley, swerved around a pile of offal from a butcher's and out into the jostling crowd on the hill and walked into the watchmaker's shop, and through it to a narrow passage. Opened the door at the end and walked up the stairs. No one had followed him.

In the street outside, Maeve had an arm round a rat-faced boy of twelve. Poorly clad, with torn and ragged trousers and a battered jerkin that was too big for him. She gave him instructions and walked away down the hill, along the bank of the stinking river, vanished into a mass of old houses past a boat yard and was gone.

In the stuffy room over the watchmaker's shop, the fire was burning. Reflections danced off the heavy oak dresser and the carved wall panels. The paint was still fresh on a small newly painted portrait of Thurloe. A coming man, the portrait said. His pale face and dark neat hair was framed with a simple collar and behind the head, a window looking out onto an orchard of cherry trees. It was a pleasing picture and not as formal as many Fox had seen.

Thurloe watched Fox from behind his cluttered desk. There was another man in the room. An assistant who was not introduced.

'You like the portrait, Sergeant Fox?'

Thurloe seemed pleased. It was flattering. Fox nodded briefly.

'It's well enough done, Master Thurloe.'

'You know about painting?' Fox nodded.

'How does a soldier know about painting? You're not an officer. You have no – family.'

'I have my eyes. As to my family it was good enough for me, sir.'

He spun away from the picture and looked directly at the man behind the desk.

'You have books about war, tactics and the like, and no doubt you read them. D'you know about war? Not being a soldier?'

'No. So where did you get your knowledge of painting?'

'In Europe I saw enough. I had a friend who began to draw when he was with me in the field, Master Thurloe. A useful skill for men such as him. And me. For keeping information about possible battle grounds for our advancing armies. He was a good friend.'

'This painter, is he still a soldier?'

'No, Master Thurloe, he lost his right hand at a small siege. Great loss for a little victory we both said. Last I heard he'd gone home.'

'Where, England?'

'Hardly. He was from The Hague. There, I suppose.'

The small man writing at a desk in the corner of the room looked up for a moment and then went on with his work.

'So, you've come for your orders?'

Thurloe steepled his pale hands and stared at Fox over them. He was almost expressionless.

'No, sir, I've come to see what you want and then to decide if I can help you.'

'And if you decide you can't?'

'Then I shall not be able to be of service. I should remind you Master Thurloe that I am not a soldier under orders. I am free to do as I wish.'

Thurloe sighed, leaned back in his chair and smiled a thin and mirthless smile

'Tom Fairfax was right about you, Master Fox. Forthright, I think he said. He admires that in you. A Yorkshire trait, he called it.'

'I call it good sense. One thing before you tell me anything – this had best be private. Between you and me and not any chatterers.' He flicked a glance at the man in the corner who appeared to be absorbed in his writing.

Thurloe shook his head.

'You have no need to concern yourself about him, Master Fox.'

'You may say so. I'll stand by my Yorkshire trait and suggest with all respect that we speak in private or not at all.'

Thurloe sighed and snapped a finger.

'Leave us. You have work to do in your room, I believe.'

The man picked up his papers and, shaking the sheet he had been working on to dry the ink, walked out looking at Fox. The door latched shut and Thurloe leaned forward, and picked up a paper from his desk.

'So, we are alone. Now may we begin?'

'Not quite – there is something you should know before you ask for my help.'

Thurloe looked up sharply. A log fell and showered ash and sparks into the room.

'Well, sir?'

'Someone has put a price on my head. I've been attacked twice. That someone wants me dead or at least out of the way.'

'Does that concern me or what I am looking for from you?'

Fox shrugged. 'You should know therefore that if you thought to have me watched, followed, observed – checked on – that the watcher may well end in a canal. I assume I am to go to The Hague to watch the activities of our dear Queen.'

Thurloe nodded.

'And . . . ?' Fox let the question hang in the air.

Thurloe shook his head.

'Nothing more. Who sells her arms, who ships them, when, and where to be landed. What she uses for money. No more.'

'My arse,' snarled Fox. 'You take me for a fool. There is more – what is it? You want her watched. Who else? What am I to

95

look for?'

Thurloe stood up, walked to the hearth and kicked a smouldering log back into the heart of the fire.

'You are no one's fool, I concede that. So I, *we* thought perhaps while watching, you might catch the drift of talk surrounding that court, sift out gossip from fact. Note the rumours and report them.'

'Rumours? Important rumours?'

'Just rumours.'

'And I'm to sniff around the skirts of the Queen's party in Holland for rumours?'

Thurloe shut his eyes in thought and sighed.

'There is talk of a small group, a cabal of influence around her. I want details of who, where they meet, what they talk of.'

'So now we get to the meat and bones of it. At last.'

Thurloe looked across the table at Fox and nodded.

'I've arranged a passage for you. Tomorrow. The Raven's a small packet boat. It will land you discreetly. Ask for Captain Traylove in Deptford Creek.'

'Captain Traylove,' Fox repeated, who had no thought of taking any boat named by Thurloe.

'There is one last matter. Any useful information can be passed to my man in The Hague. Michael Harbourson's a reliable man. Close to the court. He deals in money and the spice trade. He will pass the information on to me. You do understand Fox?'

Fox nodded.

'Tomorrow in the evening at Deptford Creek.'

Thurloe stared as if suddenly unable to remember why Fox was there. Fox stood up and walked out without a word.

The corridor was dark now but a light glimmered under the door at the end where the little forger and cryptographer worked.

CHAPTER 17

Outside the watchmaker's shop a young boy sat playing a flute. A dirty boy begging for coin is never looked at even by those who, from time to time, throw him a coin. Fox bent to drop a coin in his lap for time enough for the boy to mutter one word. Fox walked away as the boy went on playing. Rain began to spatter the pavement.

Across the city, Maeve sat on a wall outside a pie shop, eating. She was sheltered from the rain. Brick lined walks and walls on one side and a narrowing cloister along the other, leading to a graveyard and beyond it a church at Cripplegate. In front of her an open space lined with mottled plane trees with no leaves.

From where she sat Maeve could see every approach to the open space. She loved this place for its seclusion. She had not realised how deep her hatred ran for the man Fox had named. Harry Morton. Maeve's memory of him was dark. She had sworn that if she ever had the chance she'd make him dance a little before she ended him.

A figure scuttled along the cloister and ran down the steps. The urchin with the flute stood panting, a retriever with a message.

'Your man Fox come out first. I told him where to find you. Then the other come out, missus, just like you said. I follered him. He never seen me, I take my oath on that. Who notices a raggy-arsed kid like me? He went to a lodging house in the Rookery down by the Cut. There's a small cross cut into a wall near it. I can show you. I left me sister there watching it and me brother with her in case he moves on. So what now, missus?'

Maeve smiled at him and took another pie from under the folds of her cloak.

'I know the place. You've done well. Here, eat. And this is

for your pain. If I need you I'll find you. You wait on Master Fox. Show him the place. I'll be there.'

She handed the boy a silver coin which he bit to check and shoved into the pocket of his ragged shirt.

'You did well.'

He smiled at the praise. As Maeve walked into the cloister and vanished he bit into his pie.

CHAPTER 18

Fox walked slowly through the Rookeries. The higgledy-piggledy, rat-infested hovels where the poor lived miserable lives and faced vice, murder and desperation in equal measure. No hope, no chances, no money no way to escape. Only religion, perhaps, for some.

He walked on down towards the river and the stinking piles that barricaded the banks along the tidal water.

So the Queen in Amsterdam or The Hague was up to mischief. Thurloe wanted details. No doubt she'd meet her sister-in-law in exile, Elizabeth of Bohemia. Another queen in exile with a court about her that the Dutch had little liking for.

Elizabeth was a Protestant who no doubt disapproved of Henrietta's Catholicism. But blood is thicker than water so Henrietta could well be seeking advantage from her. Thurloe would want to know. He'd talked about money to buy supplies of weapons of war for the Royal army. But there was more he wanted. What did Thurloe know? What was he leading Fox into?

This rumour about a cabal of men, close to Henrietta, plotting something. What was the spymaster really looking for?

At the far end of the lane stood what had been a convent. The only remaining sign of which was a small cross cut high on one wall. Flakes of blue paint fell off the plasterwork and the cross had a fleck or two of the gold that would once have covered it.

Maeve stood in the shadows. She was alone. Fox joined her and she pointed to a narrow door that led to stairs.

'Thurloe's little man lives in the top of the house. Where there's glimmer of light. I've a spy of my own followed him. She saw the light in the top window after he had gone into the house.'

'You're sure?'

'I don't listen to fools any more than you do. It was him.'
She described him.

'Don't I know the man after all?' Fox looked down at her in surprise.

'Know him?'

'Yes. Know him. I confess it was not amusing, but he had information I wanted. There's always a price to pay. Don't look so shocked, my friend. Sure 'tis only a moment or two and done with.'

'He gave you information? Why – what for?'

Maeve shook her head.

'You never know what will tumble out of a man like that. Secrets are my coin Fox. And yours. Some we spend, some we hoard.'

She nodded. 'He's the man can unravel coded messages. Thurloe has two or three such men. If he let me have a sight of such messages merely for the use of my body what would he pass for hard gold? He's a greedy man.'

'He was there when I saw Thurloe. He might have heard us.'

Maeve nodded. 'He might. Who's buying?'

'We'll see.' She grinned.

'And then?'

'Leave – for The Hague. We'll make our own arrangements. Thurloe's plans can go whistle. We go our way. Vanish. Best way for us. Just remember Michael Harbourson is our connection in Holland. But first we have a man to see.'

The stairs were unlit and very steep. The smell of cooking cabbage and rot greeted them as they inched up in the dark, past the small landing and up again. Behind the doors on the landing they could hear the murmur of families, the occasional cry of a dreaming child. On the second landing they waited and listened. There was nothing to be heard.

Fox walked quietly to the end of the landing past the rickety wooden banisters. The floorboards creaked a little as he put his shoulder to the door. The flimsy lock snapped and Fox was in a small room lit by two candles at a desk where the cryptographer sat huddled over his papers.

He looked up and tried to hide what he was doing as he cried out in fear. 'Don't hurt me – I've nothing here. No money – you've made a mistake.'

Fox stepped into the glimmer of light.

'You, my friend, have made the mistake.'

'You – Sergeant Fox – Mr Thurloe shall hear of this,' the little man blustered.

Fox walked round the table and shoved him aside. As he thought of running he faced Maeve in the doorway with a small blade in her hand.

'You? What in the name of God?'

'Judas,' she hissed.

'But I thought you said – '

'You'd betray your mother. You thought a jump up in your bed gave you some hold – the vanity of men, Judas.'

She laughed then and he felt the blade prick at his throat.

Fox lifted up a piece of paper and read, 'Sergeant John Fox to The Hague on Parliament business.'

He read on and held out the paper.

'You wrote this? There is a description. Looking for information about recruiting and money and ships.'

He read again. 'There is talk of a cabal '

He stared at the terrified little man.

'You listened at Master Thurloe's door, didn't you?'

Maeve moved her blade a little.

'Just take that away from my throat, please. I don't understand.'

'We think we do. A message for the other side? A warning. Master Thurloe will be unhappy to know he has a turncoat in his office.'

'It's nothing to do with me. Nothing. I had to. They know things about me, I have a sister in The Hague.' He was gabbling with fear now. 'They told me if I didn't pass them intelligence from Thurloe I'd regret it.'

'Who?' Fox snapped.

'Two men. King's men. The Queen's people – '

The little man was pale with fear.

'Please don't hurt me – I meant no harm.'

Fox put the paper in his jerkin and looked through the other papers, letters, notes, reports..

'All opened and copied – you do a great deal of mischief. You could've got me killed. No doubt Thurloe will know what to do with you.'

'Please, please don't tell him. Please. I have money, in the cupboard – there is money – just let me be.'

'The name of the men? Describe them.'

His eyes flickered for a moment. Hope was there for him if he talked.

'Tell us, Judas. Betrayal come easy eh?'

She pushed him further into the room and he stumbled and stopped,

'Will you let me live?'

'Describe the men.'

He stared up into the empty eyes, glanced at Maeve and saw only the pale face framed in waves of auburn hair and the ice green eyes of the young woman

'Tall – Sir Andrew, I heard his friend call him. Moustache and pointed beard. Dark hair, cut short above his shoulders. Thick faced – red-cheeked – as if he spent time out of doors. A soldier maybe.'

'The other?' Fox had not moved.

'You will let me free? I won't tell anyone – I won't – '

'The other?'

Maeve's blade was still in her hand.

'We can persuade you. Have you ever seen the damage a red hot blade can do to a man's eyes. Don't think I wouldn't. The softer sex, is it? You know what Orientals do to prisoners they want to persuade? They hand them to their women. Men beg their captors not to hand them to the women. So – '

She smiled a little and the man began to breath too fast. His fear was mastering him.

'Thin, younger. No name. I never heard a name. I swear I never heard a name. Pale. Thin faced.'

Maeve stepped closer and suddenly he shoved her blade aside and ran along the dark landing, tripped on a rotten floorboard and crashed through the balustrade.

He screamed once and a second later, smashed into the hallway below.

The two of them waited a moment listening. Nothing moved, no door was opened, no voice raised. The whole building had been silenced.

Maeve moved to the cupboard, opened it, took up a small box and turned to Fox.

'Time we left him.'

She picked up a candle and walked out.

Fox piled all the papers from the desk in the hearth, lit them with the remaining candle and walked quickly along the landing, skirting the broken floorboard and followed Maeve down the dark staircase.

Nothing moved in the other rooms. The poor are silent.

Fox joined Maeve.

'Broke his neck. Sure he's dead as mutton.'

She snuffed the candle and stepped into the street.

'We'll wait and watch. See who comes scavenging.'

They waited an hour in the dark. A grey cat that seemed attached to Maeve mewed twice, circled her and then stepped away into the dark.

Distantly a muffled bell sounded along the river. Fog, perhaps. In the old tenement, no light showed. No one came to investigate the muffled scream and the splintering crash as the man fell through the banisters into the long drop down the well of the stairs. He'd still be there, sprawled in the hallway.

By dawn Fox knew he'd be on the sea and, as far as Thurloe was concerned, he would have vanished from the face of the earth.

He grinned in the dark at the thought of Thurloe's anger when he discovered that his trust had been betrayed by the dead cryptographer.

Maeve nudged him and indicated the passage that ran along the side of the building. A slight thickening of the dark indicated someone moving and behind him the pale face of a second man showed for a moment. The two men walked into the open door of the tenement.

Fox and Maeve waited as clouds passed over the face of the moon and vanished leaving a silver light across the buildings.

They moved back into the darker shadows. Fox looked up and saw the faintest glimmer of light from the window on the top floor where the cryptographer had lived.

It was ten minutes before they saw the two men step into the moonlit street. Between them they carried the sagging body of the dead man. The man in front seemed to find the dead weight of the body too much.

The other, carrying the dead man's legs was younger. He looked about him anxiously. They struggled across to the open drain that ran alongside the cobbled pavement and dumped the body into the slow flowing sewage. The first man poured the contents of a bottle over the body.

Without looking up, they hurried back to the passage they

had come from and vanished into the darkness.

The drain, now blocked by the dead man, began to overflow sewage and filth over the cobbles. A dead and stinking drunk would attract little attention in this place.

Two hours later, the slithering, filthy tidal waters of the river eddied and swirled into the small creek downstream. A fishing boat stood at the end of the rotten jetty. The stink of old vegetables, putrid meat and human waste as the tide floated the fishing boat off the slime and filth that was the bed of the Thames along Deptford Creek. Fox stood in the shelter of the cabin as the boat lifted clear on the tide. Huddled in the dark and tiny cabin, Maeve Aherne felt the boat rock. It stank of old fish. She hated the sea.

CHAPTER 19

Ahead of Fox and Maeve a box was weighed up on an overhead crane. It swung and turned, threatened to slip onto the cobbles below but was expertly gaffed by two men standing in the open doorway on the first floor of the warehouse. They pulled the load quickly inside and, undoing the shackles, sent the rope back for the next load.

Dutch traders brought wealth from around the world into Holland. Its true source was the muscle of the hard handed men who turned the ships about and out to sea again.

A jumble of masts, furled sails on bowsprits and spars towered over the buildings along the shore of the Nieuwe Maas. Sailors worked on dizzyingly high masts and renewed old ropes, torn, storm-damaged sails.

It was the jumble of noises that told their own story The yells of working men rolling up huge canvas sails, the rhythmic cries of the men walking to the rhythm of the ship's fiddler as they turned the huge capstans on which ropes and chains were reeled.

The squeals of pigs being slaughtered and flensed into brine tubs for the next voyage. The rattle of winches and pulleys as stores were weighed aboard and stowed below.

The harsh gutturals of the Dutch language mixed with a hundred other tongues as sailors and workers moved about the quaysides. Little butty boats skulled out to the deep seagoing merchant ships anchored in the sea lanes, ferrying stores and newly pressed men out and officers ashore.

Dutch merchants were adventurous, wealthy and greedy for more trade with the new markets of the Far East. They lived for the most part in The Hague to the north and facing the sea. It was there that they built fashionable houses along fine wide streets.

But from here, in the docks and wharves along the river, their merchant ships had access to the middle of Europe and into the North Sea. Here and in Amsterdam raw materials were unloaded from trading voyages that might last a year or more. Merchants and those who backed them had to wait for the return of their ships to realise their profits. They might increase their wealth a thousand times over or, if a ship was lost with men and cargo, it was the lost cargo that was mourned.

The overseer ticked his bill of lading and checked the markings on the next box or barrel as it was made ready to haul up into the warehouse.

Merchants were busy thrusting measuring sticks into barrels and weighing pulses. They sniffed carefully at sacks of spices from the Indies.

Maeve watched for a moment and then walked after Fox.

This was a place on the make. It was loud with commerce and vibrant with trade. Beyond the streets that served the warehouses, in the sea lanes lying off-shore, stood ships of the Dutch navy guarding the approaches to the wharves and the river mouth and also to The Hague up the coast.

Fox felt at home in this hustling bustling place. He walked on and grinned at the auburn-haired woman beside him. She turned away and vanished into a crowd of fish-women gutting fish and packing them in salt in barrels.

He walked on, whistling, without a care in the world. He turned a corner, crossed a hump-backed bridge that spanned a tiny feeder canal, and found himself in a cobbled square surrounded by fine looking houses and a few inns. He looked about then shifted his large leather satchel to his left hand and walked towards a high-gabled building with bottle glass windows and freshly painted doors. A few tables stood in front of the lower windows. It was too cold to sit out there.

Overhead the sky was that blue iron grey of the northern ports. Fox had spent time under these skies from the ports of the Baltic, across the north Prussian plains. There was an urgency here. The Dutch were eager for trade. Unlike London, it was not mired in the old stink of a sluggish river and the filth of ages.

Maeve walked across the square to him and as they approached the inn she took his arm. She had seen no one following who seemed interested in them.

'If we're not to attract comment or refusal we're man and

wife,' she said. 'This is a place where such things matter, remember. Puritanical and religious. We don't need to attract comment.'

Her eyes were alight once more. She had been sick as a cat for two days on the journey over in the tiny cabin of the fishing boat that had brought them to land a few miles down the coast where the owner of the boat was to fill his hold with barrels of brandy and schnapps soon to be buried under a catch of fish. They would have to make their own way to The Hague.

'Smuggling pays better than herring,' explained the captain. He didn't apologize for the stink of fish in the cabin. He never noticed it.

Fox walked into the inn and she followed behind him. Ever the dutiful wife.

Beyond the tiled hallway a door led into the bar and ahead of them curved a wide staircase. A fat woman came out of the bar wiping her hands on her apron and smiling a welcome when she saw they had baggage with them.

Fox took a room at the front on the first floor. She gave him a key from her pocket and took the coins he gave her without counting them and went back into the noise of the bar.

Upstairs, Fox walked the length of the corridor and checked the side window. It looked out onto a blind alley. The window was firmly locked. A narrow flight of stairs led down from the far end.

He walked back to their room and went in. Maeve was already asleep.

Fox left her and went down to the bar. The woman sold him have a plate of meat and cheese with new baked bread and a bottle of red wine. He explained that his wife needed to sleep. She had found their journey tiring.

The woman led him to a snug bar and brought his food. He ate and drank the wine and later she came to see that he had all he needed. She brought a pitcher of the wine and filled his glass.

'They tell me that that English queen is here in The Hague,' said Fox, as he picked his teeth.

'Bad luck to her,' said the fat woman. 'We don't like these Catholic tarts in our country. They make trouble and don't seem to care. I don't give a damn that she has brought her little daughter to meet her damned husband. She's a child. That queen's not welcome nor her hangers-on neither.'

'Where does she stay?' Fox smiled at her.

'Oh God knows, nothing in The Hague is good enough for her not even the New Palace on Staedt-Straat. They tell me she's forever grumbling that the city and its entertainment is for peasants. I say let her get home then and let us be. She never comes down here where the work is done which is a blessing.'

She passed a damp cloth over his table and leaned closer to him

'They say no one should give her credit. Nor her hangers on. She's on a begging mission, they say. Not a brass button to call her own, they say. Someone told me she was pretty. Well, I saw her the other day riding out near the sea. A scraggy bundle of bones in my view. And a complexion like pastry.' The fat woman laughed. 'Just your sort, I lay my oath.'

Fox smiled at her and shook his head.

'What have queens to do with the likes of you and me?' he asked.

'They say she goes to Amsterdam soon to try new pastures, new fools to gull,' she said.

Fox shrugged and took another drink.

'Your wife – ? Will she want to eat?'

Fox nodded and she bustled out of the snug and about her business.

CHAPTER 20

They lay in the bed under feather bolsters and listened to the early morning sounds from the square. Distantly the mixed sound of bells rang out over the city. They'd ridden into The Hague in the early morning and found lodgings on the edge of the city near a market square. Closer, iron-rimmed cart wheels rumbled across the cobbles with the shouts of men and women putting up stalls for a market.

Maeve stood looking out into the square and Fox looked across the room at her. She stood unconsciously beautiful, naked in the morning light streaming through the windows. She took his breath away and yet – yet he still felt guilt at the thought that his dead wife, Alison, was watching him.

Maeve turned to him

'Alison won't mind, John.'

He lay staring at her and marvelled at her skill in finding her way into his mind.

Maeve walked to the bed then and pulled the bolster away from his body.

'How?' he asked. 'How do you know ?'

'Because, Sergeant Fox, you are, inside, you are a good man and loved her. Love her yet perhaps.'

Her hands moved gently on his body, readied him and then she was covering him.

It was a quiet loving. Not like their past encounters which had been urgent, over-eager, frantic. This was gentle, calm and very deep, breathtaking in its power.

She lay alongside him and smiled not at him but to herself. Was he just another conquest? He had no way of knowing and no wish to ask.

In a corner was a bowl and a ewer of water. She rolled away from him and stepped into it and sluiced cold water over her body. The light from the uneven glass panes threw shadows over her breasts and thighs as she washed herself. He saw the taut muscles of her buttocks and the dark shadows between her legs as the water ran back into the earthenware bowl.

She poured more cold water over her head and grimaced as it ran down her body.

Stepping away she took the blanket from the bed and wiped herself dry.

'You,' she said.

He shook his head.

'If we're sleeping in the same bed, you'll be clean. You now.'

Reluctantly he stepped towards the bowl . She laughed at his attempts at modesty.

'No need for that,' she said. 'I've seen it all before, John Fox, and touched it, and more, now wash.'

He stood in the water that had poured off her and she upended the jug of water over his head. She laughed at the yelp he made when the cold water cascaded over him.

They sat in the watery morning light while around them the market began. Old women bought a few vegetables. The market was a place for gossip and for old friends as much as a place to buy food. It was, in its way, the local exchange.

Maeve drank a small beer and looked at the plate of cheese and herring pickled in salt and onions between them. Fox had already eaten.

'And now,' she said quietly, 'You wonder why you're here?'

He looked at her sharply.

'I'll tell you why. Thurloe will never tell the truth and your General Tom Fairfax won't even know it, probably. You are here to find your daughter and I am here to find the man who might have taken her. Harry Morton, to whom I owe a debt. Thurloe's questions can go hang.'

'I promised Thurloe, I gave my word to Fairfax. There is work to do.' He stared at her as she burst into peals of laughter.

'They already know the answers. They know Queen Henrietta is here on a mission to gather funds for her silly king. To buy weapons and find officers if she can. No need for you to come here to learn that. No need to put yourself in danger. Why was the forger Thurloe used frightened enough to kill himself? Not for silly rumours about buying weapons. Why are you here?'

Fox shook his head.

'This is a dangerous place. People want you dead, John Fox, which you already know. They will come after you, never fear that. So you ask yourself why. Why have your masters sent you without explaining the true reason or the real target?'

He looked about the now teeming square and listened to the harsh language as customers argued the price of a cabbage.

'They haven't even dared tell you what it is. What have they heard, what does Thurloe know, what does he really want you to confirm? Has the Queen bought arms, powder, supplies, when will it be sent and where will it be landed? They know that already or most of it.' Maeve snorted at the very idea.

'Any agent could find that for them. Everyone has their price. This is something more than secret. Think, John, think. They send you onto danger and don't even tell you the truth. You owe them spit all.'

And she picked up a herring and stripped it to the bone.

Fox stared at her and nodded reluctantly.

'You go to the heart of it. I know it is something more than who she sells to and who she buys from.'

'What is at the real heart? What is the true target that they dare not more than hint at? If I were you, my friend, I'd want to know the answer to that. I'd find out and then I might tell them and I might not. Maybe you will discover the question and the answer may kill you. There will be people guarding their secret of a certainty. It is more dangerous to discover that truth than finding out about Henrietta's plans.'

She picked up the last herring, bit one end, stripped the flesh off the bone, wiped the juices that ran onto her chin and slung the bone to a couple of cats who were watching her intently.

Fox reached out to touch her hand and she withdrew it.

'Don't, don't touch. Never do that. Never.'

He looked into her eyes and was shocked to see the opalescent green turn to blue and then almost black as she stared at him. He looked away.

'I thought,' he began.

'You thought because we'd lain together you had the right to touch me. I have never met the man who had that as a right. Never.

111

Understand?'

Fox shook his head. 'No, no I don't.'

He stood up. 'I'll pay and collect our things.'

Maeve pulled her hooded cloak over her face and didn't look at him as he turned and walked back into the tavern.

Beyond the crowded square the city was waking up. Merchants and dealers were opening their offices. In the small rooms at the head of old staircases the whirr of wheels could be heard as the jewellers and gold polishers began their work.

Fox walked out of the doorway and looked across at the table where two cats were fighting over the plate of fish bones. Maeve had gone.

He knew it would serve no purpose looking for her. If she chose to go about her own business, it was her way. Maeve had been with him from time to time, but from time to time had left him to do what he had to do. They both preferred it that way.

The Queen was in The Hague and would make her way to Amsterdam soon, according to the woman down by the dockside. Fox had two contacts in The Hague. The first had been given to him by Master Thurloe.

'He's my man,' Thurloe had boasted. 'My man in her court. He'll see you, and tell you what he knows. You'll find him in Kirk Straat, beside an apothecary's, near the town hall. But most of the time he is wherever her court is. He's Miles Harbourson.'

'Did you give him my name?' Fox had asked and Thurloe had shaken his head.

He had smiled across his steepled fingers.

'No, Sergeant. He will expect you. Tell him that the meadows by Oxford are blooming. He'll know you.'

The other contact was an old comrade Fox hadn't seen since they'd worked behind the enemy lines in Gustavus Adolphus's army when they were young men. Fox smiled at the memory. Pieter Stalhorn would be a useful man if Fox could find him.

The last time they had spoken, Pieter Stalhorn had told him he could always be found at the inn called the Two Mills on the Polder. That was three years ago.

Fox stopped at the narrow entrance to an alley between two houses, turned up it, past a bread shop that smelt of new-baked bread, turned left and left again and came back down onto the canal-side a little further on. No one followed him. It was automatic, in a strange city, to cover his tracks.

112

The Two Mills on the Polder was an ancient, low clap-board building. The weathered sign on the front had a faded picture of two mills on a dyke. The name had faded out with the northern sunlight.

Fox stood and watched the place for an hour. There was a door in the front and another at one end. Stores for the kitchen and barrels of ale went in there. The other side backed onto a slipway down to the canal where a large barge was moored.

Two girls came to the side door and stood gossiping. A man came to the door and shouted at them and they hurried back into the kitchens. The man stood in the sunshine. Fox moved out of the shadows and the man saw him. He waited and Fox was almost close enough to touch when the man recognised him.

Pieter was big, square and running to fat a little. His face was bright and open and his smile of greeting was warm as summer. They said nothing and just walked into the kitchen together. Pieter had only one arm.

Standing at the long hearth was a woman almost as tall as Pieter and fatter. She turned then and smiled.

'This is my friend,' he began.

'Sergeant John Fox.' she said softly. 'He has talked about you so often. You are welcome in my house.' Fox nodded gravely and put his bag down. 'So long as there is no talk of going back to war,' she said.

'Nothing about war then, Mevrouw. Well, not much. If a woman comes looking for me – pale faced, green eyes and auburn hair; please don't turn her away.'

She smiled at that.

'A woman is it then, John Fox?'

'Not as you mean *Mevrouw*. She is someone I owe a favour.'

Pieter's wife told one of the girls to take the leather bag to a room. 'No talk of soldiering and you are welcome.'

CHAPTER 21

As he usually did when he came to a new place, Fox began to walk the city. To learn it. It was habit. He walked the outskirts and saw the abundant market gardens that provided fresh fruit and vegetables for the ever growing population. Herds of sheep grazed the salty vegetation along the sea shore.

The huts and sheds of the dairy herds merged slowly into the inevitable hovels of the poor that ringed the outside of the city. As he moved along, Fox was once again aware of the effects of war. He had fought across Europe with mercenary armies and people moved from land they had held into villages and as they too were erased by war, people had moved again into cities and once inside, they tried to stay close to the walls the cities threw up as protection from any marauding army.

These hovels outside the city were like detritus on a beach after a storm. They stank of humanity. Muddy pools and brackish streams trickled through the passages between them. Children sat listlessly under the cold grey skies. The food in the gardens here was not for them. It was grown for the tables of the rich burghers, for the mayor and councillors, for the predicants of the church, and for the merchants who sat cold-faced and cold-arsed on plain benches in the churches dotted about the city. It was for wives who sat with ice cold faces perched over lace ruffs like cartwheels. There was not much laughter in them.

The food came by barge along canals built as defences from the sea and from armies, just as the shit of the city was carted out to grow yet more .

Within the old walls, tall merchants' houses rose to steep gabled roofs not much lower than the steeples on the grey churches. They lined wide streets and some were reflected in canals. They were fine looking brick buildings and a measure of wealth for some but for the craftsmen who lined the streets behind the quays and warehouses, ostentatious wealth was not their way.

Many were Jews who had been persecuted across Europe from Poland to Spain where the Inquisition persecuted Muslims and Jews together. So Spain lost its greatest scientists, its most important scholars. Its rich diversity was obliterated in the name of Catholicism.

Muslim scholars went from Spain to North Africa and the Eastern Mediterranean whereas the Jews came to The Hague or Amsterdam where they were allowed to practise their trades and skills.

Fox moved down into the area where their workshops hummed and rattled. Polishing wheels turned in small rooms up rickety old stairs. Gold chain, trinkets, crowns, rings, boxes, plates, earrings glittered under the light as they were polished to a lustrous sheen on the work benches of Jewish polishers and gilders.

Further down the same street small knots of men in long robes stood quietly in pairs, talking. They kept their heads down and never raised their roof gables as high as the rich merchants in the inner city. These were discreet men and more discreet women.

They were experts with stones. They could assess at a glance the weight and value of diamond, sapphire, ruby or emerald. They could see the flaw lines, know how to release the inner brilliance of a diamond, where to cut to begin the process of changing a rough stone into something of great value. Diamonds were cut into many facets under the eye-glass screwed into the eye of the cutter. These men were the aristocrats of their trade and their world.

As for the bankers and the money changers, Fox had no view but assumed they had their place. Any talk of allowing Jews back into England for their skills with money and their connection to wealth all over Europe was always resisted by the court and the Catholic Queen.

Fox had three days of walking the streets looking at dead end alleys, remembering which streets were crowded and when and where merchants gathered to eat or drink coffee. Where women gossiped.

He described it as 'tasting the temperature of the place.' He did it in the mountains on a stake out and he did it in places like The Hague.

He walked the streets at night and learned the routines of the city guardians, learned their patrols and changes, learned where they stopped to take a drink or a bite to eat. Often alone but from time to time with Pieter to guide him he went on 'tasting the temperature.'

Where the whores worked and where their clients came from. The underbelly of a city was what he needed to know. Who were the thieves and who the thief takers.

From time to time he wondered where Maeve might be. But it was likely she had her own plans. They had a common enemy, he knew that. Sir Harry, Elizabeth's husband, was a cruel man but he'd been a foolish one to make an enemy of Maeve Aherne for if she said she'd geld him she would do it, sure as spit.

Fox had two agendas, one to answer the question Thurloe had not asked and the second to find his daughter.

On the afternoon of the third day he sat with Pieter outside the inn in the watery sunshine at the end of a jetty. Even now habits died hard. No one could over hear them and no one could approach without being seen. Pieter appeared to be fishing.

'I'm not angry, not even bitter to tell the truth,' Pieter said. 'War does this to some men. I can walk, I can do most things a man needs to do. And I found a good wife when I came home.'

He stared at the oily waters and looked away into the sunlit sea beyond the wall. 'It hurts sometimes or it did until I found work. I married an innkeeper's widow, see? It's her trade and I had nothing and worse, I had only one hand.'

Fox grunted and wondered how he would have fared in the same situation. He knew he'd be angry.

'There's no gain in feeling angry. She taught me that.'

'And you found work?'

'I'll show you later. It doesn't pay much but I use the skills I have. I could draw and I used to paint a little. Now I use the skills I gained. You'll see.'

There was a moment of silence.

'Tell me.' Pieter said quietly. Fox threw a pebble into the water and took a deep breath.

'My wife – '

'Alison?' Pieter said softly

Fox stared in surprise. Pieter smiled.

'You talked of no one else. It has to be her.'

'She was burned alive.'

Pieter stared in shock.

'Her uncle wanted the land and the family house so he tried to have me butchered and he arranged to have my wife accused of witchcraft. They burned her.'

'What happened to him?'

Fox said nothing and Pieter looked away.

'And now you go soldiering again. Like we used to do.'

Fox shook his head.

'No my friend – not like we used to do. One last time for Black Tom. I hate gathering information against my own kind. English against English, brother against brother, father against son – We've seen our share of war and what it does, Pieter, you and me. But never fighting against our own people. Civil war is an abomination.'

'So. Don't do it.'

'It's not so simple. My daughter is involved. Rebecca is here in The Hague or Amsterdam with a woman I knew and her husband. I left Rebecca with the woman – Elizabeth.'

Pieter glanced at his old comrade.

'The woman?'

'We were both alone together in winter. She had nursed me. No excuses but she was lonely, Pieter. I don't believe love came into it. But she promised to protect my daughter. Her husband is an animal, it seems, and I came here to find my daughter. The work I am supposed to be doing for Fairfax opens doors for me. Connections at the Queen's court. You understand?'

Pieter nodded. Two gulls screamed over their heads and swooped down attacking a gannet just rising from the water. The gannet dropped the fish he had half-swallowed and the gulls followed it down into the water.

'This connection?

'I told your wife we'd not even talk soldiering.'

Pieter grinned.

'She knows me better than to think I won't sniff around for an old comrade. Who is this connection? Where is he? In the Hague?'

'In Kirk Straat over an apothecary's. Close to Queen Henrietta's clique. I have a message for him. He might tell me what I want to know. That will keep Tom Fairfax off my back. Can you arrange for the message to get to him? I'll see him midday tomorrow.'

Pieter grinned. 'There's a church near that street. Always open. It's quiet as the grave in there. Write it down and I'll see that he gets the message.'

'My friend. Don't get involved more than that.'

'It won't even come from me. I have my own ways, our usual means. Nothing will get back to me. His name?'

'Harbourson. Miles Harbourson.'

The two men walked up the jetty away from the screaming gulls, stopped at an ale house where Fox wrote the message.

'Shall we see the place he's staying in?' asked Pieter. 'A little reconnoitring might be wise.' He was enjoying feeling the game was on again.

They strolled up into The Hague through the main square, past hurrying clerks, beggars, churches and civic buildings. Past huddles of merchants in doorways waving papers, past lawyers and washerwomen, old men sunning themselves in the weak light, past old dogs, flowers in pots.

Suddenly, across the square came the clattering of a retinue of horses and behind them a carriage. There were fifteen mounted men, armed with cavalry swords. They wore fine clothes and their horses were almost as well bred as their riders.

In the carriage was a small woman in travelling clothes and beside her two ladies muffled against the air.

One of the horsemen was riding close to the carriage. He was black haired and sharp featured. His thin mouth had cruelty in its set that chimed well with his cold eyes.

He leaned towards the woman in his side of the carriage and spoke to her. She looked away, afraid of him. The horseman laughed and rode on.

Fox watched him as he rejoined his companions, laughing.

'The bitch doesn't listen,' he said. 'She'll come to heel, mark me.'

Fox heard him clear enough. The man didn't give a damn for what others might think. The other men in the group said nothing. They seemed uncomfortable. He laughed again and they ignored him.

No one in the square took notice as the entourage clattered across the cobbles. Fox saw a man turn and spit and then turn back to a conversation he was having with a gowned lawyer.

'Your Queen,' said Pieter. The two men didn't break step as they strolled on.

'Not liked, it seems'

Pieter grinned.

'Listen, Sergeant – we're a protestant country here and we don't like her ways. Ask my wife what she thinks of that woman and the women around her. We've seen them parading through our streets, making a show of themselves, dresses cut too low, immodest. My wife dislikes it. Our churchmen preach against their licentious ways. We want her gone and her hangers on, arrogant, loud, overbearing and unwelcome. She is only tolerated because she has money to spend or things to trade.'

Fox shook his head. 'She's here to buy weapons, supplies for her husband. If she's so disliked who'd sell to her? She's using jewels for money.'

'Our merchants would sell their mothers for mittens if it made them a profit. No matter what sort of a whore they think she is, no matter the play acting and masques and lewd dancing they bring, they also bring the stink of money if she can sell the jewels she has brought with her.'

'How d'you know this?'

'I am an intelligencer, like you. It never lets you go, Fox. It's an addiction to ask questions, to search for little bits of knowledge. It's better in some ways than a little bit of wealth. I have a friend who accumulates titbits of information. Not for money but for friendship.'

'Is she selling the jewels? Getting the money she needs to buy supplies?'

'A few will let her use the jewels as security. Most of our jewellers won't touch. You will meet my old friend. He can tell you if he likes you and if you go with me, he will like you.'

CHAPTER 22

They walked through squares and along streets. Each much like the next. Tall brick built houses lined the squares, their tall gables topped with sharply sloping tiled roofs. Three floors and more high. The homes of the wealthy ringed by the ancient walls beyond which the poor lived out their lives. It was unlike London where the wealthy had moved out of the centre of the city to avoid outbreaks of pestilence that lingered along the banks of the Thames.

A few ladies strolled from one house to the next wearing the wide pleated collars, stiff starched ruffs and white hoods or bonnets that all respectable women wore. Above all this was a respectable city where the lewdness of the estuary quaysides and the docks were kept firmly at bay.

The two men walked along a wide street where banking houses had signs and jewellers had their shops. This was a city bathing in wealth.

'This is Binnenhof,' said Pieter. 'Here in these houses the two courts live and play. '

'Two courts?'

'Your Henrietta and her sister-in-law have separate courts. Elizabeth of Bohemia who has been here a time, lives in style at Kneuterdijk and her family overflows into other houses nearby. Two exiled courts making mischief, I suppose, and not loved by each other nor the Dutch.'

They passed the lake, the Vijver in the centre of the city, passed the magnificence of Kneuterdijk. Walked on past the civic centre and down into the warren of streets radiating from the squares like the Vijverberg, crossed small bridges over tributary canals and away from the elegant business buildings.

'It's a rich city,' Fox remarked and Pieter laughed aloud

'You think so? Wait until you see Amsterdam before you talk of wealth, my friend. Now. What did you see? In the royal coach?'

Fox glanced at him. Pieter grinned.

'It takes one to know one, John – you saw something. Someone, in that carriage? With the scrawny Queen? The woman you were looking for?'

'Elizabeth. Yes and if she's here so is Rebecca, my daughter. We'll finish the business I agreed to do for Fairfax and then I'll collect my daughter and we can be done with this.'

Pieter shook his head. He didn't believe it. He knew that for Fox it was a compulsion, a drug as powerful as opium. Fox might say the secret life would be done with. Pieter knew that was as likely as a man flying.

They strolled on into Kirke Straat. It was a narrow street. On each side trees grew and the houses behind them gave straight onto the cobbles. Each house was flat-fronted with tall windows on the second floor. The roofs were steeply pitched. Two or three discreet painted signs indicated that some of the buildings housed lawyers, merchants, tailors and half way along the street, an apothecary's sign hung over a doorway.

'There?' They hardly glanced at the doorway as they walked on. Fox noted an alley that opened out to the right and, around the buttress of an old church, another narrow road entered the road they were on.

'You could meet in that church,' said Pieter as they came to a corner. Just round the corner there was a small ale house.

They walked in and Fox looked around. To his right a corner window gave a view down the road as far as the apothecary's sign. He sat down while Pieter asked for a jug of beer. It came as Fox wrote a note.

'It gives the secret words and tells him to meet me in the church near his house.'

'This afternoon,' said Pieter. 'He'll have the message by then. I can see to that.'

Pieter folded the paper and put it inside his jerkin. 'You want to meet that woman?'

Fox nodded.

'To tell her you're here and to arrange a meeting might not be easy.'

'I'll tell this man when I meet him I have a message for her.'

'Can you trust him?'

Fox shrugged.

'Can you suggest another way?'

Pieter drank his ale and put his tankard down

'No. I can't. It's a risk.'

They walked out into the bright light as the bells and carillons around the city began to sound midday.

'I have something I must do,' said Pieter as they strolled into the centre of the city. 'I work for a man called Hauer. Francis Hauer. You might be interested. He has a finger on all the gossip, all the rumours, all the trade of the city and all those who make it their business to make trades. He has a speciality.'

They turned off the wide street and walked along a narrow alley and into the back of an old town house. Then out of the tiny yard and into the passage that ran the length of the house to the front door that gave onto another street.

They walked along the corridor past two closed doors and came to the last door. Pieter knocked and a surly voice told him to come in.

The man sitting behind the desk was vast. His face the size of a pumpkin, his belly hanging in folds about his wide armchair. The robe he wore was lined with fur and draped across his huge shoulders like a sail. He looked at Fox through heavy-hooded eyes, put down his quill, tipped sand onto the page, blew it carefully off the ink and laid the paper aside on a pile of other letters. Not once did he take his eyes off Fox.

'You're late, Pieter.'

'I'm sorry. My friend and I were – '

'I don't want to know what he and you do, Pieter. I see from looking at him what he is.'

'Do you?' said Fox. 'You think you do.'

'You and your friend here, Pieter, were comrades. I am sure of that. And I know what he did, some of what he did. You, you are another matter. You,' and he looked directly at Fox. 'You will kill if necessary to find an answer.'

Fox hesitated and then nodded. 'If necessary.'

The huge face split into a wide smile and then he put out a vast pudgy hand to shake Fox's. 'And an honest man too.'

His voice rumbled up from that vast belly.

Pieter began, 'His name is – '

'Pieter – please – no names. No need for names.'

Fox looked round the room. Beyond the paper-strewn desk and the ink pots and silver sand shaker, beyond the rickety piles of books on the shelves behind the huge man were rows and rows of small drawers in a wooden cabinet that stood along the length of one wall.

In front of the cabinet, a narrow table stood and on it were long handled spoons and at intervals piles of small leather draw-top bags. The light from the only window shafted along the table.

'You're mystified?'

Fox nodded.

Pieter handed a paper to the huge man, who waved his hand

'Take what you need Pieter. Give my regards to your master. Tell him I am expecting a consignment of excellent oil next month. And some fine French varnish.'

Fox watched as Pieter checked along the drawers, opened one, and took a spoon and ladled coloured powder into a small bag. He repeated this at one drawer after another until he had twenty small leather drawstring bags piled on the table.

'You are still mystified,' rumbled the man in the armchair and explained, 'These are pigments, powder to make colours. Of quality. Pieter's master is a fine painter and needs the best he can afford. Though God knows Master Rembrandt is a profligate when it comes to money. It would please me to be paid from time to time. Tell him, Pieter.'

And he laughed at the idea and rolls of fat quivered about his face and even covered his lively eyes for a moment.

'Sit down – sit down, my friend and we'll talk a little. I enjoy it when Pieter comes. He's full of life..'

'Gossip, you mean,' said Pieter tying up the neck of another pouch of pigment.

'A man must do something other than sit. You see,' said Francis Hauer, 'I cannot walk. I have been trapped in this chair since I was twelve. Broke my back in a fall from a horse. Since then I have been as you find me. I have help, of course, and eyes and ears all over, from The Hague to Amsterdam, from Germany to the Indies. What else is a fat cripple supposed to do if he is not to die of boredom? I am a post box for titbits of knowledge. 'A snapper up of unconsidered trifles' I believe one of your writers said. It was in a silly play but is a fair description of myself.' The man wheezed, out of breath from the effort of explaining.

'The Hague, my friend is an odd city. Daily life goes on as

usual. Merchants and housewives, clerks and civil servants buzzing around the Binnenhof, near Lake Vijver. All the grand state buildings, the civic hall, the main market and exchange. The civil servants and the merchants you can find nearby. The Voorhout is there and the Vijverberg. Elizabeth of Bohemia lives in a grand house. Living as they always have off the scraps and crumbs they can glean. Or like me, sitting quietly aside from the hurly-burly and thinking. It is not a place to give out strangers' names. Why, you may ask.? What is this Francis Hauer doing saying such things? You and Pieter are, like me, acquirers of knowledge. Sometimes to be dribbled out and sometimes to be stored. Am I correct?'

Fox nodded and waited. And again the rumble of laughter caused the man's eyes to vanish behind the rolls of flesh only to remerge as the laughter subsided.

'This is a city with two royal courts. The newest is gathered abound Henrietta your Queen who says she is here to bring her little daughter to the husband she married last year. A child of ten or so I believe. She should be playing with dolls. But that's the view of a common man, eh? But the child is niece of the other queen who has a court here too, Elizabeth of Bohemia, her sister-in-law. In exile and surrounded by courtiers with more time than money and more money than they need. Here they play and dance and gossip. Here they have their salons and their intrigues. A few of the lesser lights want to dance attendance on their respective queens but are too poor, or have gone through what money they once had. Sometimes, the wisest choose to live a little apart.'

'I met a man a day or so ago. He came to buy pigments. He dabbles at painting, takes lessons from time to time. English. No painter, but it gives him pleasure. He said to me 'Happiest are those who have least to do with the courts and live apart.' Wise man. No painter, but a wise man nonetheless.'

He wheezed a little, took a drink from ornate Italian glass beside him.

'There are factions and cliques and intrigue in those courts. Too much time to plot and weave mad spells. There are rumours of bitter rivalries. Meanwhile they act in masques and their women, even the Queen of England, appear bare-breasted and dance, to the disgust of the Preachers here and of their congregations. They cause mischief and are only tolerated for the way they fritter their wealth.'

Francis Hauer sat back on his cushions gasping for breath. Pieter looked up from the pigments he was rolling into twists of paper. Fox sat on the bench near Francis Hauer who had regained his breath.

'Tolerated for their way with money. And your dear Queen is in a selling mood and that's good news for the merchants here. Her court is not liked. They're arrogant, but then the English have always been arrogant with those they think beneath them. But they need us, our merchants know it and so your Queen and her advisors will be selling at a bargain price or not at all. They need to have a care.'

'The queen is trying to sell jewels and is even willing to pawn them against a suitable advance to fund her other activity. The court is engaged in finding weapons for her husband's army about which you will know more than I do, sir, I am sure.'

Fox asked, 'I know she is buying and I know she looks for mercenary soldiers for the King's army. I want to know who she buys from and where the arms are stored, when they will go to England and where their landfall might be. I need names and places, sir.'

Francis Hauer leaned forward then and put a pudgy hand on Fox's.

'I will give you one name. Find Isaac Rosenberg in Amsterdam. He will see you. Tell him you come from the dealer in fine pigments in The Hague. He will know who.'

'He like me is a snapper up, a gleaner, and what he does not know is not worth your while to know. Apart from this I have heard there is a man in the English court, a cruel man. A friend of yours told me. I have asked discreetly about this Harry Morton. He has a vile reputation and is a very secret man, a devious man, a planner and a plotter – a dangerous man, they say. Not a man to do business with. Beware of him. You understand me?'

Fox looked at the tiny eyes buried in the fat face in astonishment. Who had told him that name? The vast bland face was suddenly closed as if he had pulled down a shutter and wished to forget what had been said.

'I understand you very well. Thank you,' Fox said quietly.

Francis Hauer looked across at Pieter

'You find what you need?' he asked.

Pieter lifted a hand.

'Nearly,' he said and went on opening drawers, scooping up powders and ground flowers, small lumps of wax and lapis, noting the weights and quantities as he did so. The light from the high windows put Francis Hauer in a dark silhouette so that only the pale face showed up against the dark heavy cloth of his gown. He explained to Fox,

'I have helped Pieter since we first met. Partly, because I was sorry for him losing a hand. Now, because we are friends and we trust each other with secrets.'

He smiled at Pieter and his eyes crinkled and vanished into the great slabs of flesh around them. Pieter went on tying up the powders.

'Have a care with that pigment, Pieter, Master Rembrandt owes me for the last pigments he had. Remind him.'

Pieter nodded and Francis Hauer looked again at Fox.

'Not that he'll pay.' He laughed. 'Now, there are other things you want to know. Gossip helps build pictures for men like you and me, sir. If I can help I will.'

'Henrietta?'

'Called by some here the Roman Harlot, I understand. She and those about her are not subtle, not discreet. They flaunt their wealth and their bodies in ways that offend the more staid burghers of my country. There is little laughter and joy about The Hague or Amsterdam. The churches see to that. So, Henrietta the wife of Charles, sent on two missions I believe. But you know the first.'

Fox nodded and said ' 'I think perhaps you can tell me what I don't know, if you choose to.' The black eyes focused sharply then. Fox waited.

'She is trying to sell jewels – hers and her husband's, she claims, though I am informed they are jewels that really belong to the State. Great carbuncles and collars of precious stones.'

He considers for a moment.

'When you arrive in Amsterdam go to the jewellery quarter and look for Isaac Rosenberg. He will help.'

He collected his breath and moved restlessly in his chair. Pieter helped him sit up and pulled a cushion into place behind him. He leaned back, sighed and went on.

'They say she wants money for arms.' Fox nodded. 'Isaac will know some of the answers. What has she has bought, who sells, where it is stored and who is buying? When will it be shipped?'

Fox smiled and nodded.

'Is that too ambitious, sir?' he asked.

'My friend, most Dutch dislike kings and queens. We are a nation who believe in money, oh yes, and our God. Our merchants

126

are usually unwilling to act unless they can see profit. Dealing with foreign princes at war with their own people is a dangerous matter. Back the right horse and you will be remembered by the winners of that battle and forever hated by the losers. Back the wrong one and kiss goodbye to any chance of trading with the winners. So, most of our merchants, most of our bankers, most will avoid her and her courtiers. However – '

He leaned forward to gather his breath.

'However, there are one or two who might supply credit against the jewels. Ask Isaac. There is one merchant who has gathered weapons from the battle fields of Europe who might be willing to sell, at a price. I break the habit of a lifetime and give you a name. Johan Haggars is your man. Find him and you may well find the stores he is putting together to sell to your Queen. He is a man of influence and a man to avoid if you can. Have a care with him. Above all as he values his life, Pieter will not lead you there. Promise you will not ask him.'

Fox nodded. 'I promise.'

Francis Hauer lay back in his chair and closed his eyes. Pieter signalled that it was time to go.

'Wait,' said Fox. 'What can I do in exchange?'

One tiny eye opened.

'Let me know should you prevent some of the weapons going to support the royalists. A good Hollander hates in particular kings who regard themselves as the elect of God like your Charles does. There is another matter. Much more important. There are rumours, strong rumours of some sort of secret plotting amongst a select group of men who surround your Queen.'

'Plotting? What – who?'

'Your masters didn't tell you? Then that's for you to discover, Master Fox. And be careful who you ask, for the rumour is that these men are ruthless. As for your daughter, you should talk to her guardian and soon.'

Fox is astonished.

'How did you know about my daughter?'

'There is, my friend, an acquaintance of mine – I have known her since she first came to this house when she was not much more than fifteen. She stayed here under my protection for a year or so. She learned a great deal. You call her Maeve Ahearne.'

'Is she here now?' Fox asked and the huge mountain of a face smiled and the eye shut. He began to snore softly.

Pieter put the twists of paper, the small boxes of semiprecious stones and the bottles of oil into two leather satchels. He topped the bags with the leather drawstring bags. Then he scribbled his name on the list he had made and put it beside the pudgy hand that lay on an open book on the table.

Fox picked up one of the satchels and walked to the door.

'Master Fox, ask yourself a question.'

The rumbling voice from Francis Hauer behind him stopped him with his hand on the door latch.

'Ask yourself why you've been sent to search out weapons and recruits and who is dealing what jewels? Why, when they know the truth already, send a man of your skill to search out information about what they already know? Or is it that other matter, the secret plotting that they dare not even tell you about? Ask yourself, sir, who they trust, your masters in London in that room over the watchmaker's shop. Which side do they fall on or do they play on both or either side one against t'other, like so many intelligence gatherers? Have a care, sir.'

He began to snore softly as they closed the door. The sunlight glittered into the room from the high windows and picked up a dab of pigment here, a dab of powder there. The pudgy hand lay on the book. Nothing moved in the room except the quiver of the man's huge lips.

CHAPTER 23

The Church had no doubt at one time been a Catholic church, but all decoration on the walls had been painted white. There were no statues, no images of saints. All was severe and plain. The wooden pulpit had a large canopy and dominated the church.

Fox was reminded strongly of the room in Shropshire where Alison used to sit each Sunday. The plain place of worship where she and the other followers of their quaint sect had sat waiting for the 'spirit to come down' which would urge them to speak.

He tried to shut out the memory of dog roses scattered across the hawthorn hedges.

He remembered Rebecca gathering flowers and laying them on the pile of cold ashes, and the twisted metal of Alison's crucifix that Maeve had uncovered amongst those ashes but dared not hold. He had it yet about his neck in a leather pouch.

Fox remembered the dry motes of dust falling across the sunlight as he looked about the white painted interior of this Dutch church and remembered Alison had begged him to abandon anger. He had tried. They had pressed her to confess, told if she did not, her daughter would be put to the test. Then Alison confessed and they had burned her.

Looking around this harsh plain church he felt a chill to his bones.

There were two doors into the church. The main one let into a huge ceremonial door and one to the right beyond a side chapel. He walked briskly to it, lifted the latch.

'It's open, John,' said a quiet voice behind him. He turned, Shea's curved blade in his hand and Maeve Aherne stood there. 'Not in God's house, John – surely.'

Fox walked to the back of the church. Behind the font two

benches stood against the wall in shadow. He sat and looked. He could see the whole church from where he sat. She walked slowly to him up the aisle.

'I saw Francis Hauer, a huge man.'

'Did he help?'

Fox shrugged.

'And now?' she asked.

'I'm seeing the man Thurloe told me to see.'

Maeve nodded and stepped into the shadows beside him.

'I saw Harry Morton. And his wife, Elizabeth. She's afraid of him.'

'Are you?'

Her eyes seemed to flatten, stilled. Her whole body stopped moving. Her green eyes darkened, her breathing slowed. She was 'seeing' something terrible, for a moment. Then –

'He'll die. I see that. I told you. Trust me.'

'Did you see Rebecca? Is she with them?'

Maeve stepped closer to him then and whispered

'I see bad things – you know how I am. I see bad things. We have to find Rebecca soon.'

Fox stared at her. He had never seen her so intense. So still, so focussed. She had powers Alison might have understood but not him. It was not open to him to know what she knew. He was, he admitted to himself, afraid of her when she was like this.

'What else, Maeve? Tell me.'

'There is a young woman living in a house near the Utrecht Canal. She's a fanatic. Cold. She is close to Harry Morton and he to five others in the court around that queen. They are separate from the others. Tight knit.'

She closed her fist close to her face.

'Secrets. There is one of their number I knew. The red-faced man we saw at that little cryptographer's house when he killed himself. You remember?' Fox nodded.

'Men tell such things when you're in their bed,' she said.

He stared at her then in shock, – disgust.

'How in the name of God? You've been here less than a week.'

She laughed in his face.

'If a man wants you, it takes less than a day, my friend. Sir Adam Stringer is his name. A minor landowner, second son of a second son. He hates his father. He hates everyone, I think. And so sure of himself. There is something about these pale-faced men who never have to shave. Have you noticed how the rich and the landed gentry are like fat priests – they never have to shave?'

She smiled at Fox and touched his cheek.

'Unlike others – '

Fox swatted her fingers away.

She stepped back from him and cocked her head to one side and looked into his eyes.

'No need for jealousy, Sergeant. None. I can tell you something else I gleaned from Sir Adam. He's afraid of Sir Harry. That man is pure evil. He is planning something, a number of them are. Something more than sending powder to the King in England.'

'Stringer is afraid. I nearly had him telling me what frightens him and then he shut his mouth. We need to know the secret, John. Maybe Rebecca knows. Maybe Elizabeth knows. We have work to do and very little time.'

'Who is this other woman?' Fox asked.

Maeve shook her head.

'Young and bound to Harry. She seems to worship him. Drinking in every word. When I saw them together – '

'His mistress?'

Maeve laughed then shook her head.

'Not her. A bride to Christ more likely. Ice cold. Fanatic. Why do men suppose always that their power lies in their thighs? Harry is ice cold, cruel. His sex is mostly about pain. He has her in the palm of his hand. I don't know why. Your daughter is the key John. Trust me. Here's your man. I will see you in Amsterdam.'

She leaned forward. She might have been praying.

A shaft of light sprang from the door as it slowly opened. Fox watched as a stocky, well dressed man waited in the light from the open door. He closed the door carefully and took off his hat as he stepped into the main body of the church. Shafts of light from the high windows cast pools of shadow and then light as he stepped down towards the pulpit. He stopped a moment, looked around. He didn't see them watching him from the shadows. He walked on down the church and sat in the side chapel then knelt. He began to pray.

Quietly Fox walked between the rows of wooden benches until he was directly behind the man.

'Thurloe sent me.' he said and the praying man looked round in shock.

'But you have words to say. A pass – '

'The name's enough. You had the message. I am here and you have things to tell me.'

'He promised preferment.'

'What he promised I could not give a drop of spit for. I want to know if she has already got weapons, who through and where they will be stored. I want to know when they will be shipped and where they are to land.'

The man started to get up but Fox put a hand on his shoulder and kept him kneeling.

'You can tell me. I know she is trading the jewels. I know she is trying to recruit young English mercenaries here in Holland. I want to know their names.'

Eventually the man spoke.

'She has bought saddles enough for a regiment, 500 barrels of powder, bullets, muskets and swords. All these from the battlefields of Europe.'

'Through Meinheer Haggar? Yes?'

'How did you know that? It's secret.'

'Not now,' said Fox dryly. 'He is the main merchant?'

'Yes.'

'Good. Where are these supplies stored?'

'I don't know.'

'You want preferment, you find out.'

'I can't. There is a group close to the Queen which arranges these matters.'

'I know there are others around her who are secret. Planning what? Who are they? Their names?'

'I can't tell you.'

'You will tell me, friend, I assure you. You know their names. Harry Morton is one? And Adam Stringer another?'

The man said nothing. He looked past Fox and all he could see was the white walls of the church.

'Yes or no?'

The man nodded.

'And what else? I know there is something else. What is it?'

'I can't tell you.'

'Daren't tell?'

The man said nothing.

'Who frightens you most, Morton or me?'

Without hesitation the man whispered

'Morton.'

'There is a girl, maid to his wife. Is she there with her mistress?'

'A maid – would I know a maid?'

'Rebecca?'

'Young? Tall? And wild they say. Her?'

'Yes. Well?'

'She was there but not for a day or so. I haven't seen her. No.'

Fox took the knife from its sheath and laid it against the neck of the kneeling man. The man shuddered. He began to cry.

'Not yet friend. Just to remind you you'll die if I betray you to your friends at court. So, bring me the answers. Early in the morning in two days. Who, what supplies, where stored, what is this inner circle planning, who are the others in the circle? You fail and they will know who betrayed them. You understand? I will be in the vegetable market at six. Be there.'

Fox sheathed the blade, turned to the back of the church and, as he had expected Maeve was already gone. He walked out of the door to the side chapel beside the font and into the brilliant afternoon light.

CHAPTER 24

The Queen was moving her court to Amsterdam. She had business to do, men to see and a masque to attend.

The carriage was guarded by a number of outriders. Inside, Henrietta and two of her ladies-in-waiting. Behind the arching horses and the trundling coach a retinue of English courtiers rode in the morning sunlight.

The gossip in the markets around The Hague was that this Queen, who behaved no better than a strumpet, was to dance in a profane masque. She had no shame nor had those about her. No respectable merchant, banker, dealer, stone cutter would allow his wife to accept invitations from her. But there were those whose self-interest was greater than their morals.

Amongst the riders were Sir Harry Morton and Adam Stringer and around them the gilded men of court.

Fox watched the approaching cavalcade and picked out the mercenary soldiers. French and a sprinkling of Germans amongst them, no doubt. There would also be English recruits ready to go back to England to fight against their own people

Fox sat on the knoll beside a small copse of trees and stared down across the road and the traffic that flowed away from The Hague and towards Amsterdam.

It was mid-day when the carriage lumbered into the yard of a substantial inn, the steps were lowered and Henrietta was handed down into the straw-covered yard.

Fox sat in the window of the inn with an ale at his elbow and watched. He was astonished at how small the Queen was. Her teeth were bad when she smiled and her skin was pale and slightly puffy.

Behind her, stepping from the carriage, came Elizabeth Morton. This woman he had lived with through a winter in the

Derbyshire Dales. They had helped each other through a lonely time.

The Queen walked inside as the outriders guarded the entrance to the yard and the door into the inn.

Elizabeth stopped a moment and looked about the yard. Sir Harry rode up to her and clearly ordered her to go inside. Elizabeth walked into the building after her Queen.

Inside there was a flurrying and a scuttering as the innkeeper tried to arrange food and drink for the unexpected guests. The escort were demanding drink and shouting at the servants.

No one would be paid for food or drink or damage. Fox was sure of that.

A girl went by carrying flagons of ale and another took a tray of steaming pies to the rooms where the travellers were waiting. One of the girls came skipping back, red in the face.

Fox beckoned to her and she stopped and walked over to him.

'You speak French?' he asked her and she shook her head.

'German?' he asked.

'*Ja.*' she said with a smile.

'There is a woman in there, in a green cloak. Tall, pale-faced. She has grey eyes?'

'Yes' she said.

'I have a message for her. Her eyes only, child.'

The maid grinned at him. Mischief in her eyes.

'Her husband must not see it?' She mocked him and Fox seemed shy. 'You are lovers?'

He nodded. 'Will you do it for love?'

'I'll do it for money,' she said.

Fox had already written out the message. To meet during the masque in Amsterdam. He would be there.

He gave the maid the folded paper and with it a coin. She almost dropped it in surprise. 'There will be another for you when you tell me she has the message.'

The girl darted off into the chaotic rooms where the noise was getting louder and the English officers seemed to be loudest of all.

CHAPTER 25

In a corner where he could see the market steps and the length of the street alongside the canal, Fox waited. He had in front of him a plate of ham and bread. His cloak was slung over the chair beside him and his wide-brimmed hat hung from the back of a chair. He seemed almost to be dozing in the morning light.

The streets around the raised market place were blazing with colour. Flowers in baskets, flowers in pots, flowers in boxes and laid on trestle tables, flowers in water, flowers in damp moss – roses, pinks, orchids from the Indies, sunflowers and poppies, vibrant with spring light. Old men and ancient crones sat beside their flowers. The Hague and the whole country was eager to turn a coin. Everything was for sale here.

Boys were sluicing water from the canal running along the side of the market square, into buckets and boxes of cut flowers.

Already the clink of coin could be heard. Beside the marketplace, canal boats were moored alongside showing yet more boxes, bags, cans and buckets of bright flowers. Some also offered brilliant green and white cabbages, earth-covered roots, carrots and herbs for sale on the cabin roofs of the barges.

They had been grown in the drained land of the polders where the sea had been held back and the sand enriched by the weed gathered from the shore and the shit gathered from the city. The stink of these vast beds of produce was the stench of money.

Small temporary bars and cafes lined the steps of the market place where the merchants gathered and the overseers of the market held sway. For despite its look, the market was no free for all. Everyone paid for a pitch and the money went into the coffers of the city to help build sea walls, hospitals and civic buildings and to help with the care of the poor and old soldiers. And some of course, went

136

into the pockets of the administrators and the officials. It was the way of the world. Even the shit was taxed.

In the shade three men sat at a table littered with plates of cheese and ham and wine glasses. They had cleared a space amongst the debris of their breakfast and played with a leather cup and dice for the price of the next flask of schnapps.

As the sun grew too warm for the flowers that were left, the traders began to pack their wares and to sell off the flowers to canny housewives who had waited for this moment to come and buy.

An hour later the market was done, the stalls were packed away in the storeroom behind the market place and most of the stall holders were eating or drinking in the bars around the square.

The three men playing dice were still there but seemed to have lost interest in the game.

Fox slept in the sun. No one had joined him. A dog lay asleep on the steps.

One of the dice players sauntered across to the table where Fox slept with his head on his arms. The dice man looked down at him, looked back at his friends and grinned. He lifted Fox's cloak and found under it a leather satchel. He took it and carefully laid the cloak back. He opened the satchel and took out a wallet.

As he did so, the other two men walked across to the sleeping figure, surrounding him. The first passed the wallet to one of the others as the second man stepped closer and reached for the leather pouch Fox wore at his throat. No one in the bars and cafes around the other side of the market square noticed. The traders were more intent on their meat and drink.

When it came, the movement was viper-fast. Fox took the man's wrist and stood up turning the hand on the wrist through a hundred degrees. The bone snapped with a noise like a pistol shot. The man fell and Fox kicked him full in the face as he lifted his cloak and slung it over the first of the advancing men. He took his sword from the scabbard on his back and raked it across the chest of the third man who was still drawing a blade from his waist.

He leaned down and kicked the first man again, full in the face. He didn't even moan any longer. The man with the wound across his chest stared down at the blood seeping over his belly, dropped the blade, turned and was ham-strung by the low backhanded sweep of the blade in Fox's hand. He dropped and tried to crawl away.

Fox turned to the man he'd smothered with his cloak. He

137

was free and held a rapier. Fox's blade was shorter by a foot and the man was no fool with the sword.

Surprise and attack were as natural to Fox as breathing. He ran directly at the man with the rapier. For a fraction of a moment the attacker hesitated. This wasn't in the book. Fox, after all, had an inferior weapon and was at a disadvantage. The attacker went in for the kill. He thrust at air. Fox had thrown himself down under the rapier arm and rolled into his attacker's legs.

The man went down on the flagstones as Fox come to his feet. He turned, stamped on the hand still holding the rapier. His full weight crushed the hand around the hilt of the sword. The man screamed as Fox, still with his heel on the hand, turned on his heel and ground the broken bones.

He leaned down then at the man writhing on the ground.

'You ? Who sent you?'

'No one.' The man moaned. 'My hand ?'

'Ruined. You'll never fight right-handed again. Who sent you?'

'I don't remember – '

'Liar. If I don't have an answer, you will be blinded. Understand me?'

The man tried to scrabble away. The sunlight glinted on the short bladed weapon in Fox's hand.

'Who sent you? '

The man said nothing. He spat. He tried to reach for his blade with his left hand. He was a brave man or a desperate one, Fox thought. He leaned closer.

'Was it Morton ?'

For a moment there was a flicker of fear in the man's eyes.

'I – I dare not – '

Fox had his answer. He leaned down, grabbed the man's leather jerkin and sat the man up.

The man stared in to dark cold eyes and saw death.

'I beg you – I beg you – listen to me. Harry Morton will have your balls. He knows about you and his wife. Everything. He beats her, thrashes her where it won't be seen. He has vowed to kill you slowly, he said. Please don't – my eyes. Don't blind me,' he whispered.

Fox waited until the whimpering man was quiet. He let the blade touch his eyelids and whispered,

'If I see you ever again, remember me and be sure you'll

never see another thing as long as you live.'

He flicked the blade and bubbles of blood came from the deep wound along the man's nose. Split like a pig's foot.

Fox went on, 'To remind you when you look in a mirror of what happens if I ever see you again. A word of advice – always know your enemy, friend.'

Fox took up his hat, the leather satchel and his wallet from the man's pocket. He sheathed his sword and walked quickly away into the narrow alleys at the back of the market hall. There was still no sign of his contact.

Along the canal side there was blood on the cobbles and in the still water old blooms were already rotting and fading.

CHAPTER 26

The evening light was beginning to fade along the street opposite the church. Shadows already lay across the cobbles and on the walls of the church opposite the house Fox was watching.

He sat in the shadow of a buttress of the church and waited.

A distant bell began to chime the hour and as it began, other bells around the city also began to ring out. Soon the city was engulfed in the sound of bells big and small, bass and tenor. The small bell in the nearby church began to sound.

As the pealing, thudding cacophony reached its crescendo two men slipped out of the door near the apothecary's in Kirke Straat. Hidden in the shadow of the church, Fox watched the men laughing together as they slipped into the alley that led away from the church towards the main square.

The two were men he recognized. One was Elizabeth's husband and the other the red faced man, Stringer. Adam Stringer whom Maeve had bedded. Fox waited. Nothing moved. The noise began to die away. Fox waited. It would be half an hour before he moved again.

As the shadows became denser, Fox slid along the road still keeping in the shadows and stepped to the house where Harbourson, his contact, lived. The street door was open and Fox vanished quickly inside the house.

As he did so, a figure detached itself from the church doorway, moved to the gate onto the street and waited there, concealed by a stone pillar.

In five minutes, Fox stepped out of the house, half closed the door and walked away past the church. The last of the bells had stopped ringing.

CHAPTER 27

It was pitch dark along the side of the canal that led to the open sea. A cluster of glittering lights marked the Two Mills on the Polder.

Two barges were tied up at bollards and light spilled from the cabins where the barge masters and their families lived. A dog rushed out at Fox as he walked towards the inn. It was brought up short by its chain. A voice from the deck called and the dog was silent.

The man on the deck raised his hand as Fox passed by and into the back yard of the inn.

He pushed at the door into the kitchen. The heat was stifling and smelt of soup and roasting lamb.

Pieter's rosy wife nodded at him as he stood in the light. Without a word she carved meat from the spitted lamb onto a platter and handed it to him with fresh bread cut from the warm loaf by the hearth.

'Before you ask, my husband is asleep. He will see you in the morning. He thinks you'll be going to Amsterdam together.'

Fox sat down at the scrubbed table and began to eat.

'Why?' he asked. 'Why will I be going to Amsterdam?'

She shrugged and sharpened her knife before slicing another platter of meat which she handed to the kitchen boy to take through into the main body of the inn.

'He must have a reason,' Fox insisted.

'Maybe it has to do with that loose woman who is, as we speak, in your room, no doubt sleeping in your bed. I told my husband I had no wish to be a place for English loose morals and whores. '

'What has she told him?'

141

'That you'll be going to 'Dam in the morning. Things have moved on, she said.'

Fox nodded. 'They have,' he said bleakly, 'They have.'

'So much for your promise not to involve him,' she said.

'Did you believe me?' her asked her, smiling.

'No,' she said. 'And he seems happy – so – take care of him.'

'He's a lucky man to have you. I'll take care. That is a promise.'

He pushed his plate aside and stood up. Without a word she handed him a flagon of schnapps.

'Get some sleep, friend. My man will call you in the morning. And remember to take your friend with you when you go. This is a godly country, Sergeant, and we can do without your English ways.'

With that she turned back to carving the turning lamb into a serving tray.

* * *

Maeve lay wide awake in his bed. Her long hair catching reflections of fire in the light from the hearth and from the three candles she had burning in the room.

Fox came in, put his satchel, knapsack, schnapps and cloak aside. Laid his sword on the chest by the bed and a knife from his boot under the pillow.

He said nothing. She watched him silently and moved across the bed a little.

After a beat Fox sat on the bedside and then lay back beside her. She seemed sad as she watched him. As if she already knew what he was going to tell her.

'You first – or me?' she asked him gently.

He got up and walked to the window looking out onto the canal side.

'Thurloe's connection is not going to help.'

The lanterns in the barge were snuffed out as they battened down for the night. A cat stalked across the gangplank and went foraging for scraps around the cabin door. Fox went on watching. He wasn't seeing much.

'Was it bad?' Maeve asked.

'You don't get used to it, do you?' said Fox.

Maeve lay watching him outlined in the pale light from the night sky.

142

'I've seen too much maybe. I thought nothing could harrow me anymore.'

He turned away from the window and stepped closer to the bed. She was surprised to see he had tears in his eyes. She lay still against the soft bolster.

'I waited for him to come to the flower market as we'd arranged. He had information for me. He was afraid, of course.'

'Of Harry, of course,' she breathed the name.

'He didn't come to the meeting place and I was attacked. '

'Yes?' she said quietly. She moved a lock of hair that had fallen across her eyes. He told her what had happened in the flower market.

'After the market was packed away. They were certainly from Harry. He knows I'm here and for a certainty he knows what happened with his wife.'

Maeve lay quite still as he went on very quietly.

'I went back to the church and waited, watching Thurloe's contact's house. I waited through the afternoon and until the evening. Patience is my business. A day, two days, a week even. In the field it's easier. In towns there are too many unknowns. Two of them came to the house.'

'Ah?' she breathed and sat up in the bed.

'I'm becoming soft. I saw them go into the house. They came out after an hour. Your friend Sir Adam Stringer was one and the other was the man I cuckolded. Harry Morton was laughing.'

Fox flung the mug holding his water at the wall. The sudden noise surprised Maeve. Fox turned back to the window.

'It's a terrible business, Maeve, we're engaged in. '

'How, terrible?'

'This morning, in the market I thought how peaceful it all was. People going about their business selling flowers and vegetables, the colours, the kind faces, the laughter – all in good humour.'

'Yes' she said. 'You are going soft, John Fox, and you must not. You'll tell me next we should stop being involved.'

'You didn't see what I saw.'

'No more I did. But I know what Harry Morton can do and loves to do. I never told you all about him and me. The detail. You'd better know. Wasn't I a child? Twelve or so living in the rocks of the west coast of Ireland. Poor as mice and living often as not on famine food we scavenged from the rocks.

'My grandmother was a wise woman. A seer of fortunes sometimes. It was dangerous for her for the priests were afraid of women like her. They preached against her. Like your dead wife Alison, never a doubt of it. I remember I was twelve and hungry and my mother was for sending me to the big house over the mountain where there were rich English who'd have work in their dairy for a child like me. It was a thirty mile walk over the mountain.

'The night before I left, my grandmother took me aside to her corner of our cabin and talked to me. She spoke the old language for never a word of English soiled her tongue.'

'Maeve,' she said, 'I have to warn you of something. I know you'll be afraid from time to time, but I tell you, you have the power I have. You know I see things. It is a dangerous gift but we can't turn it away. I tell you Maeve, have a care in that place. There is a young man, a guest – a vicious, cruel young man who has a liking for giving pain. I've seen him clear as day and I want you to be ware of him when you go there. Promise me you will be.'

Maeve looked across the bed at Fox and went on.

'I promised I'd have a care. And they sent me over the mountain with a piece of burning turf from our fire as was the custom for I would never be expected back. It was like a funeral wake. I was twelve and the spring flowers were in the hedgerows and it was a great adventure. It's how it was.'

Two of the candles guttered out and the soft night sky lit the room in parts. She went on quietly and without emotion. As if somehow what she told about didn't touch her any more.

'The long and the short of it is that a man was staying in the big house maybe a year or so after I got there. He made the young man of the house hold me while he hurt me. He loved to hurt animals and people. He used fire on me, John, as you'd brand an animal or a criminal. Will I show you ?'

And she stepped out of the bed, stripped off her shift and pointed out a circle of puckered flesh. On her inner thigh.

'He branded me. Laughing he was, then you may imagine what he did.'

'Jesus wept.' Fox hissed the words and she reached to his face and gentled the murderous rage she saw in his eyes.

'Hush now, John. His time is coming and he is mine. You understand me?' Fox nodded.

'I ran from that house then and since I have lived as I have lived.'

He touched her face and saw in it only sadness.

'Tell me what you saw,' she said after a moment.

'I went in an hour after they left the house. The place was empty. Then in the back of the house, in the kitchen I found poor Mark. I heard him first. Mumbling. He was still alive. What was left of him. He couldn't see me, of course, and he couldn't speak for his tongue was cut out and he couldn't move and they'd gelded him and left him bleeding. They knew I'd find him.' He turned away from her.

'He has Rebecca. That animal has her. I'm sure he knows whose daughter she is.'

Maeve reached up then and took him in her arms and for a moment she tried to comfort him.

The cat mewed in the night as the shadow of a hunting owl floated across the darkness of the sky.

'I killed the poor man in the house for mercy's sake. But Morton has Rebecca. I have to find her.'

CHAPTER 28

Fox and Maeve rode in silence towards Amsterdam.
It was early morning and the bright northern light sparkled across the land and over the sea to their left. The sand banks and dunes that cut off the land from the tides were sparsely covered in sea holly and marram grass.

From time to time the sea broke over the dunes, ran down into the small pockets of reclaimed land and sucked away the top soil the peasants had made from sand and seaweed and the night soil from the towns and villages behind the dykes.

It was a hard and forbidding landscape.

Fox sat his horse and stared ahead along the track that led towards Leiden. He was angry, and for the first time he could remember, he was afraid. Rebecca was in the hands of the husband he had cuckolded and he was afraid for her.

Their path curved to the right and skirted Leiden. Smoke was spiralling straight up into the pale sky from the hearths of roadside cottages. Over the city of Leiden the sky was paler yet and through the early morning haze, spires and towers poked over the huddle of sloping roofs that clustered around centre of the city.

They left Leiden behind them, riding past a small lake on their right. Beyond it the sky lightened over the Ijsselmeer, the huge inlet from the North Sea and the reason for Amsterdam.

At the southern extension of the Ijsselmeer was the sheltered Markersee which provided safe harbour for traders from across the world. Merchant ships lay at anchor here.

Bigger ships stayed in the lanes beyond the entrance to the Ijsselmeer protected by men of war bristling with cannon on three decks. Here was the core of Dutch worldwide trade. Trade routes to the Baltic and into Northern Germany attracted traders from across the world, sea routes down the North Sea and south to Africa and the Indies. The Ijsselmeer was flat calm and pale jade green to the horizon where the land seemed to lift into the rose pink sky.

They rode past Haarlem and below them off the causeway were laid out the market gardens that served Amsterdam. The night soil barges travelled by night along the canals from the city and left behind a stench hanging in curtains and carpets whatever the good ladies of the city tried to do to hide it.

Barges brought dog waste for leather curing, poultry waste for the gardens and human waste to feed the vegetables and flowers growing in neat ranks on small plots of fine soil.

Maeve, locked in her own thoughts, watched her companion anxiously.

Pieter had set off much earlier. He had matters to see to, friends to alert who wanted to help Fox to locate his daughter and Harry Morton.

He and Fox had talked until late in the evening.

'Can you find me four or five men? I can't pay much. But what I can pay I will pay.'

Pieter shook his head.

'These will be men from Black Tom Fairfax's regiment. They'll be pleased to help an old comrade.'

Fox nevertheless passed him a heavy bag of coin. Pieter let it fall on the table.

'They will need to eat and drink, Pieter. Take it.'

Pieter hesitated and then took up the purse and tucked it away.

'They are to search out and follow Morton. Not to warn him. They need to have a care. I want to know where he goes, who he sees, where he sleeps.'

Pieter grinned.

'Don't let my wife know I'm working. I made a promise remember, not to get involved.'

'You don't have to do anything, friend. Just gather the men together. I can brief them. You have business to do in Amsterdam, I think.'

They'd gone to their rooms after that. Maeve lay in the dark. By the light of his candle he saw her eyes glittering, alert.

They lay in the big bed together and Fox turned his back on her. He had his own daemons to confront and better do that alone, she knew. She slept.

They rode on and Amsterdam appeared on the horizon.

Fox reined in his horse and turned to her.

'Were you ever in Amsterdam?' he asked her.

She shook her head. Before them and a little to the east lay the haze of a city. They had another fifteen miles to ride and would be swallowed into the outskirts by early afternoon.

'We're meeting Pieter in Damsquar. There is an arcade to the left and in the middle, a large building with a coat of arms. He will be waiting there.'

She nodded. She knew the dangers of anger and impatience at times like this. Francis Hauer, the fat man, who sat amongst his paints and pigments had warned her that the motto of a good intelligencer was 'festina lente.' Hurry slowly. These two knew the value of hurrying slowly. They rode steadily towards the city.

Past the old walls, across a network of canals towards Damsquar and the civic building that dominated the square. The small gabled building in the centre was a little exposed.

Around the square stood fine houses and under them a long arcade concealed the fronts of expensive shops and workshops.

Fox and Maeve had left the horses in the stables of a small inn on the outskirts of the town, and now walked round the square in the shadows of the arcades, stopping from time to time, pretending to look into the shops and workshops as if discussing a purchase. Sometimes the proprietor of a shop might call them in to look at a display of jewels, some fine leather clothes, a range of shoes.

All the time they were discreetly checking the people who moved across the open cobbled square beyond the arcade. Groups of men stood talking, arguing about the price of a shipment of tea, or the insurance value of a ship lost at sea.

A man clapped another on his back and laughed aloud. Others shook hands and went on their way. It was the same as in any trading centre where the price of copper or gold, the value of a spice cargo or a foundered ship was traded daily.

Fox loved these places for they offered every chance of concealment. People were too busy making money. No one would notice a man and a woman strolling by.

The men were dressed in dark browns and blacks. Their cloaks might be collared with ermine or bear fur from Russia. Some wore gold chains wrought by local craftsmen from gold brought from a Spanish treasure ship recently captured by a Dutch man o'war, Here the talk was of ducats, doubloons, pounds, silver, gold and notes of promise being enacted or paid out.

Amsterdam was the centre of Dutch trade. Here above all was the place were silver, precious stones, exotic spices and stinking hides were transformed into money as a deal was done and a promise made by the touch of hands between these men with sombre faces and black hats.

A few women walked together arm-in-arm across the cobbles towards the church tucked against the corner of the square. They wore long full skirts and high, ornate lace collars goffered into great white wheels. They took little or no notice of the men and the children on the square.

A few market traders stood on the cobbles alongside barrows with fresh produce for sale. A white horse dragging a sleigh with a large bundle on it crossed the square.

Beyond the civic building near the church, were tree-lined streets and canals. The pale brick-built houses of the rich merchants stood almost with their feet in the still waters. The high curving gable ends that fronted the houses were reflected in the water of canals that surrounded the main square and radiated out into the rest of the city.

Pieter was waiting.

CHAPTER 29

A clock ticked in the back room of the inn. Pieter had introduced the men he'd recruited.

Fox looked over them. Maeve sat on a settle near the door and watched. The men were typical of their sort. Soldiers down on their luck, mercenaries waiting for the next contract to come their way. Each claimed to know of Sergeant Fox as a man with a fine reputation and a man they'd be happy to work for so long as the price was right.

For the moment they were Fox's men.

Hans Schneider, a German, sat at the end of the table, smiled and drank too much. Marco Francetti, an Italian, said very little. Maeve watched his darting eyes as he leaned back against the wall where he had chosen to sit. He may have come from Milan but Maeve was not so sure and he talked too much.

Norbert Aignan, a tall, thin, bony sort of a man who said he was Breton and was certainly hard to understand when he tried to speak French. He seemed not to be listening as Pieter explained that Fox would want them find Harry Morton and Rebecca. Maeve watched their faces bleakly. She trusted no one.

She had objected to the meeting when Pieter had suggested it. She had argued with Fox that it was not necessary. They would find Harry Morton themselves and follow him. Maeve had no wish for more people to be involved.

'There is more that can go wrong. There are more people we have to take on trust. This is not good and I am against it. I know your friend Pieter is an honest man but the others – what do we know of them?'

Fox had dismissed her suspicions.

'How long will this take with three of us in a city we don't know? Think. It takes more than three to mount a proper surveillance. We have neither the time nor the skill not in a city we don't know.'

Maeve knew it was fear for Rebecca that drove him to take chances. Normally he would never have wanted to use these men. She watched the faces round the table.

The three men left to begin their search. Pieter stayed for a moment.

'John,' he said, 'Do you have a drawing, can you draw your daughter?'

Fox shook his head.

'You have a picture of her? Something?'

Fox shook his head again and then drew out from his shirt a small suede bag on a drawstring. He opened it and onto the table spilled a twisted piece of silver. Maeve saw it and shuddered.

Pieter put out his hand to move it aside and found his hand gripped. 'Don't touch!' Fox said. 'Don't touch.'

Maeve knew it for what it was. What was left of the crucifix his wife had been given when they burned her in a field above her village below The Devil's Chair.

She shut her eyes.

Fox took up a small framed drawing in a pearl frame.

'This is Rebecca,' and held it out to Pieter who said

'I need to keep it. For one day.'

Fox shook his head.

'None of us know what the girl looks like, John. They need to have an idea. I can see to that. I can have copies made.'

'Who by?'

'My master. I see him tomorrow with the pigments. Him.'

'Will he do it?'

'Yes. He'll do it. She's beautiful. He has an eye for beautiful women. I promise no harm shall come to it.'

After a moment Fox dropped his eyes and scooped up the bent burned metal into the amulet bag and put it back inside his shirt as Pieter slipped the pearl framed image into his pocket and stood up.

'We'll go to see Isaac Heinemann tomorrow. He is a man who knows the city and everyone in it. He might help.'

'I don't see the point.' Fox argued.

'He will know about Sir Harry,' Pieter went on patiently. 'He will have had dealings with your money-grubbing Queen and may even know where she and her people are storing the weapons they intend to send to King Charles. You need to see him. He is a stone cutter. One of the best. An artist. Trust me.'

He left them then to argue and to sleep.

Fox lay on his back and didn't sleep. Beside him he heard Maeve move restlessly, stop breathing and wake. One minute she was asleep and the next wide awake. She sat up, walked to the window and looked into the dark blue sky and stared at the huge moon. She shook her head.

'Why send you here? I keep asking myself, John. Why send you into danger to look for something they already know? I don't understand.'

Fox shook his head.

'D'you have an answer?' she asked, without turning away from the window.

'No,' he said. 'Someone said something about rumours of something. Vague, useless and probably nothing whatsoever.'

Without changing her tone, raising her voice or moving away from the window, she said 'There's a man standing in the corner by the chandler's store. Watching. He was there an hour ago when I looked.'

'You were asleep.'

'No, you were asleep. I always wake on the hour. It's habit, John Fox, and it's kept me alive so far. That watcher was there an hour since.'

'For me?'

'Maybe. Maybe one of the men you talked to tonight. Maybe he has a loose tongue.'

'Pieter stood for them. Honest men, he said.'

'They're hungry men. Never trust a hungry man. They'll swing in the wind like a corpse on a gibbet, my grandmother would say. The Italian as sure as spit is too hungry.'

Outside a cockerel crowed and the sky began to lighten.

'Gone now.'

And she smiled.

'So, we begin now. It's something truly secret. The stuff Thurloe deals in. Real secrets and we're to tease them out for him. Don't you feel it John Fox? Dangerous games.'

He stared at her and she smiled at him as she tossed back her loose mane of hair.

'I have a man to pay. I feel the time is coming when he'll

discover what it means to brand a child, to spoil her.'

Her smile had gone now and Fox shuddered at what he saw in her eyes. Gut-wrenching hatred. There for a moment and gone.

'Just remember, John, Harry is mine.'

As he sat naked on the edge of the bed he almost pitied the man she was hunting. Hers were the instincts of a feral cat, cruel, vengeful and eager for the kill.

'I will tell you something that I never thought to say to anyone,' he said. 'When my friend Shea died I never found another man I wanted to guard my back. None of them could do it as he did. When he died it was as if I'd lost a limb.'

He looked up at her and said simply

'I never believed I'd find another I trusted so well. And now I've found another.'

She put her hand out and touched his face.

'We'll find Rebecca and then we'll find that man.'

Outside the cockerel crowed again and the light began to spill into the room. She began to pack her few things into her leather bag.

'We'll move on, John. Why make it easy for them? We'll find another place. Pieter will bring the bags to us. Be armed.'

'Are you?'

'This!' she said, and in her hand appeared a glittering thin blade of Toledo steel.

CHAPTER 30

Isaac Heinemann was small, bustling and from his demeanour, amused by the world. It was only when he was still, that gravity and sadness showed in his eyes.

They came to his house on the Nieuwe Dohnstraat. There was a view of the Amstel from the lower windows of his three storey brick-built house. It was the house of an unostentatious man who had arrived, who was accepted for what he was. He was more than he seemed.

Pieter had said that he was a fine craftsman, a master stone cutter and polisher and a kind master who had five apprentices.

Pieter introduced Fox. Maeve was left outside in the hall as the men went into the small half-panelled room. Isaac went back into the hall and asked her to join them. His were the manners of old fashioned courtesy and kindness.

He lived as he found and, in Holland, he had found a nation that accepted him and his for what they were. Talented and skilled with business connections across the whole of Europe. Men who added to society and were never regarded with hatred and suspicion except by the most vehement of Protestants and the Catholics of course.

He offered his guests wine and biscuits and fluttered about the room like a brown moth. He wore his hair long and curled and a small cap on his head.

Maeve had turned her back on the men as they drank and was looking at a small painting of an interior. It glowed with light from the window on the left of the image which caught the couple who were holding hands and looking at each other. Isaac saw her staring at the picture and was delighted.

'You like it?' he asked.

'I never saw anything quite like it, sir,' she said.

'The painter is a friend. I want Vermeer to make more of these interiors. Did you see this by Heda?'

It was a small still life. Simple, but beautifully executed. A pewter jug, a goblet and a lobster on a dish.

'Please, be free to look if they please you.'

Maeve nodded and turned away from the others and continued to look at the other pictures hanging in the room. Isaac walked back to Fox and Pieter.

'It's a surprise to meet a young woman with a good eye. You like pictures, Master Fox?'

Fox shrugged.

'No, of course. Now, you want to know a few things. I have no idea of the details but Pieter knew I'd be interested to help a friend of his. It was Pieter who introduced me to his master, Rembrandt, who works rather larger than these. I owe him some favours.'

He turned to Pieter.

'Pieter please show the young lady the pictures in my cabinet.'

Pieter and Maeve moved into the next room as the two men sat at the small table gleaming with polish. On it a bowl of exotic fruit in a simple earthenware bowl. Fox began,

'We understand the Queen is selling her jewels. Does it go well?'

'It's not easy for her. Most of them are too big or in settings that make it hard to value them. I personally won't touch them as I know their provenance.'

Fox waited for this eager man to go on. Isaac Heinemann grimaced.

'Not hers to sell, I believe. My friend, if they belong to the state and if the parliament men win and I have a connection to helping the losers, what then? I hear that the parliament men are not averse to Jews and might even ask them to return to England. I know, I know that's of no concern to you, sir. But to a merchant like me, to my children, it might be important to be able to move on freely.'

He smiled gently at Fox. It was as if he was explaining to a child.

'We Jews have a history of being made to move with nothing but the clothes on our backs. Will I block another safe haven by an act of greed? Most of the Jewish cutters won't touch the stones she offers. Some younger ones may, but otherwise it's the non Jews who will be tempted to buy.'

He went on quietly, 'Henrietta is not finding it easy to sell and some of her people are not well favoured. One called on me not a week since. Harry Morton found it hard to be civil to me. His contempt was almost palpable. He hated dealing with a Jew, selling him something. My refusal made it worse, I think.'

Isaac smiled then and darted across to a side table and took the wine pitcher to Fox and poured a little wine.

Fox sniffed it, tasted it and nodded. Isaac, the stone cutter, smiled.

'She knows pictures, you know wine.'

'I used to buy it when I was younger, sir. In Bordeaux – '

'So, we are both traders?'

'I think you are more than a trader, sir. I am told you are a fine stone cutter.'

'You are also told I am a great repository of information? Rumours, yes?'

Fox shrugged.

'I met a man in The Hague. A large man,' he said.

'Ah. Hauer. He knows where the bodies are buried. I know them before they are buried. Yes? He's a good man. Is the young woman here the one he cared for?'

Fox nodded.

'I see. Have a care with her, my friend. She is wild – wild.'

Fox nodded.

'I know. There is one more question, sir. If the Queen is selling jewels and buying weapons, where would she buy those weapons and where would she store them?'

The darting Jew was suddenly stilled.

He sighed and turned the single diamond ring on his little finger.

'Now we are dealing in matters that are state matters, political matters. This is more sensitive.'

He stood and walked to the window, glanced out at the street and the Amstel river, making up his mind.

'Can I trust your discretion?'

Fox swirled the last of the wine about the goblet and put it down.

'I have never betrayed a friend, nor a source. If I came here in ten years' time and needed a little guidance and I had betrayed you, would I get the guidance?'

'We understand each other. Good.'

He came back to the table and sat gathering his dark robe about him as he gathered his thoughts. When he spoke he spoke softly.

'You must understand, John Fox, that I loathe these merchants of death. They are wealthy, they have power and they care not a spit for the lives of others. Children torched, women raped, men gutted. Jews have seen it all and in my mind it can be laid entirely at the door of those who profit from the sales of weapons and their political clients. They sicken me.'

He sat huddled, suddenly smaller, in his velvet robe.

'So, what can I tell you? There are two or three merchants who deal in such things.'

'The biggest, the most important?'

'They are secret, ply their trade at a distance, are never seen to have had anything to do with the merchandise. It comes to them from all over Europe. The warehouses filled with weapons from other wars, collected, conserved, cleaned and stored and traded now.'

'These men are ruthless men who will sell to whoever has the biggest purse. Maybe at the moment it is your Queen Henrietta. Haggar is a name of one dealer and Trip is another who has friends in Sweden who make and refurbish weapons. They could be the suppliers. But I have never mentioned their names, never connected you to them. Never.'

He leaned closer to Fox across the polished table.

'I understand.' Fox said.

The stone cutter leapt to his feet and swirled across the room. It was as if he was a spring forever coiled, unable to stop the energy surging through his body. He laughed at Fox's surprise and danced across the black and white tiled floor to his guest.

'Now, tell me what you truly want to know. Not this trivial stuff anyone with an ear to the ground could tell you. Tell me why you have really come here.'

For a moment Fox sat silent and then he admitted, 'I'm not certain that I know.'

To Fox's further surprise the springing man rubbed his hands in delight.

'Good. Then perhaps we may help you. Tell me what you

157

know for a certainty and then I will try.'

It was Fox's turn to stand and to walk about the small room. Isaac went on as Fox paced.

'I have to advise you that it is unwise if you are dabbling in politics here, my friend. There are two royal courts living between Amsterdam and The Hague. Your Queen is amongst a rabble of English courtiers. Some of them came with her and others were already gathered, not sure what to do about England. Waiting the call, I think. And the other queen is her sister-in-law in exile from Bavaria. With her courtiers about her too. And between them, the Dutch dance an awkward jig and mostly want neither living here.

'Their courtiers have nothing to do except play games and make trouble. None of them are well liked by the good citizens of Holland. They attract the riff- raff of the European wars looking for engagements with the royalist armies. Henrietta has men scouring these mercenaries for English speaking officers to hire for the service of her husband.'

Fox nodded.

'But you already knew that my friend, so again I ask why are you sent here?'

Fox waited. In the inner room he heard Maeve's laughter at a muttered comment from Pieter.

'Go on,' he urged.

'There are rumours about the city. Bankers talk, merchants discuss, we humble craftsmen listen. I will tell you what we are hearing. But first I will show you something.'

He sat at the table and pulled open a drawer. He took out a velvet bag and emptied the contents onto a small piece of black velvet. Fox watched astounded by the glittering cold light from the three or four dozen cut stones that lay on the velvet catching the light from all their facets.

'These are what I deal in, mostly. But they are truly like these,' he said as he dipped his hand into his pocket and took out four dirty pebbles and put them beside the cut diamonds.

'This is my skill, my friend. To release these from these raw pebbles. What is inside may be beautiful but once their true nature is clear they are also dangerous.'

'Those are diamonds as well?' whispered Fox pointing at the dirty pebbles. The stone cutter smiled and nodded.

'You cut and slice and saw them to make these. From nothing you release this beauty. But it's in the beauty that their danger lies. Diamonds, my friend, are like cruel men. Scratch off their cover, reveal them for what they are and show what they can do,' he said and swept them into the velvet bag.

'People die for them, kill, fight and covet them. What are they? In the end, they are only stones from the ground. Yet – ,' He shrugged and put the parcel of stones back in the drawer.

'You leave them in a drawer like that – loose. Unprotected?'

'Not exactly. I know the stones. I can recognise the stones I have cut from a thousand others. And anyway I have my people here in the workshops and in the house. Not everyone can come in and no one sees what you have seen. I showed you for one reason. I wanted you to understand that I trust you. I value discretion above all things except knowledge. Like your Francis Hauer, your fat man in The Hague. He told me I could trust you and so what I will tell you is not fact but gossip.'

Fox sat, tense, waiting. Maybe this little man would show him what his true mission was.

'Gossip and rumour are in the air. Catching, small whispers here and here and here.'

His hands darted about his head as if catching flies.

'If you are a man who lives to catch the first hint of danger, threat, you will learn why in a moment. We need to know when to take up the small packets of stones, the tools of the trade. 'There is always warning, my friend. Always a hint in the cosmos. Something.'

Fox nodded. 'A friend used to say to me that if you felt something, if something inside you warned you, if there was an instinct that told you of danger, it was a fool who ignored the warning.'

'Exactly so,' said the small, darting man. 'So. There is a court inside the court of Henrietta. A secret group. When that man, Sir Harry came here he was accompanied by two others. They are the sort of arrogant English who assume all foreigners, particularly Jews, have no brains, no ears, no feelings and no eyes. They wanted to sell me a parcel of stones and I refused them. They were not pleased.'

'I told them the stones were too big and the mounts too difficult. I had neither wish for them nor any use. They were of no interest to me. The little man, their leader shouted at me and lost his temper.'

He smiled.

159

'How dare a little Jew tell him no, refuse him what he wanted? He told me then that he was going to be a powerful man in England one day and I would regret refusing him anything. He would not forget, he said, when matters had changed in England and real men were in power. He called me names. It's not unusual. His friends stopped him talking and they quickly went their way.'

Fox could hardly believe his ears.

'Him. Harry Morton in power? He said that? Power?'

'Yes. In anger of course, and only to a filthy Jew you understand. We are of no account to men like him. Only useful when they want a loan. But it only added to the hints and rumours we already hear about 'Dam and in The Hague. You have only to know where to listen. The true listener knows when there is something dangerous about any man. I know you understand that.'

Fox nodded and watched as Isaac twisted the diamond ring on his little finger and smiled.

'He is nothing to me. We learn to bend with the wind about such men.'

Fox asked again.

'He talked about power? Him? He's a country land owner. Nothing.'

'He seems to think otherwise. I confess I did not like the man. My only daughter came into the room at that moment. She is a child. I saw him look at her and I told her to leave us. There was something indecent there. I have seen few men like him. He's a cruel man without either good manners or charm.

'I have warned my friends in my trade. Maybe the young will agree to buy the stones or to offer a loan against them. I would not. There is something more here. Something which sounds like a broken bell. You understand me? Something wrong. This word power? Was it this you were sent to find?'

Fox stared at the gentle man who was no longer darting about the room. His eyes were quite still as he watched Fox think.

'Thank you Master Heinnman. If this is as it sounds then there could be danger for England in it.'

Maeve came back into the room with Pieter and saw the look on Fox's face. She walked across to Isaac and smiled.

'It is a remarkable collection of paintings, sir. Thank you for letting me see them.'

'It's a pleasure to share them with you. Your protector in The Hague, taught you well I think.' and he bowed gracefully as if giving her a gift.

'One thing I have noticed,' Maeve said. 'They are all small works. You only buy small ones. Is there a reason?'

He nodded.

'My mother came from Russia and my father from Turkey. They lived for a time in Prussia and then in Spain. Each time they settled, the Jews were turned out. We learned to keep only small things. That way you can pack up and begin again in another place, the next time.'

'Next time?' she asked.

'We never know, my dear girl. We never know.'

In the silence that followed nothing but the ticking of a small clock could be heard in the room. Isaac twisted off the ring on his little finger and held it out to Maeve.

'This is a little thing. For you. I have enjoyed meeting your friend and also you. When you see my old friend Francis in The Hague give him my respects. Here. Take it.'

Reluctantly she took the diamond ring from his outstretched palm and put it on her finger. She looked at it and then at him and Fox saw she had tears in her eyes.

'Thank you,' she said and wiped her sleeve across her face. 'No man ever gave me a gift and didn't want anything in return. Thank you for that.'

She smiled at Isaac as he watched her gravely.

'Once' he said, 'I had another daughter. The plague took her. Five years ago. So, go now in health and have a care.'

Outside in the sunshine the street was empty. Fox looked to right and left, stepped out and walked briskly away with Pieter at his side. Five minutes after the two men left, a hooded woman stepped out into the narrow cobbled street beside the house, waited a beat and then walked slowly away among the shadows.

161

CHAPTER 31

In the studio beside the red brick house on Amstel Straat, Fox and Pieter stood amongst easels, drapes and curtains, old bits of armour, helmets and flags. A long table with pots and jars, brushes in oil, brushes in bundles, pigments in bladders, sheets of glass, bottles of oil, varnish, cloths, charcoal, pencils, graphite, broken frames, torn canvas, a drawing of a Madonna and child, torn, a lantern, candles, broken knives. The detritus of a working studio.

On the easel in the centre of the room stood a huge canvas on which crude charcoal sketches marked out the positions of figures and the battlements of a castle.

'It's a work commissioned by the City, for the new halls. He is doing something about the guards of the city. See the lanterns here and these figures carrying pikes and wearing helmets and armour. See, see, all here ready for the first under painting.'

Pieter was as excited by it as if it was his own work. He looked round as a small door opened and the portly figure of a fleshy-faced man stood in the light thrown from the window beyond the door.

'Pieter,' he said. His voice gruff as if he had only just woken up. He walked slowly into the room and looked Fox up and down.

He grunted, nodded at Pieter and walked to the canvas on the easel. He spoke without looking round. Pieter translated.

'He wants you to stand over there in the light. He thinks you're a model for a soldier. You're to stand just here.'

Fox stared at the painter as Pieter explained his mistake. The painter laughed then and spun to look at Fox.

'He's a friend, sir. From my old life. A soldier.'

The painter shrugged and went on. Pieter translated the Dutch.

162

'I see that he's a soldier. What's he doing here?'

'I left you with a small drawing. You said you might be able to help,' Pieter reminded him.

'Of course. Pretty girl. They're over here somewhere.'

He went to the table covered in yet more glass bowls, spatulas and grinders, brushes and paraphernalia. He shoved stuff aside with his stubby hands and found what he was looking for.

He held out the small pearl framed original image.

'Your daughter, sir? She is beautiful. I'd like her to sit to me when she has a moment. Ask her. From the set of her face she's a wilful child.'

He handed the frame to Fox.

'And here are four copies. I assume friends are looking for her.'

'Yes' said Pieter.

The painter handed over small pieces of heavy paper. On each a sepia ink copy of the original.

'And the more fool you for losing a daughter like that.'

He put his hand gently on Fox's arm. A bell chimed in a distant church tower. The painter turned away from Fox.

'Now, Pieter we will get on. There's work to do.'

'Can I pay you, sir?' The painter hesitated and then shrugged.

'No, no it's a gift for my friend.'

He turned away impatiently and began to look for the brushes he wanted to use. Fox murmured to Pieter, 'Give the pictures of Rebecca to the three men we have searching. Tell them we have little time to find her.'

CHAPTER 32

It was raining when Fox walked through the city. Everywhere on the edges of the city was evidence of new building. A wide canal arced around the outskirts, joining a network of other canals. He turned away into the main square and stepped into a shadowy brick cloister with small shops and workrooms along its edge.

In a shop selling shoes he picked up a pair of boots, put them down, walked briskly past the cobbler working at his bench and without a word, stepped back into the damp arcade.

In a cutler's workshop he glanced at the blades and knives on racks and in the window that opened onto the street. Behind him the roar of a small bellows whipped up heat as the cutler forged a new blade and then the hiss as he thrust it, pulsing with heat into a barrel of water.

Fox left the shop and walked past a hooded figure crouched on the ground at the end of the cloister. The hood covered the person's face. She had a bowl at her feet and two small coins in it.

He bent down and put a coin in the bowl.

'There's a small inn at the back of the church,' he said and walked away.

A carillon of bells began to sound and as it did so, another began and then another and another. The city was pulsing again with the sound of a thousand bells.

Behind the church the small alleys and narrow roads were no longer lined with rich houses. In the ale house, Fox looked around the crowded tables and the huddle of men at the rough bar in front of two barrels and a shelf of rough earthenware mugs.

The barman was talking to two men and was deep into a long story as Fox waited patiently.

The place had fallen silent for a moment or two as the

stranger walked in. The men at the back looked at his clothes and the slouch of the battered hat. Nothing about this stranger gave them cause for concern. He was not part of the City Watch, nor an official. He was certainly not rich and there would be no point in tapping him for a drink or a handout.

As the moment of silence ended and the hum of conversation began, a hooded figure joined him. They walked past the end of the bar and into a quieter room at the back with benches and scrubbed tables.

As they sat down, a pot boy walked over to them and waited by their table. 'Wine,' said Fox and the pot boy walked slowly away. He wasn't going to hurry for a stranger.

'Well?' he asked Maeve.

'I was right. There is someone watching.'

'Who?'

'The Italian friend of your old army comrade. Him. There are two others. They work together. What makes you so important? No one knew you when you came here except Thurloe and Fairfax. Everyone knows what the Queen is doing. So why are they now more interested in you?'

Fox shrugged. 'Harry Morton has reason. He knows that his wife and I were together in Derbyshire one winter. We know he is looking for revenge.'

'And your daughter is with his wife and if he knows who she is, he has you by the balls.'

Maeve stared at the table as the pot boy slammed down a pitcher and two cups. Fox threw a coin onto the table which he snapped up. He walked away with a smirk.

Three men walked in and sat on the far side, drinking. They took no notice of Fox and Maeve. She glanced across at them and smiled at Fox. A shift in her eyes directed him to the group and he nodded at her.

'Do you trust Black Tom Fairfax?' he asked her for no connected reason.

'As much as I trust most men which means very little. Why?'

'And Thurloe?'

'No. Not him. Not one inch. His whole life is about dishonesty, disloyalty, deceit, secrets. Searching for the weakness in others.'

'Is he serving himself or the parliament or who?'

'Who knows?'

Fox swirled the poor wine around in the brown earthen cup. Sipped it. The three men on the other side of the room laughed aloud and poured more wine.

'A sorry business if we can't even trust the intelligence gatherers. Whose side are they on?'

Fox shrugged.

'It's the usual dilemma, interpreting who wants what and why and where it may lead.'

'And what to tell them when you make your report.'

Fox nodded.

'So – all this from our little Jewish friend. He must've liked you to be so indiscreet.'

'It was you he liked, Maeve. He was warning us there is more to this than meets the eye. He talked about power.'

'Who talked about power?'

'Morton threatened Isaac that when he had power he, Isaac, would regret refusing to buy the stones or to advance money on them. He would regret it when he had the power, is what he said.'

'He boasted about power. Who has the power?' Maeve was puzzled.

'The King says he has power, through God. Henrietta loves him, it seems. But he seems weak to some around him, perhaps.'

Maeve swirled a puddle of spilt wine on the table top.

'Maybe she is irritated by Charles forever listening to the wrong advisors. Maybe the obstacle, as she sees it, to beating back the parliament men is the King himself.'

Maeve was still drawing in the puddles of wine on the table and didn't look up but went on.

'Maybe the men around her see him as an obstacle to beating back the parliament men and to their ambition.'

Fox agreed.

'The Queen listens to them, trusts them.'

She scoffed at the very idea.

'Who can anyone trust in these times?'

Fox looked at her .

'You know I am sick of these people. I'll find my daughter and the rest can go hang.'

Maeve shook her head and stared up at him. Her grey-green eyes clouded with pity for the man.

'You can't escape it, John Fox. You are locked into this

166

now. If they discover that you are thinking as you are, they'll be afraid you'll expose them. They would have to shut your mouth in case you have discovered anything. They have to pull you in like a hooked fish to the priest, my friend, and they have the very best of bait. Who are they, John? The people here who'd kill you, or those who sent you? Who trusts who now, John?'

'Then we have to let them pull me in if that's the way to find out,' said Fox quietly. She stared at the patterns she had made on the table.

'Thurloe is a bloody snake to lead you here, my friend. What will you do?'

'I'll give them reason to think I know more than I surmise. Can you get a message to Elizabeth for me?'

Maeve shrugged and looked away glancing at the men on the other side of the room for a moment.

'And then?' she asked.

'I'll bait my own trap. Tell Pieter, I want to know where Sir Harry meets the other members of his secret cabal. It's time to trail my coat.'

Maeve nodded and leaned closer as she rose to leave.

'You should know there will be a masque for Henrietta in a hall near Hoff Straat. I'll be there. There is a garden at the back of the building. I will get a message to Elizabeth that you too will be there.'

CHAPTER 33

The English Queen had married the sickly Charles when they were both young. Charles was short, coughed a lot, had weak legs and only rode because of his stubborn determination to overcome his frailty. Nothing though could conceal his size and like so many small men with power, he abused it.

God had ordained him king so no man could say him nay. Henrietta was also small and also arrogant. No one was to be allowed to usurp the royal prerogative and if Charles was not man enough to stand up for himself then she would do it for him.

She was surrounded by men and women who saw her as the means of gaining favoured status about the royal court. No one did anything but flatter the little stiff-backed Queen.

In this stuffy provincial Dutch republic, Henrietta's royal court continued to live the life they had hoped for in England. When the King had won and the Parliament force of petty lawyers and little landowners was defeated they would expect to be favoured amongst men and women. Meanwhile Henrietta was woman enough to bask in flattery and listen most to the flatterers about her.

Courts in exile were thick with plots and petty arguments, discussions and downright hatreds played out between the arrogant and the ambitious.

Henrietta was surrounded by a whirlwind of advice, rumour, suggestions and, away from her husband, could see that sometimes his lack of decisiveness was bad for his interests. Maybe she had begun to believe that she was the real power behind the throne. And there were those about her who would play on that belief to their own advantage.

Boredom was a constant problem. How were they to be entertained in this old fashioned, fusty society? It was essential to make their own entertainment and indeed Henrietta saw no reason why she should not do so even if it scandalised the local burghers.

Why should she give a fig for the local people with their puritanical vision of a Christian faith that it was stripped of glory, colour, pageantry, music and the smells of incense and the sound of altar boys ringing bells?

Those about her knew that her favourite entertainment was the masque and that, above all, she liked to have an active part in it. And if her part required her to dance in costumes that were cut to delight and seduce rather than to appease local disapproval she would wear them.

In a small hall near Hoff Straat the masque was entertaining the court in exile. Trumpets sounded and great clouds wafted across the room on pulleys and trolleys. Children, near naked, with painted faces and golden hair peeped from behind them as the usual allegorical figures joined in the fanciful tales of gods and goddesses, Roman heroines and classical heroes –

Gods and giants, dwarves and fiery chariots swept about the hall and at every tableau the court and their guests marvelled.

The scenery makers surpassed themselves when a noble figure of Venus appeared on a chariot drawn across the sky by cut-out horses with silver wings. When she stepped from the chariot and moved amongst her courtiers, they saw it was Henrietta.

Her dress, cut low across her breasts, was sparkling with jewels and cut-glass sequins as she gave her hand to a favoured courtier and then, as the music changed, she began the dance.

It was a fine revel at which the recently arrived courtiers displayed their new clothes and the members of the court who had been in exile for years tried to hide the fact that their clothes were outdated and threadbare.

The wives tried to out-do their neighbours with the lace and gold and glitter of their collars and their décolletage, their sparkling eyes made up and cheeks rouged, their best jewels glittering like fiery ice across their heaving breasts as the music swelled.

In the shadows outside the hall, Fox sat on a stone wall and waited. The glittering light of a thousand candles shone out through the tall windows. The chatter of men and women inside could be heard over the music.

It was deserted in this garden. Local people were not invited and had no wish to join these foreigners and their ungodly festivities. The sound of the music and laughter rose as a door opened and closed near Fox.

He watched as a grey-robed woman stood in the doorway. Behind her Sir Harry stared into the night and then touched the woman and she turned back into the bright light of the hall. It was a face Fox knew but could not place. The door shut. Why was this woman there with Sir Harry? Who was she?

The door opened again and another woman stepped out into the garden. The door closed behind her. She hesitated for a moment and then, as her eyes adjusted to the dimmer light in the gardens, Fox stood up and Elizabeth walked slowly towards him.

She stopped. 'John?' she whispered.

He stepped closer and she shrank back and shook her head.

'I'm sorry, John. Don't – don't touch me.'

She looked up at him and he saw the bruise across her neck and over her breast. Fox had no need to ask who had done it.

'He'll kill me. He said he would kill me. I'm afraid of him. So frightened.'

They moved into the darker part of the gardens. This was a woman he had once felt very close to. Now he pitied her with all his heart.

'You could leave him?'

'No John. You don't know my husband, what he owns, he owns. I'm lost. Someone in Derbyshire that winter we were together betrayed us. I don't know who but when he came home he knew you and I had been together.'

Fox tried to touch her hand.

'John, he knew everything. He has beaten me time and again. Punishment, he says. I wish to die. Truly.'

'No' he whispered. 'Leave him.'

'I have nowhere to run where I'd be safe. He'd find me, destroy me. I have nothing left, John. He insults me, makes me stay, mocks me. I think – I think maybe he is mad but – he knew I had a child – a son. He died before Harry came home. But he knew everything.'

'Your shepherd told me,' said Fox. 'A son.'

'He was taken away. I was told he died.'

'Our son?' he asked eventually and she nodded.

Fox said nothing. He stared at her tired, worn face and felt rage. Not love, only sadness.

'They know you are here. They know you are spying for Fairfax. They boast of what they will do to you.'

'They? Who are they?'

'There is a little group of them. They are very close to the Queen. Harry flatters her. He says she is stronger than her husband, that she is the King's backbone. She seems to love Charles very much. But she is flattered. Harry says he admires her very much.'

'Strange to love a man who'd make war on his own subjects.'

Elizabeth shook her head.

'Maybe, maybe not. What is a woman to make of what men do? My husband has a friend, a young woman. She seems to be very religious. A strange companion for my husband but he flatters her, praises her, gives her gifts, pretends he believes as she believes. He's using her.'

'Name? Her name?'

'I don't know. She calls herself Mary. I don't know. All of them keep her close. They don't touch her, you understand me?'

Fox nodded as she went on, 'It's as if they are teaching her something, something secret. She is very young and very proud. Arrogant even. As if she held secrets. She is not allowed to talk with me.'

Elizabeth stood with her eyes on the ground. She was unable to look him in the eyes. This once proud and lovely woman, so full of life, had been beaten down, cowed, ruined. Fox could offer her no comfort.

'If you stay, you'll be killed. Please, leave Holland. Go.'

'And my daughter?' he snarled. 'What about my daughter? You swore you'd take care of her. Where is Rebecca?'

The woman shook her head.

'I don't know. I honestly do not know. She left about a week or ten days ago. He took her away to be a companion to this strange woman, he said. He laughed in my face when I begged him to let her come back to me. He knows who's daughter she is. I'm sorry, John.'

'Bait,' he said. 'She's bait. Her father will come and jump to my tune – '

Elizabeth looked up at him then and he saw the tears and the fear, the misery in her face. He reached out to touch her cheek and she backed away as if he'd struck her.

'Please – don't touch me – don't .'

The music in the hall rose up again and in the garden the moon was covered by a thunder cloud. Apart from the lanterns dotted about the garden, it was dark.

'What is he planning, this husband of yours and his secret little group?'

She shook her head

'And the strange girl?' he asked.

'I don't know. He boasts to others from time to time that when he has power – when they have power, things will change in the world and England will be free of rebels who'll hang off every tree and tower when he has his way .'

'When he has power – what are they planning to do?'

'I don't know.'

'Where do they meet, this secret group? Where would he take Rebecca?'

She shakes her head.

'I'm sorry, John. I can't help you. I don't know. When he has drunk a little he has talked about a man called Haggar. He has boasted about weapons and supplies stored somewhere. I don't know what it's about, John.'

She felt under her cloak and took out a small package.

'He – he asked me to give you these.'

Fox stared at her in shock then reached for the blade he wore slung across his back.

'He knew we were meeting?'

'He knows everything John. I was to give you these to prove he had Rebecca. I have to do as he tells me. I'm sorry. He wants you in his power. He'll torment you with it. Delight in it.'

She held out the package to Fox.

Reluctantly he took the package and felt the touch of her familiar hand for a moment.

'I shan't see you again, John Fox. Remember those weeks in Derbyshire sometimes. When it snows, perhaps. As I will. Please. They were such happy times.'

And she stepped out of the pool of lantern light, turned and swept away as a door opened in the portico of the hall as if someone was waiting for her.

Fanfares of trumpets and the masque ended, final speeches were made and the chariots retreated behind the clouds leaving only Venus on her throne.

Fox stood in the darkness as the door thudded shut.

CHAPTER 34

Fox and Pieter walked along the earthworks that marked the outer edge of Amsterdam. Clods of freshly turned earth lay in a great arc around the northern edge beyond the old walls as further defence against the sea. Men scurried back and forth carrying earth in baskets up the slopes.

Other men took the soil and spread it on the seaward side to reinforce the defences against any surge of the sea that sometimes happened in winter storms. Further up the wide trench came other men lining its walls with clay and stones. Yet others making the foundations of locks, measuring, checking, measuring more, a vast enterprise to circle the city with canals.

Pieter explained as he walked with Fox.

'The plan is to build an arc of canals. Produce can be brought into the city on the wide-bellied barges. Tobacco, and spices, gold and cloth, pottery and china brought directly from around the trading world into the city. Supplies of cordage, sails, stores of flour and bread, dried fish in casks with salt, prepared for the next journey across the Dutch Empire.'

In the distance, the tall masts, spars and rigging of the merchant fleet which provided the wealth of the city stood stark against the steel blue sky.

'Is there any news?' Fox asked eventually.

Pieter stopped and leaned against an old willow tree that had yet to be torn out of the way of the digging labourers.

In the distance they could hear the shouts and yells of the men, someone was singing, somewhere else two men were arguing and others were encouraging them to fight. Close by two women cooked a mess of oats and wheat over a fire to make a breakfast porridge for any man who cared to buy. The women watched the two men and laughed at something they said. They went on stirring their porridge.

Pieter spat. 'Haggar and his Swedish friends are gathering weapons. The dealers know Henrietta is desperate so are driving the price of diamonds down. The way of the world, my friend.'

Fox looked bleakly at the one-handed soldier.

'Go on,' he said.

'Harry Morton is negotiating directly with the weapons merchants. He has struck up a friendship with the most important.'

'Haggar?' asked Fox.

'And Tripp. Yes. Stores are being brought into the city.'

'Where?'

'Not sure. Not yet.'

'Find out.' ordered Fox. 'And Pieter,' he went on quietly, 'I want to see our Italian scout.'

Pieter looked at Fox.

'A problem?'

'Just bring him. Tell him we need to discuss plans with him.'

Pieter waited. 'Is something wrong?'

Fox looked at him.

'I have been followed ever since we talked with them. I want to see the Italian and I want him to think we are all meeting. Planning together.'

Pieter shrugged and looked away at the mounds of dark red earth piled across the flat land. Behind them the houses and churches, the squares and alleys of Amsterdam.

'Somewhere quiet?' asked Pieter softly.

'Yes. Somewhere quiet.'

'There is a place. Along this track a little. There is a cutting they have made there. A few trees around. Work stops here at dusk. No one will be about. Would that be quiet enough?'

'Yes,' said Fox. 'Dusk then. I have two things to do. I have to find Sir Harry before he comes to me. If he comes to me, he comes with strength. He says he has my daughter, his wife says he has my daughter.

'If he comes to me, it will be to demand my obedience. I need to get to him first, to take him by surprise. I need to have seen him, observed him without a spy on my back. I need him to be afraid he has lost sight of me. I need him to think I know what is going on.'

174

The old soldier scratched at his wrist above wherever his hand had been.

'It itches sometimes – my hand. Odd isn't it? You want to vanish?'

Fox nodded. Pieter grinned.

'Like old times behind enemy lines. To be absorbed – lost in the city. I can show you where this death dealer Haggar lives. It is a beautiful new house near the southern canal. He is a powerful man. Dangerous.'

Fox nodded.

'I was told. It's not him I want.'

'You'd know this Harry Morton's face?'

Fox smiled then but his eyes were like black chips of stone.

'His portrait hangs in a house in Derbyshire. I saw it every morning through the whole winter I was there. Yes, I will know him.'

He wiped the heel of his boot free of the clinging mud and stepped back onto the path. 'We'll go and see this quiet place and then you can show me this death dealer's fine house, Pieter. If you see the Irish girl, tell her I have a parcel from Harry Morton. I don't want to open it.'

The two men set off along the track to the dip in the ground where the workers stored their tools for the next day's work. A rough shack had an old sail for a roof to provide shelter on the worst of days. Fox and Pieter looked down into the workers' camp, a place with no semblance of order. A stray dog looked up and then skulked away into the shelter. The workmen had already gone for the day.

Fox nodded. 'This will do,' he said. 'A killing ground.'

Pieter shuddered as he saw the look in Fox's face.

'Are you sure he's betrayed you?'

'Just bring him here. In an hour. For a meeting. Can you do that?'

Pieter nodded and turned and walked away along the track.

Fox stepped down into the hollow and walked into the shelter. There was no one. He worked his way past a cage of tools, past a barrel of clean water with a cup tied to a string alongside it.

Up the far slope, on the top, was an old willow, bent with age. The trunk, twisted and gnarled was the width of a man.

Fox watched. This was what he knew about. Be in place early and stay still – vanish.

175

Bells were beginning to sound across the city as the day ended. Far away over the flat land towards the grey horizon he heard the sound of a curlew mewing. Like the Somerset levels he remembered from his boyhood, this was sad land.

He heard the horses first. Then as two riders breasted the ridge opposite him he saw the Italian and Pieter. They were talking together and the Italian was clearly suspicious, edgy. It had begun to mizzle with rain,

Fox stepped briskly into sight on the far bank close to the willow. He ran down the slope and raised his hand in greeting.

'Pieter , good man – on time for once. And you my friend, come down out of the drizzle. We can light a fire while we wait for the others.'

He turned to Pieter. 'You told the others where to find us?'

Pieter grunted and dismounted. The Italian slipped off his horse and smiled at Fox.

Fox noted the rapier at his side and under the cloak the silver wire decoration on the dagger he wore. He turned his back and walked into the shelter of the sailcloth roof. He stood there as the rain dripped off the edge onto the muddy ground.

The Italian walked quickly in out of the rain and slung his sodden hat onto a rough wooden table and sat on the bench.

'Well?' he said.

Fox said nothing. Pieter stood in the doorway leaning on an old pick handle he had picked up from the stores.

The Italian looked up at Fox and was puzzled by what he saw.

'Where are the others?'

'How much did they pay you?' Fox asked him quietly.

'I don't know what – pay me? Who?'

The Italian looked from Fox to Pieter and stood up.

'You know who and you know how much I'm worth,' said Fox quietly.' Are you supposed to kill me as well as to follow me?'

The Italian stood and moved away from the bench and the table to give himself room. Pieter waited at the edge of the shelter.

'I want to know who paid you.'

'Paid what for?'

'That too, I want to know?'

Fox looked towards Pieter and as he looked away, the Italian made the mistake Fox wanted him to make.

The dagger came first from under the man's right arm and

the rapier next. This was a man who knew the game. Fox turned as he heard the rasp of steel on steel. He had nothing in his hand.

'You're dead, Fox.' The Italian advanced like a fencing master in a class. 'Stay out of this, Pieter, or you'll be next,' he hissed, as Pieter stepped into the space.

The Italian smiled. It was an easy kill for a man like him. A thrust of the sword and then step close to his unarmed victim and rip him with the razor sharp dagger. Easy. The blade circled a little and the dagger provided cover for his chest and abdomen. Fox was quite still. It was the perfect fencing school situation and the enemy was naked. The Italian smiled and advanced fast for the coup de grace.

Pieter threw the pick handle across the open space between the two men. Fox ducked the thrust of the long blade and caught the wooden pick handle. The Italian was off balance with the power of the thrust and his legs were spread. Fox swung the pick handle low and fast into his groin. The Italian screamed and fell. Fox kicked the sword away and looked down at the writhing man.

'Never assume a man is defenceless, friend,' Fox observed to Pieter. 'Always a mistake.'

He looked down at the man in the mud.

'So, now you will tell me or I will have to break your knee cap and then you may never walk again. Now, who ordered you to follow me and to tell him where I went, who I saw? Were you paid or was it a promise?'

For a moment the Italian hesitated and then Fox smashed the man's knee cap and leaned on the axe handle. Shards of bone ground together and the man screamed until Fox leaned back.

'A man – red faced – tall. He came first. He spoke good Italian. '

'Blond hair? Called Sir Adam?'

The Italian nodded.

'Please, Help me. I can't get up.

'And – who did you tell? Harry Morton?'

'He'll kill me if I say anything. He swore he'd hunt me down and kill me.'

'Where did you meet him? Think on this. I don't have to hunt you down. I can snuff you out like an old candle on the instant. Where did you meet him?'

'I don't know. A mill, no, two mills. I don't know. I can't trade with you, Fox. You'll want to trade when you hear what he intends for your daughter. Revenge, he says, for what you did with his wife. Nothing to do with me. But he won't let that go, I promise you. He has your daughter. A fiery girl – spirited. Ready to be tamed. You kill me and you'll lose her. Sir Harry told me he'd tame her and then she's for anyone who wants her. Me even. You can't kill me, Fox. You'll never find her if you do. And she'll be dancing jigs and the beast with two backs with anyone who wants her. She'll be begging for more when Morton has finished with her. Jig, jig, jig.'

The Italian laughed, almost gloating, until he looked up. Fox leaned over him with the dagger in his hand. The mocking man stared up into Fox's dead eyes and began to scrabble at the earth trying to lever himself away.

Fox reached down, put his hand across the man's terrified eyes and hauled his head backwards. Then the blade sliced down and across the sinews of the taut throat.

The dead man's legs twitched once, twice, and stilled.

Across the flat sea marsh where a mist was rolling beyond the ridge of the canal, the mewing curlew sounded.

CHAPTER 35

Rain dripped from the trees in the deserted garden in incessant tiny explosions of water on his face and hands. Fox was waiting. It's always waiting, patiently waiting, not allowing anxiety or fear to gnaw at you.

Waiting in the field and watching. Noting every detail of the target, waiting. Forgetting the personal doubts and fears. Watching and waiting. Not allowing anything to disturb the watching. Nothing. Waiting, watching, merged into the surroundings. Waiting.

Night had fallen five hours ago. He hadn't slept. He lay behind the large beech tree in the garden of a deserted building near the line of the new canal. In front of him the target. The house of Haggar, the weapons dealer.

Two men patrolled the house back and forth with huge fighting dogs on leashes. They crossed each half hour in front of the house, exchanged a word and moved on.

Pieter had said very little. Fox knew he'd seen enough and when he had suggested he rode home to The Hague and a warm bed, Pieter had been relieved.

'Killing that man was a mistake,' he said. 'You'll never find Rebecca now.'

'He should not have threatened my daughter. Mocked me. You go home, my friend, just tell Maeve where I am. Then go home to your good wife in The Hague and forget we met.'

The sun came up and the ground steamed with sudden warmth. A horse's bridle jingled behind the ruined house. Fox looked across at the arms dealer's house. Nothing was moving there. The doors were shut and the gates were still locked. A pebble hit Fox and he looked behind him.

Maeve sat concealed behind the ruined doorway of the

house. Fox crawled between overgrown bushes and flower beds to join her.

'Nothing and no-one has moved out of the house. Harry Morton came here yesterday afternoon. He is still there. He was with that strange woman,' Maeve said quietly.

'You're sure?'

'I've been here for two days,' she said.

The chains on the gate rattled and one of them swung open. From their cover on the terrace they watched as Harry Morton rode out. He wasn't alone. A grey cloaked and hooded figure rode at his side. A young woman, from her hands on the reins of her horse. Taller than Rebecca and with black hair falling free under the hood.

Harry leaned across to her and said something. She pulled aside her hood the better to hear him. He was close to her but did not touch her. She shook her head without looking at him. They rode on.

It was the girl Fox had seen before, with Morton. Pale faced and almost as grey as her robe. Two well armed men appeared from behind the house and joined them. An escort.

The group moved off.

'We'll lose them,' Fox snarled.

'I brought horses. We shan't lose them.' Maeve said.

The road followed the gently curving line of the waterway. The land offered little cover but already there were travellers moving in the early morning. Traders with panniers of vegetables on their sturdy ponies, merchants with three or four clerks riding purposefully towards the city. A carriage or two clattered by on the road towards The Hague.

A huge barge moved slowly along the wide waterway to their right heading for a small basin and a lock gate. Other, smaller boats, moved quietly along under sail or oar. Two boys in blue trousers skiffed their little boat across the canal to an old lady who wanted a ferry over the water.

The washed-out sky promised more rain later. Maeve and Fox followed the distant quartet of riders ahead of them. The path ran along the high bank for as far as they could see. Anyone travelling was a silhouette against the pale sky.

Maeve leaned across to him.

'What happened?'

Fox shrugged.

'I made a mistake. The Italian betrayed us.'

Maeve nodded.

'So? Did you kiss him farewell – or what?'

'I asked him about Rebecca and he told me. He told me what Harry Morton promised for her. He said he'd been promised her after Harry had finished with her and he laughed at me. Sir Harry was looking forward to taming her, he said.'

Maeve spat between her teeth and looked along the crowded road. In the distance their target rode on. She glanced at Fox and her smile struck him like ice.

CHAPTER 36

In the afternoon the sky over the sea began to darken. Thunder clouds began to build and the sky changed from blue to silver grey. The people on the road began to hurry. They wanted to be in shelter before the approaching storm hit land.

Even the barges on the nearby canal began to crowd on sail, heading for the haven of a basin near the next lock.

Fox and Maeve crossed a small canal that led into the main water through a single lock. Men in two barges that were already moored hurried to get tarpaulin covers over their cargo and to give it and themselves shelter.

Ahead of them a haze of rain came closer and the four people they were following vanished.

The sky opened and when the first squall cleared, the sun broke though and the road began to steam. Fox and Maeve peered ahead. There was no sign of their quarry.

They rode on over a slight rise and there, before them, was a huge basin with many boats moored up.

They moved back into cover and watched the storm gathering. To their right a stepped cobbled track led down to the side of a lock gate. Beyond the lock lay a smooth stretch of water at the far end of which two barges lay.

Towering over the calm water were two huge windmills. Their sails were turning fast as water was pumped from the lower stretch of canal to the pool below the lock.

A line of ponies was being led carefully along the track. Beside the barge a pile of boxes, panniers and hessian sacks lay waiting to be loaded. A wide gangplank led onto one of the huge barges. The mast was stepped along the length of the deck and across the shallow hump where steps led into a cabin.

Sir Harry Morton and the young woman were standing at the head of the companionway. Harry watched as two men began to unload the panniers from the ponies. Three others were already taking stores from the pile on the bank. Boxes like coffins.

'Muskets!' breathed Fox.

The men carried the boxes onto the barge and along the deck where they were lowered through a cargo hatch into the hold. Fox counted forty boxes and then watched as the men began carefully to lower small wooden kegs which Fox knew to be powder kegs. He counted over a hundred.

Harry Morton checked these off on a list. Bundles of pikes and sheaves of swords were passed down into the hold with lengths of rope, baskets of saddles, stirrups and leather, more heavy baskets of ball and shot, more coffin-shaped boxes, more barrels.

Harry urged the men to hurry but to be careful. The storm clouds were coming closer off the sea.

Fox went on counting as more weapons were stowed through open hatches on the forrard deck.

Two men were lashing canvas covers across the wooden hatches to keep the cargo below dry.

An hour later, Sir Harry had gone and with him went the mysterious woman and the men who had been loading the barges.

The late afternoon sky was black and distant thunder rumbled. Dark grey and gold clouds towered over the low lying land. They rumbled and roared and lightning fizzed over the sea.

When it came the rain would be torrential. Suddenly the wind died away and it was still.

The windmill's sails had been anchored. A warning of the power of the wind that would come when the storm broke.

The light began to fade as Fox slithered down the bank and joined Maeve.

'I'm going to see what else they have.'

Maeve pulled her hood over her head and said nothing. Fox touched her shoulder.

'Are you alright?' he asked.

'I'm afraid – I'm afraid of thunder,' she said and lay still.

'I won't be long.'

A streak of lightning lit up the barge basin for a moment and Fox ran as the rain began to pour across the land, hissing over the basin.

No one was going to guard a dangerous cargo like this, Fox

was sure. When he climbed across the gangway onto the boat it was a matter of seconds to find the hatch to the small cabin, to loosen the canvas cover and to slide down into the gangway to the cabin, down the steps that led to the lower deck where the cargo was stowed.

What light there was flickered through the portholes along the line of the barge. Fox could see along the hold where the stores were neatly stacked.

He opened one of the small kegs, plunged his hand in and found the black powder he was expecting. Carefully he lifted the opened keg and, walking down the line of the hold, laid a narrow trail of powder from the cabin hatchway around the stores.

Boxes of muskets, lead bullets, cannon balls, old harness, saddles, swords and pikes from a dozen armies who'd fought across Europe over the past decade.

Weapons gleaned from old battlefields, refurbished and sold on to kill the English. At the hatchway he laid a pile of powder and then lugged three small kegs into place over the powder. Then he smashed the bung out of each barrel and took a reel of slow-burning fuse he'd found beside a box of muskets.

He pushed the end of the fuse into the black powder. As he stepped slowly up the steps back into the cabin he unreeled the fuse and carried a half-full keg of powder under his arm.

He slipped out of the cabin and still unreeling the fuse, moved along the deck towards the gang plank. Kneeling, he put the barrel down, took a flint and steel from his jacket pocket and was about to kneel to strike a spark.

'I don't think so, Sergeant.'

Fox looked round and saw the gangway blocked by three men led by Sir Adam Stringer, the florid faced friend of Harry Morton. He was grinning as he moved closer to Fox with his cavalry sword at the ready. Fox knew he was a ruthless man who'd already tortured one of Fox's contacts to death in The Hague. Fox moved away and to the side of the barge.

Stringer had a pistol in his left hand pointed directly at Fox.

'Well, well – Sergeant Fox, isn't it?'

Fox said nothing. He turned and flung the small powder keg onto the quayside then pointed at the pile of powder on the fuse he'd laid.

'I wouldn't fire that friend. Or we might all go up.'

The florid faced man shrugged and stepped closer to Fox.

He was smiling still.

'Back, Sergeant. Get back.' The others closed on Fox.

'You really are a careless man. It's a litany of errors,' Stringer mocked Fox. 'Not covering your tracks, losing your daughter. Sir Harry had such a fate in store for her.'

'Had?' said Fox, 'Had?'

'She has spirit, I'll give her that, Sergeant.'

Fox didn't speak.

Behind the little group of men he saw a shape move in the dark shadows of the bank. The small powder keg had gone. He smiled then.

'You were going to watch your daughter suffer. He was going to avenge himself for what you did with his wife. And Elizabeth will suffer of course, again and again. I think we'll save him the trouble with you though. But first you should understand that when he catches your daughter again he'll mark her well and truly.'

'Gone, you said?'

'Sliced him with a blade she'd kept hidden. And ran. There's a man been sent to hunt her down. She won't last long, a girl on her own.'

The shadow on the bank came closer now.

Fox reached across his back and took the curved blade from its scabbard.

'Which of you wants to die first?' Fox asked quietly. He needed to keep their attention on him and away from the canal bank.

'You're a bigger fool than I thought,' mocked Sir Adam. 'You can't take on all of us. Impossible.'

'Adam Stringer, well met, ' said a voice from the darkness of the bank. The rain squall had passed by. 'I'd have a care if I were you. I have a gift for you here.'

The men looked and saw Maeve with a glowing length of fuse in one hand and the small powder barrel in the other. It was clear what she meant to do.

'Back off,' she said, as she moved up the gangplank onto the deck. She held the fuse close to the barrel.

'You men. Get below. Get below.'

'You'll die if you let that touch the powder,' said Sir Adam. 'You wouldn't dare.'

'If wishes were deeds, my friend.' said Maeve, and she

laughed in the face of Adam Stringer as she stepped closer. The men backed away from her instinctively.

'Now – get below. Or I swear I'll touch this to the powder and take my chance on heaven or hell. Drop your sword, Stringer, drop it! And the pistol.'

Stringer stared into her face and slowly lowered the sword and dropped it. Maeve smiled then.

'And the pistol.'

Stringer aimed the weapon at Fox and squeezed the trigger. Nothing happened. Two of the men behind Stringer turned and jumped into the water.

'Loyal friends,' Maeve mocked

'Wet powder, friend.' said Fox and he stepped to the remaining guard. 'You can jump and join your friends and take your chances.'

The guard hesitated and then jumped. Fox took up Stringer's sword. 'Now you get below.'

Adam Stringer hesitated.

'What are you going to do? You can't kill an unarmed man.'

Fox laughed then.

'This is not a gentleman's game Stringer. Remember I saw what you did to Michael Harbourson before he died. I'll have no problem killing you. Believe me. Now get below.'

Stringer still hesitated.

'Maeve. You and I...we made love. You can't let him do this.'

'I can,' she said and stared at him without an expression on her face. 'Think of that man you left blind and gelded in The Hague. Think of him.'

And Fox shoved him hard and he fell back down the companionway. Fox quickly slipped the hatch across the opening and slammed the metal bolt into place. Maeve laid the last of the powder from the barrel onto the hatch and around the fuse that led into the cabin. She brushed powder through the gaps in the planks and added fresh dry powder to the pile. Then Fox touched the smouldering end to the fuse which at first sputtered and then sparks began to run along the cord spurting on the small piles of powder.

Maeve and Fox ran for their lives.

The fuse burned down through the hatchway and began to move faster.

As the two of them reached the top of the bank and threw

186

themselves over it the heavens erupted as the storm roared into life. Sheet lightening lit up the landscape for a moment and then the thunderous explosion of the barge cracked about them in a long roaring crescendo and the stores vomited up in a raging sheet of flame.

CHAPTER 37

Beside the canal the anchored windmills could not pump water out of the ditch beyond the heaped spoil from the cutting of a new canal. The explosion of the barge had breached the new sea wall and the sea was pouring into the gap. It was hardly light.

Already a vast curve of water flooded in a crescent five miles across. At the edge of the land where the horizon met the sea' a darker line marked the end of the defences that would become a barrier against the unrelenting sea.

Fox stared at it all and marvelled. The Dutch engineers were making land out of water – a miracle. But now the sea was reclaiming the land.

In the early morning light Maeve and Fox rode towards the city which was a haze of blue buildings. The storm had abated but the wind still promised more turbulent weather.

The glint of sunshine on grey slate roofs and beyond the sea walls of the city. Pale colours, greys and greens, sad ochre and burnt out greens, pale yellow and deep browns – a painter's palette.

They rode slowly across the wet landscape and down into the outskirts of The Hague where the streets were sheened with drying water. Both soaked through and cold,they rode immersed in their own thoughts.

Francis Hauer, the fat man, lived at the end of the wide road. The house was still shuttered against the night. As they rode towards it, a maid stepped out and began to take down the shutters over each window and watered the pots standing on the sills. She took no notice of the riders until they stopped and dismounted.

Then she recognized Fox. 'Good morning,' she said.

'Is he at home?' asked Fox.

'He has been waiting for you. He never sleeps. I'll see to the

188

horses,' and she urged them to go inside as she led the horses along the side of the house to the stable at the back.

In the house there was quiet. In his room behind the wide flat desk the man sat with his eyes closed. Just the soft puffing of his fleshy lips gave any sign of life. He didn't open his yes as Fox and Maeve stood in the doorway. He spoke.

'Your man came to The Hague. He had a girl with him.'

Francis opened his eyes.

'Your daughter?'

Fox stared. 'No,' he said. 'Who told you?'

'No need for you to know, my friend.'

'I need to know.'

'Pieter – my eyes about the city.'

Hauer lifted his head a little then and waited.

'The girl?' said Fox, 'Tall girl, grey faced, eyes like stones?'

The man smiled at that and nodded.

'Yes. From what I have heard she seemed to be sleepwalking, Pieter was told. The man who saw the two of them said she had the look of an old saint about her. A Madonna looking up at Christ on the Cross was how she was described. Curious thing to say. Harry Morton seemed to be in a hurry to leave Holland with her. She seemed important to him.'

He glanced across at Maeve and held out his hand. She went to him quietly and took his hand and kissed it. He held her hand and looked at the diamond that gleamed there.

'Isaac?' he asked and she nodded.

'He likes you. You reminded him of his daughter. He wrote to me.'

He smiled at her indulgently and glanced at Fox through the pudgy slits where his eyes were buried,

'My daughter too, you see. Almost. You travel a hard road, Maeve.' He said.

Maeve shrugged, 'To be sure, nothing changes' she said and walked away, looking into the drawers of pigments that lined the walls. 'Is there anything new here?' she asked.

'Some fine lapis lazuli for grinding. Makes a fine blue'

'Why was he hurrying? Did your eyes say?' Fox asked.

Francis shrugged.

'I don't read his mind, John Fox. He has urgent business maybe. He was looking for your friend – my friend with one arm. You told him to go home?'

189

Fox said nothing.

'Morton's a vicious man and he hates you. With reason?'

Fox said nothing.

'Not that it matters, my friend. He is looking for a passage to England. No one will sail today. There is promise of another storm. He is offering gold but no one is fool enough to risk their lives for him.'

'Is Pieter safe?' Fox asked.

'Pieter took his wife to the country. Her family farm, I think. She is not pleased with him.' Francis grinned. 'Your daughter?'

'Running. Afraid, I suppose. He has sent men to hunt her down.'

'So she knows something he'd rather keep close,' murmured the fat man. 'Well, well – I'd give that lapis to know what that was. Is this the secret that you were sent to find for your master, Thurloe?'

'You know him?'

'His name swims by from time to time, John Fox. People in Europe talk to a man like me, who can do nothing. I am a little like a posting house, messages pass from time to time. Secrets come to me too from time to time. I am a discreet man, Sergeant.'

He leaned back against the cushions.

'Thurloe has a net of men, like you, or men who live lives of total respectability. Sleeping in their homes. gathering threads of traces, ravelling and unravelling secrets. Passing some to this man, some to that. I am a man made by circumstance to be what I am, John. You are a man of action, eager, fired up, ready to act. I am as you see me, bloated, filled fat with secrets. Find your girl. I have no doubt she holds the key. Maybe one day you will tell me what it was. If you live to tell the tale, of course. Men in your work have cheap lives, my friend. Trust no one.'

His hand lay like a fat pastry on the desk in front of him.

Fox walked away impatiently. Maeve said nothing. Fox turned to her.

'I just need to know where she'll run. Where?'

He stepped briskly to the door.

'I'll find Pieter. Maeve, we'll stay with him tonight and try to find word of her tomorrow at first light. Pieter may have heard something.'

'No' said Francis softly. 'You will leave him alone. You stay tonight here. You'll only put him in more danger. He's my legs and eyes and I won't have him harmed. You stay here. There's a room ready at the back of the house.'

Fox was about to refuse but he went on.

'Think before you act for once, John Fox. You'll never find her by going off like a firework. If you don't find Rebecca first, his hunters will. I dread to consider what they might do when they find her before they return her to their master. Don't show yourself. Your man, Morton has eyes about the town so it's best you are not seen. You have to think, my friend. Think.'

He closed his eyes then and his fat pudgy hand slid off the desk top into the folds of cloth that covered his belly.

'Oh, bye the bye, my friend.' he whispered as an afterthought, 'Did you have anything to do with an explosion yesterday evening? I hear that the weapons dealer, Hagaar, has yet to be paid. He is not pleased.'

He held up his pudgy fist.

'No, my friend. Don't tell me.'

He closed his eyes, smiled softly and slept.

CHAPTER 38

Fox stared out of the window and down into a small garden. He could see a row of lettuce and some leeks standing in a long pale green row in the moonlight.

Maeve watched him from the bed. She had never seen him so tense since he had targeted the man who had killed his wife and that man died in fire as his wife had.

She made no judgements. You did whatever the cards turned up and you lived with it. It was never going to be any other way for her nor, she knew, for Fox. She pitied him. He was trapped by his own nature. When Alison, his wife, was murdered he took his vengeance and rode away. He had chosen a life of secrecy and uncertainty. For the first time since she had known him, Fox was lost and afraid . She knew she could help him but at terrible cost to herself.

'John,' she called softly, 'Come here. To me.'

He stared at her, mistaking her.

'No, John, no. Not that, John. Give me your amulet. Give it to me.'

She held out her hand. He shook his head.

'I can't ask you – no!'

'It frightens you, John. You're afraid of a few words, A few words?'

She held out her hand and locked her eyes on his.

He stared at her and could feel his heart beating faster. Her face was pale in the moonlight.

He shook his head. 'I have seen what happens to you, Maeve. No.'

She pushed aside the blankets and walked light-footed to the open window and stared into the night. She shivered, though it was not cold.

'You were given a package when you met Elizabeth. A gift she said from her husband. She'd finally betrayed you, John.'

'No!' he barked, and stepped closer as if to hit her.

'It's the truth, John Fox. Elizabeth fears her husband so she betrayed you. I don't say it to blame her. Remember I know what that Harry Morton can do. And remember something else – he is mine when the time comes. Give me the package you're afraid to open.'

Fox slowly lifted the leather pouch he wore about his neck.

'You're right. I was afraid to look.'

'Give it to me, John. Don't touch me. Don't touch me when – don't touch me.'

Slowly she opened the leather pouch and tipped what was inside it onto the stone window sill. A small twisted piece of metal that had been melted by a fierce heat. It still held the shape of a cross. Maeve ignored it. She pushed an oilcloth-wrapped package across the sill.

'This was what she brought. Open it now.'

Fox reached for the package Elizabeth had given him. He broke the seal.

Two things lay there. One, a simple miniature portrait of a young and beautiful girl. Fox hesitated and wiped the back of his hand across his face.

'Alison,' he said.

'Yes' Maeve said. 'And the other ?'

A single curl of deep red hair tied with a small silk ribbon.

Fox stared at it and now he began to fear what he saw.

'Rebecca's hair?' asked Maeve quietly.

He nodded and walked away leaving the two objects there.

Outside the moon lay on its back with both arms pointed at the sky, horns. Fox remembered he'd seen a picture of the Virgin in Spain perhaps or Germany. He wasn't sure but he remembered that the Virgin was standing with her feet on the curving moon.

He heard the harsh intake of her breath as Maeve reached for the lock of hair. He dared not look. He was afraid. She was right. What he knew would happen was terrifying and primeval, the work, some might say, of the devil.

Instantly Maeve began to shake. Her body convulsed, stretched, arched and her mouth opened in a silent agonising scream.

Then she fell like a tree in a storm. And her body arched off the ground, her heels thundered on the cold stone slabs, her eyes opened and her pupils vanished into her skull, her hand holding the curl of hair stretched up and away from her body and then hammered onto the ground .

Her mouth opened again and she shrieked and tore at her shift, ripped it open across her breasts and lay for a moment in the pool of moonlight on the floor. She reached up and shook with terrible bone-crunching force. The shaking slowed to a stop and she breathed deeply. Then it began again.

'Evil – vile man – evil – I see fire – fire. I see secrets. She is running across a wide, wide land and behind her – men. She has something they want – something she knows – something. She is running and afraid – hiding near water – near a hut by a river and a bridge.'

The words hissed out of Maeve. She breathed again and spoke again in a deeper register.

Her body convulsed again by the wracking tremors of her vision.

'A fishing village – vast river with bird – a bird – a bird with black feathers and a grey collar – I see it pecking the eyes out of a fish – pecking – and the bloody guts of a herring. And a boat – she is running – they're losing her – maybe – she is afeared as I was once – Holy Mother of God, help Rebecca. '

She lay back panting with the effort, her body convulsed once more and then she screamed.

'There's a girl – in terrible danger. I see ice. I see cold – I see vengeance and danger and hatred. Jesus singing, and flames and a crown – she has a long pole and a crucifix. Not love – hate and fire and death – Holy Mother of God, have mercy – '

And as suddenly as it began, Maeve slumped still and let the curl of hair fall from her fingers. She lay quiet now, breathing deeply. Fox picked her up, laid her on the bed and covered her.

He put the things back into the pouch, took his curved blade and slung it across his back, packed his leather bag, stepped quietly out of the room into the corridor. He left her sleeping. He knew now what he needed to know.

CHAPTER 39

Light showed under the door where Francis Hauer sat. Fox sat opposite him.

'Well?' said the fat man. 'She is a remarkable young woman. Has remarkable gifts.'

'Yes. She has. I know where my daughter is running now. Maeve found her.'

Francis grunted as Fox went on.

'There was a place. When I was a younger man I used to help a friend. We smuggled between Cornwall and the French coast. He had a small fishing boat. We met again a few months ago. He has a wife in France, on the Brittany Coast. He has another in Cornwall.'

'Well?'

'I used to tell my daughter's mother stories about those times and the young Cornish man and his boat. She told Rebecca the stories when she was little. She will know where we worked from in Normandy. He still has a boat. Still plies his trade.'

'How d'you know it's there she is making for?'

'Maeve saw a bird black with a grey collar. The Cornish call it a chough. The name of his boat is *The Chough*.'

'If Maeve mistook what she saw?'

'What choice do I have? There was something more about a girl with a crucifix and a crown. Confused. I don't know what it was. Maybe nothing. A crown and fire and hatred. I don't know.'

The fat man said 'You have to go. Find the men who're hunting her down. Find the secret those men want to stop up. I'll take care of Maeve.'

He nodded his huge head and stretched out his pudgy hand. They parted, the one to stay in his prison and the other to take horse

195

under the horned moon away from Holland to find his daughter and the secret she carried.

As Fox rode away, the kitchen maid slipped out into the silent streets. She ran then to a house on the side of the Damplatz as she had been told and knocked at a window as she had been told. The window opened and she leaned into the room as she had been told. Some coins were thrown at her and the window slammed shut.

CHAPTER 40

Huge clouds gathered as Fox rode alone across the flat land. He rode through four days of storms. Nothing much moved except the figure on the horse making his way steadily over boggy roads and muddy cart tracks.

Passing through towns and villages, it was as if these places were dead. Windows shuttered against the winds and the rain. Even the smell of baking bread was not on the air as fires were dowsed by the water that poured into chimneys and along gutters.

Leaden skies lowered over the lonely figure as he rode remorselessly, steadily eating up the distance to the Seine which he would follow to the small village on the bird-filled estuary he remembered from those old times.

Fox had been on the road for ten days, heading towards Caen and on past Mont St Michel, into horse country. Between the cities and tiny villages were miles of forest and rolling hills. There were few houses. The land was barren of people.

He had slept where he could, living off his fat and what he could scavenge off the land. Ahead of him stretched a dark line of trees as far as he could see to right and left. Over it the thunder clouds towered over the land and rolled across the sky.

The way to the fishing village he was looking for lay beyond the deep forest that clothed the hills and valleys. If Rebecca was heading for the village hidden at the end of a narrow valley leading down to the sea she must have come this way.

He reined in his horse and looked under the soaked and sagging brim of his hat to left and right. To the right, across a few poor fields, he saw a glimmer of light. He turned his horse towards it and the lone cottage at the end of the rough, puddled cart track.

As he came closer, two dogs come skittering towards him,

snarling. He rode steadily past them and they began to run alongside him, snapping at his feet. He stopped at the door of the cabin and waited. The light was snuffed out. He didn't move.

The sky over the forest was beginning to lighten and the rain began to slacken. Fox watched the door of the cabin and waited. The dogs snarled, daring him to dismount.

A cockerel crowed in a shack that leaned against the cabin. The lightening sky had tricked the bird into thinking dawn was coming. Fox waited.

The door opened a little and a small boy in a ragged shirt that was too big for him, stood in the opening and stared up at the man on the horse.

'Is your mother there?' Fox asked in French.

The little boy shook his head.

'Your father?'

The little boy again shook his head.

'You're alone?'

The door was pulled wider and standing in the doorway was a girl of around eighteen. As filthy as the boy, with long matted hair and the same pale, starved face.

'Shove off, my father's on his way home.' she snarled.

He shook his head.

'I need to talk to you? Will they bite my arse if I dismount?'

He gestured at the snarling dogs.

The little boy laughed.

The young woman grinned too. 'You'll find out, won't you?' she said.

Slowly, stiffly he swung down to the ground. The dogs came closer. He leaned down and gently held out his hand. The dogs came closer, he stroked each head and glanced at the young woman and the boy. He smiled at them.

'I could always do that with dogs – since I was a child. It's a gift, I suppose.'

He turned his back on the calm dogs as he stood and undid his saddle bag, reached in to it and took from it a dead rabbit and two fat birds.

He held them out to the girl.

'Can you cook?' he asked.

Two hours later the cabin was warm from the cooking fire where the rabbit turned on a small spit. The girl had made bread with some of the flour he gave her from his other saddle bag.

The little boy was almost drunk with the smell of the roasting meat.

Around the room Fox's clothes were drying out and he was wrapped in an old cloak.

Outside the weather had changed. The rain clouds had moved north and the land was steaming under the sun.

They told him that they had buried their mother three weeks before. Their father had gone to the city to find work months ago and had promised to come back for them. He hadn't come. They were alone and afraid and had no idea what to do.

'There are wolves in the forest, Monsieur,' said the boy. 'And we have nothing left. Not a sou. Papa took it all. What do we do now?'

Fox had no answer for them. Nor comfort.

'Go to the nearest village – find the priest. Ask him for help. That's his job if he's a decent priest and if he's not then God rot his bones. It's all you can do. You're both strong. You can work. Find something. Anything. Don't wait here to rot.'

'Our father said he'd come back for us – we have to wait. To sow the crops – look after the cow and the hens. It's all we can do.'

Fox nodded. It was the answer he expected.

'I have a question to ask you.'

'Ask' said the young woman chewing on a bone.

'Did a girl come by here? A few days ago?'

'Yes, Monsieur. On a horse. Better than yours. Stolen, I'd say.'

'Robert!' The young woman looked at her little brother and silenced him.

'Why?'

'She's my daughter. I have to catch up with her.'

'She said maybe there would be people looking for her. We promised to say nothing.'

'We promised to say we'd seen someone going away from the forest.' The little boy burst out.

'Has anyone been following – ?'

'Only you.'

Fox took the pouch from his neck, opened it and took out the tiny miniature of his dead wife. He showed it to the girl.

'This is her mother. Did she look like her?'

The young woman nodded.

'About four days ago. We warned her not to go into the

forest. It is dangerous. We told her there are still wolves. We never go there. We're not allowed. It's owned by the king for hunting. We'd be hanged if they found us there.'

Fox began to put on the half-dried clothes. They watched him.

'If anyone comes after me. Tell them you saw me. You understand? I want them to follow me. Tell them I went into the forest.'

They nodded. He took his leather satchel and opened it and took two coins and held them out to the young woman.

'What is this for?' she said.

'Food and the knowledge you gave me.'

'We don't need to be paid.'

'Then take it for friendship.' And he handed the coins to the boy. He took a small silver coin and put it in the young woman's hand, picked up his bag and the curved bladed knife and walked past the two dogs out into the bright daylight.

Hens were rooting about the muddy yard, a cow mooed in the byre. There was work to be done.

Fox mounted, lifted a hand to the two figures in the doorway of the cabin.

'Remember, if anyone came after me. Tell them I was here. And hide the birds – I stole them off your king.'

He grinned at them and turned away and rode on down into the forest.

Once in the cover of the forest he rode along a small side track between ancient trees and dense bushes. He stopped a small distance from the main track, tethered his horse and worked his way back to where he could see the line of the only bridleway away from the forest towards the cabin in the distance.

He settled down to wait. He was cursing himself for a fool. He was the lead they needed. If they had to silence his daughter, all they had to do was to follow him. He was their guide to where she might be. Sir Harry Morton was no fool. He'd set men on his back. They'd let him lead them to Rebecca and silence him and her.

He could see nothing on the road. No sign of followers. He'd wait for the trackers he was sure would be following him. He slid the throwing knife he'd taken from the Italian from his boot, and moved away from the edge of the tree line and back into the woods.

In a clearing he hefted the knife and felt the balance of it. It was perfect. He threw it underhand across the clearing into the trunk of an old sweet chestnut tree. He did it again and again and when he was satisfied he slid the blade back into his boot and laced it in place.

He crawled back into his observation post on the edge of the forest and waited. The sun rose higher and the flies began to bite.

For a moment he saw Maeve's agonised face and heard her scream. 'The girl, and a crown and a long pole and fire.'

Was it nothing, was it just a wild waking dream? Fox was frightened by what she did. Was it magic or a force? He had no idea but he knew Maeve had strange gifts and stranger powers. Many disbelieved but they were the fools. Fox knew that it hurt her terribly when she used these powers.

The heat of the sun was burning off the damp ground and a soft mist lay low over the track.

They came at dusk. As the light began to fade, two figures appeared on the horizon. They rode slowly towards the cabin and Fox saw the young woman standing talking to the men. They did not dismount. She pointed along the track in the direction Fox had taken.

The riders moved on together more purposefully now they had a target. These were soldiers, well used to looking after themselves. They were wet and possibly cold but they rode on into the forest along the wide cart track.

They rode past Fox and moved on deep into the woods. He let them go, moved back to his horse, fed it a handful of oats from his saddle bag, checked the rapier in its scabbard, took the saddle off the horse, tethered him lightly and pulled together a pile of bracken. Wrapped in his cloak, he slept.

CHAPTER 41

He woke in the dark. In the distance a wolf howled, broke off its call and was answered by another and then another.

It was the smell that betrayed the two men. They'd cooked a bird and they had a bottle between them as they sat huddled close to the fire as much for protection as for warmth.

From the shadows of the forest, Fox watched them. He recognized one of them. He'd been one of the group of guards about the Queen when he watched them on their ride from The Hague to Amsterdam.

The other was neat, quiet and not drinking. He refused a pull at the brandy the other man offered from time to time.

Fox waited and watched as they fell asleep then glided past them, found their horses tethered and gentled the two horses as he freed them.

He heard the voice before he saw the man.

'You're too old for this game, friend.'

Fox said nothing as he turned about. His hands were clear of his body. Behind him he heard the horses move steadily away into the trees.

'Following you, we were. Simple little exercise. You made it easy, friend. Like I said, 'you're too old or too stupid.''

His cavalry sword was held low. He had the advantage.

'You and me are going to have a little talk, friend. Just step easy – ahead of me where I can see you.'

Fox did as he was told. The heavy sword was inches from his back and he'd no wish to feel it slice into his back. The blade was rough sharpened. This soldier was an old hand.

'We was gonna let you lead us to your girl and take her back for Sir Harry. He'd taken a fancy to her it seems. He likes them young does that one and he likes them fiery and your daughter is that alright. He owes her for a sliced face. She'll pay for that and more. It'll be slow and nasty for her, friend. And he will break her. So all we have to do is warm your feet a little and you'll tell us where to find her. Save us a lot of trouble. Like I said, you're too old for this game, friend.'

Fox stumbled and almost fell. He pushed down on the damp ground and almost stood, grabbed his left leg and staggered. His right hand swept across his chest and back. The soldier behind him took the throwing knife in his throat. He went down like a felled tree.

Fox walked back to him, turned him over and retrieved his knife, wiped it on the man's jerkin, put it back inside his boot, picked up the cavalry sword and walked back to the remains of the fire.

He kicked life back into the ashes, laid the jagged blade of the sword in the heart of the flames and then slapped the face of the sleeping man.

When he saw Fox standing over him, he looked around for his companion. He scrabbled back and away from Fox and opened his mouth to call out.

'Waste of breath,' Fox said quietly. 'Your man is dead. He was getting too old for the work. Now – you.'

'I don't know what you mean. I was out hunting with a friend. Dead?'

Fox nodded.

The man began to laugh. It was fear. He sat up.

'Who the devil are you?'

'You know who I am. Her father. Rebecca's father. You know her?'

The man nodded.

'You have to silence her?'

The man said nothing.

'You will tell me. I saw what you did to that poor man in the apothecary's street in The Hague. Enjoy it, did you? I saw what was left when you had finished with him. It was you, wasn't it?'

'I do as I am told. I'm a soldier, me. It's how it is.'

'Torture a weak man? Kill a girl? You call that soldiering?'

'Don't you? It's what we do.'

'And you want the same, do you? I'm a soldier.'

The man stared at him and saw in Fox's eyes a remorseless

emptiness. 'No tongue, no eyes, his balls slashed. A hand severed. Where did you start? His fingers was it?'

The man looked away. Fox waited.

'I don't know what you mean.'

'Ah yes, Sir Harry wants her silenced. Tell me or be blind. It will happen to you, I promise. He wants her silenced?'

'Yes. Yes.'

'He told you, you could do what you wanted with her so long as she died?'

The man tried to stand up. Fox kicked him full in the face.

The man's nose was crushed to gristle.

'For even thinking what you thought. Now, why was she to be silenced? What does she know?'

The man felt the blood on his face. He spat it from his mouth and looked up at Fox.

'Believe me. I don't know. There are plans. Not for me to know.'

'You're a bad liar.'

Fox lifted the blade from the heart of the fire. It glowed red hot at its tip.

He smiled at the man as he cowered back on the ground, watching the dull red end of the blade coming close.

'The eyes first was it? For that man in the Dutch house?' he asked quietly.

'No. Please. I didn't do anything. It was the man you killed. He enjoyed it. He'd do it for Harry. Sir Harry watched from time to time.'

The man was whimpering, trying to squirm away from the approaching blade.

'The secret?'

'He drinks sometimes. He forgot she was in the room. I don't know. He made a mistake and she overheard him . He knew. She had to be silenced then. She took a blade to him. She'd hidden it in her hair. Then she ran. I swear I don't know what the secret is.'

'That other girl? The girl in grey?'

'The fanatic – he – he has her under his thumb. She believes in him. She will do anything for him. I don't know anymore. Please believe me. They talk secrets. I don't know any more. Trust me.'

An owl screeched in the darkness of the forest and a small animal screamed as it made its kill.

CHAPTER 42

Along the grey stone quayside of the old fishing village a few small boats were moored. The men were unloading their catch into baskets. Further along, on a shelving strand, a team of men and women were hauling in a wide net alive with small flapping fish. Overhead, gulls wheeled and turned, swooped and fought cruelly for discarded fish.

The salt marshes where the river opened out to the sea lay flat and pale and glittering under the early morning light. A bittern boomed in the reed beds. Here Fox found Hawken's French wife.

'Too late to find your girl,' Therese Hawken told him. She was a woman of middle age with salt-stained clothes and hands cut and scarred by nets and lines and by salt water. She had dancing eyes and was amused by life, it seemed. And kind, too.

The Chough had set out the moment the storm dropped and the sea settled.

'She was so afraid, Rebecca. Afraid of being followed, afraid of being seen – afraid of shadows. We all thought she had lost her mind but she begged Hawken to take her away. For her father's sake.'

She had begged and begged him to put to sea. She said she was going home to some place she called The Devil's Chair on the Long Mynd – some such names. Therese was sure of it. Her husband had sailed with the frightened girl.

'He's taking a cargo to Bristol, he tells me,' she said, smiling and giving the child at her knee a hunk of bread. 'Going to see his other wife in Cornwall, I have no doubt, monsieur. '

He looked sharply at her then.

'Poor man, he thinks I don't know. But he's kind to us and what does the other one matter to me?'

Fox said nothing. The woman fondled the little boy's hair, grinned. 'He thinks I don't know, but that's a man for you.'

Fox smiled for a moment and nodded.

'Your daughter was so frightened. I have never seen anyone so terrified of any man. She'd not let my husband near her, not even to comfort her. She shied away from his hand like a broken dog. We did our best but she begged and begged us to help her get away. Like I said, *The Chough* was going to sea with a cargo for old friends in England. She went too. Still afeared. She had a secret place she knew, near this Devil's Chair, A secret place to hide. She was going there she said, and no more. I liked her and I've been afraid for her ever since she left.'

Fox left with Therese's brother on the next tide . He too was afraid. Evil was in the air. He had to find his daughter and the answers she held. Answers some men would kill to silence.

CHAPTER 43

Great grey slabs of stone towered over the ridge. Beyond them the blue haze that was Wales. Fox had come up the valley from Bristol on familiar paths towards the village where he had been born. He rode through at night. Nothing stirred apart from an old dog. These righteous men and women slept the sleep of the god-fearing and the innocent. The very people who had let the Witchfinder burn his wife.

These were troubled times and even the godly fell into sects and secret associations. There was a man in Bristol whose followers claimed he was the second coming of Christ and firmly believed it.

Others, who thought no man should claim to be anointed by God and others who believed there was no place for a King who said he was anointed by God and had the right to rule through God's direct intercession. This was a time of image breakers and fanatics for their faith.

Some would sit each Sunday in their worship house and wait for the word of God to come on them and then they spoke. Sometimes. Others ranted and raged about the Fire next time, the Devil's fundament, sickness and pestilence, death and the horsemen of the Apocalypse. Fanatic, misguided – misled.

It was dawn when he rode up the craggy path to the field where Alison had been burned for a witch. He walked across to the centre and found what he expected to find – A wreath of fresh wild rose-pink hedge roses on the place where Rebecca had watched as the Witchfinder burned her mother.

He stared at the simple flowers and felt the pain again. He turned away and headed up and up into the tumbled grey rocks. The Devil's Chair. He knew Rebecca had come home and he knew where she would hide.

He left his horse and walked up onto the chair-shaped, smooth stone. He stood as he used to stand when he was a child and later, when he was a young man uncertain of what to do with his life.

He had always known the village was not for him. The placid life, the turn of the seasons, the slow pace of growing crops, arguing with neighbours.

The sun was beginning to light up the land below. He stepped off the rock and to a secret place he'd used as a boy to hide precious things. He pulled aside a stone and found a single old coin. He put it back and replaced the stone. He looked once more along the ridge and then stepped down a track towards a row of stunted hedges and old stone walls.

Before he came to them there was a single tree, an ancient hawthorn laid almost flat by the wind. A crow lifted off a branch of the tree as he walked slowly down to it.

He stopped for a moment and looked at the pile of stones that he'd used to cover the old woman, a friend of Alison's, a wise woman.

They'd hanged her at the same time they had burned Alison. It was done out of spite and fear of powers they either did not understand or believed to be the work of the devil.

He turned away from the tree and the pile of stones. Maeve was standing in the crudely fashioned doorway of the cave where the old woman had lived.

Maeve had her finger to her lips and walked away past Fox to the edge of the little ridge. She sat on a rock partly concealed by bushes and a length of stone wall around an untended field. To her right, the high view over the vast swathe of England below them.

'No one comes here now,' she said. 'People are afraid of the old woman's ghost. They think this place is cursed. Your daughter was right to come here for safety.'

'She is here, then?'

Maeve nodded. 'She's sleeping. I gave her something to help her. She will sleep for a day or more. She has been terrified and not of ghosts. She has been talking about – about matters that concern us. Later – we can talk later.'

'I want to talk to her now.'

'No.' Maeve shook her head. 'She needs time, she needs rest and healing. Later, John after you've done your work.'

Fox sat beside this strange woman. He didn't ask how she

208

came here. He didn't ask anything for he knew he'd get no answer if Maeve didn't want to tell him.

'I have brought enough food here. There is a spring the old woman used for water inside the cave. Rebecca must live quietly for a time. It will be best for her. Trust me.'

Fox nodded. The sun began to warm his back. He felt tired but he had more to do. Thurloe wanted an answer to a question he had not even dared to ask. Why had he not asked the question about plots and plans and secrets and only sent him looking to confirm what he already would have known about supplies and recruits? What did Thurloe really want?

Had he wind of a plot – a serious plot? Did he need to help ensure that the secret plans remained secret? Had he sent Fox to ensure that the plot was not going to leak out? Was Thurloe involved too? Questions, questions.

'She has talked?'

Maeve nodded. 'Yes.'

'Tell me?'

'Sure I will. That's a brave girl in there, but fragile now. I will tell what she told me. I don't want her to go through it again. When she is ready I will take her to your friend with the boat in Bristol. He can take her down to Padstow in Cornwall near a place I know for peace and to restore her.'

Below them a blackbird sang for the sun, a robin hopped across the stones and pecked sharply at the ground then skittered away as Fox stretched out his hand. He got up.

'I'll go and see her. I won't wake her.'

He walked into the dim cave where the old woman had made a bed and a few shelves by cutting niches in the rocks. There was a small fireplace with a chimney made of stone and clay near the doorway.

A blanket covered the bed and the slight form of his daughter lay deep asleep. Her hair tumbled about her pale face and as he watched she almost woke, cried out and then slept again.

Fox cursed the men who'd terrified her. He thought for a moment of Elizabeth whom he'd trusted with her. He felt no anger but only pity for her.

He poured water from a pitcher by the bed into a small beaker and left it close to his sleeping daughter. If anyone could help her now he knew it was Maeve who was sitting in the sun outside the cave.

He walked out into the light. He had work to do.

'She needs to sleep, John. She has heard too much and no doubt Harry and his people wish her dead. But so long as she can be kept out of their way and so long as no one acts, their plan will go on. They are terrible ambitious men, John Fox. Terrible ambitious men.'

'Tell me, Maeve.'

'She was in a fever when she came here. It was night and she came as I expected her. I knew she would come. You told me how her mother used to visit the old woman who lived here. Her only friend. To keep her company when she felt lonely. Rebecca came here. Home, she said. And secret.'

Fox sat and stared across the landscape and said nothing.

'She was afraid to speak at first. She had been badly damaged by the fear she felt by the cruelty she had seen. He'd beat his wife in front of her and Elizabeth had no one to turn to who'd dare to stop him. He enjoyed the hurt he did. Rebecca knows what he can do. It takes a massive piece of your soul, that any human being can be so cruel, so careless of anyone else.'

He looked round at her and she refused to catch his eye.

'So, there is a plot to kill someone whose death would reverberate about the land and destroy the Parliament cause. Your general's cause. Fairfax's cause.'

'Who?' he asked. 'She must have told you.'

'Who is believed by some people to be the anointed of God? He believes it himself.'

Fox stared at her.

'The King? No. I don't believe it.'

Maeve watched Fox and waited.

'It can't be true.'

'It's what your daughter ran from. Having that knowledge meant that killing her was necessary. It's true, John. She knows where and how, but she didn't tell me that.'

'There are those say he's God's anointed.'

'And they believe it. That woman in grey does not. She believes he blasphemes. Betrays his God. Rebecca told me. She believes whatever Harry Morton tells her. She believes she comes to herald the new King, the new Christ. Morton tells her so. Tells her she will redeem the world. She believes it.'

And suddenly Fox saw the young woman again but this time in Bristol. Not beside Sir Harry Morton at the Masque in

210

Amsterdam, nor at the arms dealer's house.

In Bristol she had been by the gate when he come into the city. A woman in grey carrying a cross and leading a group of women. Martyrs, they had called themselves. Martyrs for God and the Second Coming. He stared at Maeve as she went on.

'Kill the King and what have you done?' Maeve asked him.

Fox thought for a moment and then shook his head.

'It would be a curse. For some would believe that killing the King would be killing the anointed of God, a terrible, terrible sin. If they kill the King and set the blame on the Parliament they'll set the whole of England alight. It will bring even worse chaos. Vicious fighting all over England. To kill the King. Like killing God.'

'But we know it has nothing to do with God. It's about ambition, John. Their ambition. They don't care, John. They see the King as weak. Sir Harry was laughing about him to others in the plot. Rebecca told me she had seen him mocking that small puny sickly half-man half-dwarf, stuttering in the clutches of a few favourites with no more backbone than he has. The King listens to the wrong counsels. Sir Harry mocked him to his friends the plotters. Rebecca heard him. He told the woman in grey that the King stood in the way of God. Rebecca heard him. The woman believes anything he tells her. Anything.'

'And who will take his place?

'Rebecca said they see the Queen as having the stomach for a real fight. And she will have the stomach also to rule when they have destroyed the Parliament men. She will rule with their help, of course. In the name of her young son. With their help. Rebecca kept on talking about Henrietta. She was afraid for her too.'

Fox slept through what was left of the day. He woke in the night to find Maeve had covered him with his cavalry cloak. She sat beside Rebecca.

Fox sat in the mouth of the cave and watched the sun rising over the ridge. Maeve joined him there and handed him a hunk of bread and a rabbit leg. 'Eat,' she said. 'There is work to do, my friend.'

He ate and she sat quietly by the cairn of stones over the old woman.

'You'll see she's safe?' he asked quietly and she nodded once.

'If they kill the King, there will be terrible retribution.'

'And who would suffer the worst from it?'

Fox stood up.

'We have to warn Tom Fairfax and Thurloe.'

'Would they believe you?'

'Why not ?'

'Think, John. Would you believe it? Really believe it and if you did, what would you do.?'

'Warn the King, of course.'

'If you could get to him. Would he believe you?'

He stared into her dark green eyes now and knew she was right. He wiped his hands over his tired face and thought for a time. She said nothing. The crow sat in the hawthorn tree.

'No one will listen even if you're bringing them a message they want to hear. No one.'

'Who's the assassin?'

Maeve shook her head.

'Rebecca and I talked a time and she may know but she will not say and no one can tear it out of her. It's too much. You have to make up your own mind what you do, John Fox. I'm taking her when she is well enough to your friend Shea's inn in Bristol. He will hide her until Hawken comes back and he will take her on – secretly, safely.'

'And me?'

'Find the answer to the question that Thurloe never asked you to discover. Find the assassin. He'll be near the King in Oxford.'

Fox rode away from the Long Mynd. Maeve carved at a stick with a fiercely sharp-bladed knife. She'd taken it in the night when she covered Fox with his cloak.

She weighed the knife and flipped it into the hawthorn tree, She smiled. The balance was right. She looked down the track And watched Fox as he dropped from her sight and went to do his work in Oxford.

CHAPTER 44

Fox had been in Oxford for a week watching the King and those around him. The people suffered what any people suffer in a garrison town.

Discipline was easy for most of the army gathered about the King. Officers rode about the city, requisitioned stores and beds and made themselves thoroughly unpopular. The citizens of Oxford had no choice but to accept their lot.

The ancient colleges supported the King and had donated silver cups and chalices, plate and jewels for his war chest.

To Fox's surprise the regularity of his movements made the King vulnerable to attack. Charles rode to church across Christ Church meadow every day. Every morning the little figure came down from his rooms accompanied by a small troop of favoured young officers.

Fox watched him as he rode through the crowded streets past men and women going about their daily business.

He would ride from church past Magdalene College towards the River Cherwell through the outskirts of the city. In the morning he would inspect his soldiers as they drilled in squares along the river bank. He would then ride back through crowded streets from the parade ground beyond the walls.

The King was a man of habit. Fox was astonished to discover that the young men tasked with guarding him were obviously not professional soldiers. The King's routine was merely a social round.

Everyday, with his favourites, Charles took the same route to the parade ground to review his troops. From time to time he went hawking after church. Fox knew that the early morning routine made the task of an assassin easy. For Fox the problem was to know when the attack might come and from where.

A multitude of alleys and narrow lanes criss-crossed the regular route back through the town up to Christ Church Meadow.

Each day he watched the royal progress. Fox saw women and children waiting in crowds, watching as the King and his men rode by. They'd raise a cheer and the King would ignore them. How easy for an assassin to hide in the crowd. But for most of his progress the King was shielded by the young courtiers riding beside him.

Fox walked the route looking for suitable killing grounds, watching the progress and assessing the weakness of this daily journey.

The route narrowed only at one point where the outriders had to ride in single file down a short passage and into a small market place. The King rode, naturally, at their head, alone. Once in the market square the guards formed up, surrounded their King and rode on.

It was here, when Fox was watching one morning, that a peasant woman ran to the King as the riders formed up. The guard tried to stop her but she reached him and tried to touch him. She was begging him for his blessing believing that touching him would cure her of scrofula.

The King's horse skittered away from the woman who, within a minute, had been pushed aside and the guard reformed. The King was exposed for one minute. Enough.

The outriders dragged the woman away and the King rode on from the square. He hardly looked at her.

Fox looked about at the buildings on each side of the small market square near the place the peasant woman had approached the King.

It was only a moment but for that moment the King would have been vulnerable if the woman had had a weapon about her. Or if someone was waiting with a cross-bow in a high window. One minute was enough time for a killer. Fox tried to assess where an attack might come from if the King was approached in that place again.

He waited and watched in that square for three days and saw the same procession and the King enter the square alone before the body guard gathered around him again. By now Fox was convinced that the small square was the perfect killing ground and he began to look more carefully at the buildings and the houses along the

214

regular route. Where could an assassin shoot a cross-bow or a musket, at the small bejewelled figure? Most of the larger buildings were connected to the colleges and churches that filled the city. Hardly places from which to launch an attack on the King.

Fox followed the King from church to the daily review of his soldiers. He watched with other townsfolk as the King rode up and down the lines of men and officers. He might speak to an officer he recognised, smile at something the man said and then move on past silk standards, ranks of soldiers and raised hats.

These soldiers cheered their monarch as if they were eager to get to war, thought Fox bitterly. He wondered how many of them had seen service and also how many would be alive to tell the tale when the sorry business was over.

It was a Thursday when he first saw Sir Harry Morton talking with a group of officers as they rode by after the king's guard. He was laughing and gesticulating with great good humour to the men about him. They rode single file through the small alley after the king's guards had ridden through the market and down towards the river to inspect the troopers.

They clattered on across the market square where the peasant woman had approached the King. Sir Harry stopped behind in the square as the others rode on.

Fox watched him dismount and leave his horse with a stall holder. He walked briskly across the square and back along the alley that was the only approach to the north of the square. It was down this narrow alley that the king rode back towards Christ Church Meadow each morning.

Fox strolled through the stalls and looked along the alley. There was no sight of his target. He'd vanished.

On the corner overlooking the point at which the alleyway opened into the market was an old, boarded-up gate house.

Fox watched for a time and still saw no sign of Sir Harry. He walked back to the market as the King's party came back across the square. Sir Harry appeared suddenly from the gate house on the corner of the square. He waited in the shadows of the building. Fox watched as he turned back and a woman in grey stepped out of the doorway to join him. The two figures stood together on the edge of the market square.

Sir Harry was talking urgently. The woman was the pale-faced, tall woman Fox had glimpsed briefly at the masque in Amsterdam. He knew now where he had seen her before. In Bristol preaching hate and anger.

Fox went on watching while pretending to inspect some meat on a stall. Morton went on talking to the young woman. She listened and nodded, glanced round at the building behind her as Harry Morton explained something. He put his arm around her and she moved away from him. It was clear she disliked being touched.

They walked across to the door in the front wall of the closed gate house on the corner. Morton pushed it and the shuttered door opened smoothly. The two went inside. Fox looked up and saw a flicker of movement behind the shutters in the narrow embrasure on the upper floor. From the room behind those shutters anyone would have a perfect view over the square.

Fox waited. No one came out of the front door.

Up the alley alongside the building a dog barked. A clock in the town struck twelve. The stall-holders began to take down their stalls. The market was over for the day.

Fox moved into the alley and found a small door recessed into the brickwork. He pushed at it and it remained firmly closed.

He found a place where a buttress provided a means of getting over the wall. He checked the alley behind him and then quickly climbed into the neglected garden.

There was a second door at the bottom of the tower. It had clearly been used recently. The weeds about the door had been trampled flat. The killer had a clear means of escape. Here was the killing ground.

In the evening groups of soldiers roamed the streets, some looking for a drink, others for a woman and a few for a fight. Fox sat in the back room of a small inn, drank his ale, ate a plate of cold meats and thought.

There was no point in trying to alert the King nor the men around him. No one would take notice of an old soldier talking about a possible attack on the King. They'd throw him out or worse they might arrest him.

He walked through the streets as dusk fell. He pushed through groups of singing men, drunk by now but still amiable enough. It was dark when he returned to the inn, outside the town, where he had stabled his horse and kept his few belongings. As he stepped quietly into the empty bar room the pot boy was clearing up tables and pots and jugs of stale ale.

'There's a friend come to see you, mister.' He grinned as he made the usual signs for a shapely female. Fox didn't smile. He picked up a long-tined fork from the table at the back of the bar.

'You're the careful one. It's only a girl. She said you'd asked her to join you – I don't ask questions. You'll pay for the extra costs of a woman in the room.'

Fox grunted assent and the pot boy mocked him.

'She's only a girl and no threat to a decent working soldier.'

'Maybe. But I'm a working *living* soldier, friend.' Fox walked out of the room and up the narrow stairs to his room. He opened the door, walked in very quickly and turned to check the space behind him as the door slammed shut.

A single candle lit the room. Fox saw in the shadows the quiet, pale face of Maeve sitting in the only chair. She didn't move as he came into the room. She waited while he closed the door and bolted it. He turned to her, put down the long-tined fork and waited.

Her pale face was framed by her long dark auburn hair. She looked at him with her pale green eyes that changed colour by the minute. The candlelight flickered.

'Rebecca's safe, John – before you ask me. And I have business here.'

For a moment he had it in mind to refuse her. But he knew it might take two to prevent what was likely to happen soon in that market place.

They talked and planned into the night. He drew her a diagram, explained why the gate house was important and what he believed would be the course of events.

'She will stop the King. Beg for a blessing. No one will expect her to be other than yet another poor supplicant. She will be close enough to stop him. In the moment he is exposed, Sir Harry will use a cross-bow from the window of the gatehouse.

'Sir Harry has her trained. Rebecca said she believed all he told her, didn't she?'

Maeve nodded. 'A cross-bow? How d'you know that?' she asked.

'I went up to the room. There is a box there and a saddle bag. Under some old sacks there is a bow and a dozen quarrels. Deadly. Once the King comes into the square he becomes a target just for a moment before the guard gets back into position. All she has to do is stop the King for a moment in the open.'

'She's a fanatic. Believes the King and his wife will deliver the country to the Pope. A Pope she believes is the Devil himself.

She will help Sir Harry kill him to prevent that. Maeve sat silent for a moment.

'And the girl, what about her?'

'He dare not leave her as a witness for they'll get the truth from her one way or another. She'll be betrayed by Sir Harry. Slaughtered in the chaos before he makes an easy escape.'

Fox sighed and sat back on the bed.

'Simple. Then foist blame on the Parliament men. The people will be disgusted and terrified by an act they will see as killing God's power in the land. Which leaves Henrietta as regent for her son and Morton and his people prepared to take power.'

'By the time the panic is over he will have vanished into the alleyways and courtyards of the old town?' Maeve said.

Fox nodded.

'So, we have to get to her before she gets to the King.'

'And him?' Maeve asked.

'Sir Harry is yours, Maeve,' said Fox.

CHAPTER 45

Two days later Fox was watching the inn where Sir Harry Morton was lodged. The woman stepped out into the street with him at her side. He was talking to her intently and she, from time to time, nodded her head. They walked on. She walked through the crowds towards the small market place. She hardly seemed to notice them. Fox followed at a distance.

A clock struck the half hour. The King would be on his way to church.

Maeve followed the King's procession as it made its way towards the market place where Fox was begging. She skirted the crowd and cut through the narrow side streets ahead of the procession. She found Fox with a bowl in front of him close to the door of the old gate house. His hat was pulled well down over his face.

He stood when he saw Maeve and she joined him.

'The King is on his way. Where's the woman?'

'She's not here,' he said. 'She was there one minute and gone the next. Somewhere in this press of people. Sir Harry vanished too.'

Maeve nodded. 'We know where he will be, John. The King's party is on its way so you'll have to find the woman. I have some unfinished business.'

She walked quickly into the milling crowd and vanished.

The clatter of horses' hooves and the jingle of their harness signalled the arrival of the King. People pushed and shoved to get a view.

Fox was close to the entrance the King would take into the square. He couldn't see the woman for the press around him.

There was the usual shoving and pushing and then applause

as the little King rode out of the narrow alley. He was alone for a moment and the crowd looked at their King.

Fox stared across the crowd and saw a flicker of movement near the door of the gatehouse. The guards were already emerging from the alleyway and beginning to regroup around the King's horse.

As they did so the young woman in grey stepped past the guards, past the horses and close to the King. She had a blade in her hand.

Fox threw aside the two men blocking his way and as the woman lunged at the King he slammed into her. She turned snarling at him and slashed at him with the knife. He stepped close, took her wrist and slung her away from the King. Her dagger flew across the cobbles. No one moved for a second and then she began to get up.

The bolt from the cross-bow took her in the throat and she flew backwards.

By now guards and horses were milling around. Women screamed and men yelled. The crowd only had eyes for the young woman and for the King, who was already being hurried away by his guard. Fox walked away from the dead woman and through the crowd into the alley alongside the gatehouse. He pushed at the open gate in the wall, ran along the garden and into the back door of the house.

He raced up the stairs, taking the blade from his back and into the room overlooking the market square. A cross-bow was propped against the wall. Sir Harry Morton was facing Maeve who had a dagger in her hand and her heavy riding cloak over one arm. He flicked his rapier at her, smiling.

'Mine!' shouted Maeve as Fox stepped onto the small room. Sir Harry glanced at Fox and then moved a step closer to Maeve.

'I'll kill you after I've killed this bitch,' he snarled and Maeve laughed in his face.

Sir Harry lunged at her. She parried the sword with her heavy riding cloak and as he tried to pull the blade from its heavy folds, Maeve stepped into a close embrace with him and slid her blade into his belly. She pressed down and opened him.

'I owe you for so much,' she whispered, stepping back from him as he stared at the handle sticking out of his belly, plucking at it before he fell to his knees.

He looked up at her and shook his head in disbelief.

'Dear God it hurts – it hurts – '

220

Maeve leaned closer, 'This is for the girl you tortured and raped in Ireland. I was fourteen and you laughed in my face as your friend held me. It is for all the others, too.'

And she leaned close to the dying man and spat in his face. She walked out of the room.

CHAPTER 46

Over the watchmaker's shop near the stinking Thames, Tom Fairfax paced the room. Thurloe sat tapping his desk with the signet ring on his right pinkie. Events were beginning to overtake them and they could do nothing. There was word about London that an attempt had been made to cause trouble in Oxford. No more than rumour. No detail.

The rumour was that a woman had been killed in an Oxford market place. A young woman who was a religious fanatic, some said. Two women had come out of the mob to claim her body and had taken her away. No one had any idea who they were or where they came from.

Thurloe was angry and so was Fairfax.

'Killed by a bolt from a cross-bow. She was carrying a blade. Got to within a hair of the King. Not another word, no more information. Nothing'

Fairfax turned on him.

'How many agents do you have in Oxford? Are any of them worth a spit in the wind? Who was the woman? What was she doing there? What's being said?'

'The King's party are only saying she was found dead in the market place some time after the King had paraded to church. Nothing more. Officially.'

'Officially!' Fairfax spat. 'Officially! For the love of Christ, what happened there?'

'Nothing,' said Thurloe softly. 'Nothing happened.'

'You know what that woman said to me? Fox's woman? What she said? She said there was a plot. To kill the King.'

Thurloe looked at Fairfax sharply and shook his head.

'Not true.'

'How the pox do you know if it's true or not?'

'Put it another way, my friend. If it's true it never happened. Never.'

'Maeve Aherne said to look in the room over the gatehouse on the corner of the square.' Thurloe said nothing and watched as Fairfax went on, angrily. 'This was an assassination attempt which as near as damn succeeded, according to my source.'

'Fox?'

'No. The Irish woman ? '

'What else did she say?'

'I told you, she told me to look in the gatehouse. She said that the circle about the Queen – the Catholic circle you might call it were planning to proclaim the young son as King and make themselves Regents in his name. Take power. They were apparently contemptuous of Charles as a weak-minded fool. Fanatics for their religion, it seems.'

'And willing to plunge us into war with Spain and France at the same moment we have a civil war unfolding here. Fanatics are fools by definition, Peter. Will your Irish woman keep her mouth firmly shut?'

'I have no idea.'

'Where is she now?'

'She was at my lodgings a day ago. Said she'd stay. Next morning she was gone. She took two horses from my stable and some food. No one saw her go.'

Fairfax went on angrily.

'There's no appetite for war, Master Thurloe, except with Parliament's officers and the King's. Armies thrive on war, do they not? You ask the people and most would opt for a quiet life at home around their hearths.'

Thurloe dismissed the very idea with a wave of his hand.

'Too late for that. But if they learned their King was near as spit assassinated by the hand of a Parliament agent – think what would happen then.'

'I know. If they learned there were those who'd assassinate the King and they could lay it firmly at the door of the Parliament men the country would be up in arms against Parliament. There's a foolish loyalty to fools even when they call themselves kings. King Charles dead would have tipped the people behind the throne. He has to stay alive for all our sakes. For the moment.'

Fairfax stopped pacing then and looked at the pinched face

behind the desk. The cold eyes stared back. Thurloe raised an eyebrow in question.

'For the moment? You'd remove the King?' Fairfax breathed the question.

Thurloe said nothing.

'Or do you play on his side as well?'

Thurloe smiled then.

'You soldiers, Tom. Such simple men. We here are pragmatic.'

'So you play both sides?'

'I'm not a bloody martyr, Tom. Not what I am made of. Let us say I keep my channels open. You should do the same. You are known as a general who takes rash decisions. Sends men into battle without an escape route. Learn from it. Always have a way to escape. Always. The manuals of war tell you. Listen to Lady Anne, your wife, who I understand is less inclined than you to Parliament's side.'

'My wife is my business, sir. Keep her name out of it. You hear me?'

Thurloe smiled and sighed as he reached for a paper on his desk. He read from it.

'I am not inclined to support the Parliament cause blindly as my husband might seem to do." She said as much a month since. It was sent me for the files.'

Fairfax started forward and snatched the paper from Thurloe's unresisting hands.

'You bastard.'

'Perhaps. I have eyes and ears everywhere, Tom. Perhaps I shore myself up as surely with words and paper as you do with swords and muskets. You'd do well to do the same. Listen to Lady Anne and bury this attempt on the King in your heart. It never happened.'

After a pause Fairfax nodded. He'd say nothing against the official line even though it disgusted him. He picked up his hat and headed for the door as Thurloe spoke without standing.

'Something to make you feel easier. We looked in the gatehouse. Nothing there. Your informant lied to you. Nothing happened in Oxford. Some pickpocket was killed. No more. The King's people and ours are agreed. Tell the Irish girl and your man Fox. He needs telling. Should either attempt to say anything, they will be silenced. It's the way of the State. Trust me for that.'

Fairfax stood at the door and said nothing. Thurloe waved a dismissive hand.

'Where is he? Where is the girl? Find them if you must. Warn them for their sakes.'

Fairfax stared at him for a moment then turned and left the room. He didn't shut the door.

CHAPTER 47

Fox left Bristol early. 'I can't wait to get the stink of cities out of my nostrils,' he told Patrick Shea in the back room of his inn.

'It's no better out there. All we hear in Bristol is war and all they hear out there is war again.'

Fox rolled up his blanket, tightened the leather thongs around it and tied it to his saddle. Patrick's wife had put flour and salt into the pannier and dried fruit too.

'A soldier's rations,' he'd said and she nodded and cut the meat off a ham bone to wrap with two chicken. 'A soldier's rations,' she repeated and then she turned to him directly.

'Stay, John Fox. My man would be delighted but dare not ask you. There's work and plenty about an inn like ours – stay and welcome. Bring your daughter back here.'

Fox smiled at her and shrugged.

'She – she chose to go with Maeve Aherne. She'll be well protected. She's been hurt and needs healing and Maeve can do that. She has the skills for it. I don't. What use is a soldier for a father?'

'So stop. Just stop here. With us. Make a life here.'

He shook his head, tightened a stirrup.

'I can't. It sickens me and what is happening here, now sickens me the more. Brother against brother, father against son. Men and women dying. I've seen enough of it friend. I'll go and search out Maeve and Rebecca and maybe find peace with them.'

Fox rode away from the city looking for the high ground, fresh air and clear skies He turned across the fearful country and down to the west towards the sea. He was hurrying now to be with Rebecca.

High on the moors by the hill called Rough Tor looking

across to the seaward north coast, over the bog and waste of the ancient land called Avalon by some, Kernow by the natives and Cornwall by their rulers, two figures stood and looked down past Camelford and its castle. The deep lanes cut across the land and flowers bloomed in the spring hedgerows.

Trees shaped and bent by winter winds and storms off the sea concealed the paths and ways that were thousands of years old.

Huge standing stones carved with strange runic signs, a land of mystery and the promise of risen kings and Merlin buried under stone slabs on outcrops far into the mossy pools and black peat waters, protected, hidden by nature and fierce loyalties to older times than these.

Two women stood together quietly. The clouds behind them forming and reforming into thunderheads and storm clouds further inland. Over to seaward, bright almost white light and the thin green line where the sky met the sea.

They turned and rode down the slopes and into the deep hidden lanes leading west. It was a quiet going these two made.

There is a small stone hut on a saddle of rock between two headlands known as Dinah's Head and the rock pillar known as Trethias. The land behind the sands is marram-covered and barren. Sea thistles guard the approaches and the long stretches of sand rise up to short runs of slate-grey cliffs and the soft curves that lead down to the jut of Dinah's Head and the rolling Atlantic.

Watching from Dinah's Head, a boy lay against a bank of pale pink thrift flowers and grasses. Over his head waved fronds of tamarisk. Peter watched the two strangers as they dismounted by the hut, led their tired horses inside the stone-walled field and turned them loose.

The waves came almost soundlessly onto the sands and folded backwards pulling the sand and small stones and shells in a rippling movement across the swerve of the bay. On Trethias the single stack at the end of the island was throwing up spume from the deeper boom of the waves.

Later, smoke curled from the slate chimney. One of the figures lay on the soft grass inside the small rock-built walls surrounding the isolated stone house.

Inside the smell of baking bread. Outside, the shriek of gulls and across the rocks Maeve walked carrying in one hand a string of sea bass and in the other a large, foaming angry crab held by its back legs.

She pushed aside her hair which sparkled with silver fish scales and the salt of the sea. She laughed at the girl lying on the grass. Sitting beside the girl, Peter read slowly from an old book he'd found in his mother's house down along St Merryn way. Maeve grinned at him.

'Food!' she said. 'Can you cook crab?'

Peter got up and walked into the small room past the stone-lintelled doorway with Maeve. The girl on the grass smiled after them, leaned back and looked into the pale sky, heard the sea and the yelping of gulls. Rebecca shut her eyes and slept.

Armies were moving across the land while in a secret room over a watchmaker's shop near the Thames in London, a new man broke seals on messages, forged letters and Thurloe complained about the cold.

Up on the moors Fox rode past the stone circle near Rough Tor and down towards the sea and his daughter

12th January 2013
Kew.

228